# MICKEY FINN
## 21st Century Noir
## Volume 5

Michael Bracken, Editor

# MICKEY FINN
## 21st Century Noir
## Volume 5

Collection Copyright © 2024 by Michael Bracken
Individual Story Copyrights © 2024 by Respective Authors

All rights reserved. No part of the book may be reproduced in any form or by any electronic or mechanical means, including information storage and retrieval systems, without permission in writing from the publisher, except by a reviewer who may quote brief passages in a review. Without in any way limiting the author's [and publisher's] exclusive rights under copyright, any use of this publication to "train" generative artificial intelligence (AI) technologies to generate text is expressly prohibited. The author reserves all rights to license uses of this work for generative AI training and development of machine learning language models.

Down & Out Books
3959 Van Dyke Road, Suite 265
Lutz, FL 33558
DownAndOutBooks.com

The characters and events in this book are fictitious. Any similarity to real persons, living or dead, is coincidental and not intended by the author.

Cover design by Zach McCain and Margo Nauert

ISBN: 1-64396-386-4
ISBN-13: 978-1-64396-386-0

# TABLE OF CONTENTS

| | |
|---|---:|
| Introduction<br>Michael Bracken | 1 |
| *The French Toast Special*<br>Sean McCluskey | 3 |
| *Burned*<br>Hugh Lessig | 21 |
| *The Boxer*<br>Bill W. Morgan | 39 |
| *Red Dust Express*<br>K.L. Abrahamson | 53 |
| *Sister*<br>Eddie Generous | 67 |
| *Quackers*<br>Nils Gilbertson | 77 |
| *A Rose for a Rose*<br>Stacy Woodson | 91 |
| *All Apples*<br>Andrew Welsh-Huggins | 99 |
| *Gone Fishin'*<br>James A. Hearn | 123 |

| | |
|---|---|
| *Ronnie Mercer is Back in Town*<br>Joseph S. Walker | 145 |
| *Three Sorry Langers*<br>Caleb Coy | 159 |
| *No Request Denied*<br>Travis Richardson | 173 |
| *Rhapsody in Blood*<br>Robb T. White | 185 |
| *Dinky Dau*<br>Michael Chandos | 203 |
| *Unlucky for Some*<br>Alan Barker | 219 |
| *Solid Six*<br>Alan Orloff | 239 |
| *Broken English*<br>Sam Wiebe | 249 |
| *Barstow*<br>Tom Milani | 267 |
| About the Editor | 285 |
| About the Contributors | 287 |

*For Temple*
*My Love, My Muse, My Everything*

# INTRODUCTION

*Noir* stories often feature characters who have, either by their own hand or due to the whims of fate, fallen into darkness. As they struggle to return to the light, their efforts prove futile, and they fall further until even the concept of light eludes them.

But this isn't the only definition of noir. Critics of the genre often mention cynicism and moral ambiguity as important elements. Other critics mention setting, mood, or a particular writing style. Each year, as I sift through submissions, I try to keep these many and varied definitions in mind, and the stories in this volume represent every shade of black.

As in the first four editions of *Mickey Finn*, I restricted the stories to the twenty-first century, challenging contributors to write modern noir stories that don't rely heavily on the technological restrictions of the past. The eighteen writers included herein more than met the challenge.

So, be prepared as you turn the page. Not only is it dark in here, there's also no light at the end.

—Michael Bracken
Hewitt, Texas

# THE FRENCH TOAST SPECIAL
## Sean McCluskey

Crenshaw hoped the cops wouldn't arrive before he finished his French toast. It was the best he'd ever had. Three slices, fried perfectly golden, sprinkled with powdered sugar. He wasn't a fan of sweet foods for breakfast, but this diner was famous for the stuff.

He was at the counter, close to the middle, so he could see out the north and south windows by turning his head. Last time, the cops had parked on the north end of the lot, near a *Welcome to the Famous Roscoe Diner* sign. Last time they'd arrived at nine, which would be in two minutes. Crenshaw cut his last slab of toast into cubes.

As the final bite went into his mouth, a Chevrolet Spark rolled into the lot. Same car as last time. It looked like a minivan whose mother had taken thalidomide, grimy with road salt and painted an astonishing shade of green that General Motors called *Jalapeño*. It swung into a spot by the sign, splashing through slush puddles. The cops, right on time. Crenshaw finished his coffee.

Two guys exited the Spark. Crenshaw recognized them from last time. They were federal investigators with the Manhattan US Attorney's Office, so no uniforms. Wrinkled khaki slacks, pullovers, and winter coats. Both on the downslope of middle age. Cops, but not street cops anymore. Like dependable knives, gone a bit dull. They stretched, backs cramped after a long drive in a small car.

Crenshaw lifted his phone from the counter, beside the check he'd paid when he sat down. A cheap burner, with one number programmed. He opened the text app, tapped two asterisks, and hit *Send*. The reply appeared: a plus sign. He dropped the phone into his coat pocket.

The cops tromped in, shaking off the cold. Mid-November in upstate New York—probably a shock to these city boys. They had their pick of tables. Hunting season had started a week ago, so the breakfast rush kicked off at five a.m. and was done by sunrise. Just a handful of regular old-timers now.

The cops picked a booth by a window on the north end, so they could see their car. They dropped gloves and hats beside the menus the hostess left them. Then they headed for the bathroom. Middle-aged guys, bladders full of the coffee they'd drunk on a two-hour drive. Crenshaw stood and followed, in no hurry. He pulled on a cloth COVID mask as he went.

The Roscoe Diner was a good-sized place, so the bathroom was, too. L-shaped, its door opening into the shorter leg, across from a bank of sinks. In the long section, around the bend, a trio of urinals stood opposite three stalls.

Crenshaw put on his gloves. Then he took a heavy rubber wedge from his pocket. He set it under the door and pushed it in hard with the toe of his boot. Gave the handle a tug—plugged tight. He turned the corner.

The cops were at the urinals, on both ends of the row. Men's room etiquette forbade Crenshaw to use the unoccupied one in the middle, if other options were available. Feet were visible under the door of one stall. The other two were empty.

"Looks like sitting room only," said Crenshaw.

The cops glanced over. Neither gave the quip so much as a polite chuckle. That was okay—it wasn't for them. It was for the guy in the stall.

The stall door bashed open, and Gordon lunged out. He

grabbed the cop closest to him. Urine sprayed as Gordon hauled the man backward.

As the second cop turned, Crenshaw pulled a COVID mask from his pocket. An N95 respirator, high-end. He clapped the mask over the cop's nose and mouth. With his other hand, he grabbed the man's sleeve and yanked his arm back to keep it from his gun.

The cop thrashed. He was big, but most of it was fat. Crenshaw was a bit younger and much leaner, his body roped with the unobtrusive muscle of swimmers and distance runners. He clamped the mask down hard and dragged the cop backward into one of the stalls. The mask was impregnated with sevoflurane, an inhalation anesthetic, and the man was already weakening. He gave one last desperate wrench, then slumped. Crenshaw set him on the toilet.

In the next stall, Gordon's guy was putting up more of a fight. Solid kicks to the door and walls. Something clanged across the tile.

"Do not kill him," Crenshaw said over the din.

"I know, I know," Gordon grunted. "We're fine." More kicks, weakening, and then the guy quieted down. Thumps and scrapes as Gordon wrestled him onto the seat.

Crenshaw looped the N95's straps over his cop's ears. He shut the stall door and locked it. "You good?"

"Yeah," said Gordon, sounding only slightly winded. "Figures you get the easy one."

Crenshaw looted the cop. Phone, wallet, badge case, car keys, Glock. No spare magazines, no handcuffs. A knife gone dull. He undid the man's khakis and yanked them to his ankles, then pulled the N95 down. The cop's eyes were shut, mouth open, breathing steadily. Sevoflurane had a good safety record, but accidents happened. Crenshaw held the guy's phone up to his face, unlocked it, and replaced the mask.

Gordon's canvas work coat hissed on the tile as he slid out under his stall's gap. Crenshaw lay down and pulled himself over.

Saw Gordon's guy masked, pants down, chest rising and falling. Most importantly, not dead. Crenshaw dragged himself out into the restroom and stood.

Gordon adjusted the Confederate flag neck gaiter over his lower face. His eyes were a pale gray that reminded Crenshaw of heat shimmer. "You figure these guys always go to the bathroom together?" he asked. "Like girls?"

Crenshaw tugged his gloves off. "It's what they did last time."

Gordon snorted. Cracked his knuckles. Took a deep breath.

Crenshaw knew what was coming.

"You know it's better to kill them," Gordon said.

Crenshaw shook his head. "We're not having this conversation again." Gordon was a freelancer Crenshaw used occasionally, with a narrow skillset. *Revoking birth certificates*, he called it. Like a trained dog, he was useful if managed.

Gordon looked at him for a few moments. His pale eyes were flat and calm. "Your call, man." He crossed the room to retrieve the coat hook his guy had kicked loose. "I just work here."

Crenshaw opened *Settings* on the phone he'd taken. Tapped *Display,* then shut off its auto-lock feature so it wouldn't seize up on him. "Give me your guy's phone," he said to Gordon. When he did, Crenshaw reset that one, too. Gordon dropped the coat hook into a waste bin by the sinks.

Crenshaw dropped the phones into his coat pockets as he walked to the door. He worked the wedge free and pulled it open. An old man was out there, stooped and scrawny, in a flannel shirt and creased blue jeans. He'd turned to walk away but stopped. "What's a'matter with the damn door?" he groused.

Crenshaw shrugged, stepping aside so the man could shuffle past. At the sink, Gordon pretended to wash his gloved hands.

Crenshaw walked out. A waitress was setting two coffee mugs on the cops' table. He went straight to the front door. The only cameras in the place were aimed at the register and the entrance, so he kept his mask on, chin down, collar up, and wool cap pulled low.

"Have a wonderful day," said the hostess, not looking at him.

Outside, flurries fell from a sky the color of dingy laundry as Crenshaw hiked across the parking lot. He blipped the Spark's doors open with the key fob and settled into the passenger seat. He pulled off his mask to scratch at the goatee he'd grown for this job. Having facial hair. It made him look like his father. He hated it.

A folder was wedged between seat and console. It was a case file, like the hundreds Crenshaw had read back when he was a cop. He pulled it out and opened it.

The file was about a man named Dale Stoller. He'd been indicted in Manhattan nine months earlier for securities fraud, then released on bond. Stoller lived in Albright, an affluent suburb of Buffalo, so his pretrial release was supervised by federal probation in the Western District of New York.

The night they'd fitted him with an ankle monitor, Stoller cut it off and took his sailboat across the Niagara River into Canada. He'd run aground in the dark and wound up in a Montreal jail. While the feds worked on getting him back, investigators on the fraud case found a ghastly trove of bespoke child pornography on one of Stoller's hard drives. He'd been indicted on a federal Sexual Exploitation of Children charge, returned to Buffalo, and remanded without bail.

Last week, he'd been driven to Manhattan to meet with his attorney and prosecutors, then brought back to Buffalo that same day. Today, he was being transferred to a federal jail in Brooklyn.

Cold wind swept through the car as Gordon dumped himself into the driver's seat. He pulled down his gaiter, doffed his Giants cap, and hit the starter. The dashboard vents, already on high, whooshed lukewarm air.

"That old guy did his business and came out," said Gordon. "No fuss."

"Good." Crenshaw passed him the cops' phones. "Keep an eye on these. Give me your guy's ID."

Gordon handed over the other cop's badge case. Crenshaw took out the one he'd stolen and opened them both on his lap. The credentials were two-piece affairs, stacked like magazine centerfolds. The top card identified the bearer as an investigator for the United States Attorney, Southern District of New York. The bottom had a photo and a signature. Gordon's guy was named Lonigan. Crenshaw's was Keats. Crenshaw pulled two new bottom cards from his breast pocket. They had pictures of him and Gordon with fake names. He tucked them into the cases.

At the diner's north window, the waitress came into view. She looked at the cops' empty table, then drifted off.

Gordon had a phone in each hand. One buzzed. He looked at it. "'*Two minutes out*,'" he read. "They're early."

"Outstanding." Crenshaw handed Gordon his new badge case.

They sat quietly for a bit. The flurries increased to snow.

"If those guys wake up…," said Gordon.

"They won't."

"They do, we're fucked."

Crenshaw pointed at the window. "We'll see the commotion. Drive away, ditch the car. No harm, no foul."

"No money."

"God grant serenity, courage, and wisdom," said Crenshaw.

"Two heroin overdoses would'a done it. No suffering. Feels great, actually."

"Killing cops draws heat. I only do it for a lot more money than this."

"I'm just saying, if they wake up—"

"Then you'll get to say *I told you so*. That'll feel great, too."

They sat quietly.

Not quite two minutes later, a dark SUV crunched into the lot. It was caked with salt and slush—worse weather up north. It gunned over, splashing to a stop beside the Spark. Crenshaw put on a pair of eyeglasses. He grabbed the file and got out.

The SUV driver, gray-haired and rangy, swung down. He wore a canvas coat over jeans and boots. Maybe the Northern District

## THE FRENCH TOAST SPECIAL

US Attorney's investigators were the frontiersmen of the bunch. He eyeballed Crenshaw, in khakis, pea coat, watch cap, and glasses. Crenshaw nodded to him. He knew he still looked like a cop.

The driver walked over, looking at the Spark and shaking his head. "That car, man. That's pure NYC."

"Woodland camouflage," said Crenshaw. "For when we come up to the sticks." They bumped fists. Showed IDs.

"Bill Marsh," the driver said.

"Ron MacLeod," said Crenshaw. "Nice to meet you, Bill."

Marsh looked in at Gordon. "No Lonnie today?"

Crenshaw figured that meant *Lonigan*. "Popped hot for COVID. He forwarded me your texts."

"That sucks. He loves the French toast here."

"He's right. Best I've ever had."

"Good." Marsh brushed sleet from his hair. "Let's get your package before the blizzard starts." He walked to the SUV's passenger side. Crenshaw followed.

"Any problems with him?" Crenshaw asked.

"Slept the whole way." The schedule in the file said Stoller was picked up by Western District investigators that morning and driven to Ithaca, then passed to these guys. Four hours and two hundred fifty miles so far. A regular Cook's tour.

Crenshaw glanced at the diner. The waitress and hostess were looking at the cops' empty table, talking. The hostess shrugged.

"You know what he's charged with, right?" Marsh asked. "Some real Jeffery Epstein shit."

"I've read his file."

Marsh's partner exited the SUV. Younger, buzzcut hair, tactical pants with kneepads stitched in. "Morning, sir," he said to Crenshaw. "Got the paperwork?"

Crenshaw handed over the writ and transfer order. The kid attached them to a steel clipboard with a gun manufacturer's logo on it. Peered at the form. "You're Keats? Or Lonigan?"

"I'm MacLeod. Lonigan's got COVID."

The kid looked at the Spark. "That's Keats?"

"That's Taurino. Keats is quarantining because he works with Lonigan. Who has COVID."

"Also," said Marsh, "it's snowing."

The kid frowned. "Paperwork says Keats and Lonigan." They weren't all dull knives.

"So cross it out," said Crenshaw. "Or keep the package. Either's fine with me. I got my French toast." He exchanged looks with Marsh. Two veterans, weary of this administrative nonsense. Marsh rolled his eyes.

"It's okay," said Marsh. "I checked his creds." He opened the SUV's door.

Dale Stoller was pale, short, and skinny, his thinning hair longer than in the file's mugshot. He wore red prison scrubs, which meant he'd been segregated for protection from other inmates. It's what they did with guys accused of raping children.

Stoller blinked rapidly. "You're from the city?"

Crenshaw nodded. "Come on out."

Stoller eased down, awkward in handcuffs and leg shackles. The kid grabbed his elbow and hauled him around to the Spark, just in case the middle-aged financier tried to dash away with his ankles chained together. Marsh rolled his eyes again.

"God, it's cold," Stoller gasped.

Crenshaw opened the Spark's rear door. "Nice and warm inside." The kid pushed Stoller in.

"I need the bathroom," Stoller said.

"Not here," said Crenshaw. "At the State Police barracks down in Liberty."

"I really need to go."

"I believe you." Crenshaw shut the door. He turned to the kid, took the metal clipboard, and scribbled a signature on the prisoner receipt. The kid took it without a word and stalked back to the SUV. Marsh and Crenshaw watched him go.

"Thanks, Bill," said Crenshaw. "Have fun with GI Joe."

Marsh chuckled. "The enthusiasm of youth." As he walked away, he patted the Spark. "Drive safe in the Green Monster."

The SUV rumbled off. Gordon let them get out of sight. Then he dropped the Spark into gear and pulled out of the lot.

The diner was quiet. The old man from the bathroom was leaving, scowling up at the clouds.

"Guess they didn't wake up," said Gordon.

Crenshaw took off his glasses and stuffed the file back. "I never say *I told you so.*"

"How far to that bathroom?" Stoller asked. Crenshaw and Gordon ignored him. Gordon turned on the radio. Crenshaw pulled the phony cards from both badge cases, then dropped the credentials into the center console. The cops' guns, phones, and wallets all went into the glove box. He yanked the batteries and SIM cards from the burner phones he and Gordon had used and put them in his coat.

They drove north on Old Route 17. They passed a weathered brick house with an American flag on a pole out front. Its signs read *Justice Court* and *New York State Police Substation.*

"Can I use the bathroom there?" Stoller asked. Crenshaw and Gordon ignored him.

Gordon turned at a firehouse whose sign declared it *The Home of the Fightin' 29th.* They cruised through a small retail strip. Ahead, the road passed under the new Route 17, a six-lane expressway. The ramp's sign read *New York City, 117 miles.* Gordon drove right past it.

"Uh, I think that was the turn," Stoller said. Crenshaw and Gordon ignored him.

The road ended at a T intersection with County 129. Directly across, a cracked asphalt strip curved away into the woods, beside a weather-beaten sign that said *Campbell Inn.* There was no traffic in sight. Gordon gunned across onto the potholed track.

"Officers, where are we going?" Stoller asked. They ignored him.

The low-slung car juddered and scraped, gravel ricocheting in the wheel wells. Around a bend, a chained cattle gate blocked the road. Gordon stopped short of it.

"Listen, I want to know where we're going," Stoller said, trying to put some steel in his voice. "Right now."

This time, Gordon didn't ignore him. He turned. Gave the smaller man a blast of those heat shimmer eyes. "Sit back and shut up." He didn't raise his voice. A narrow skill set, but he was very good at it. Stoller sat back.

Crenshaw got out and walked to the gate. Earlier, the chain had been secured by a padlock that proved childishly easy to pick. Now it was just looped around itself. Crenshaw unwound it and shoved the gate open. Closed it again after the Spark rattled through.

Another quarter-mile, and the driveway ended at a ramshackle three-story hotel. The Campbell Inn, built at the turn of the century and defunct for thirty years. The siding had faded white, but the shutters were still a green only slightly dimmer than the Spark's.

A rusty, mud-spattered pickup truck sat by the porch. Gordon parked next to it and shut the engine off. Crenshaw got out and opened Stoller's door.

"Mister Stoller," said Crenshaw. "We work for Banks & Stokes. That's the law firm representing Emmett Shea, your codefendant in the securities fraud case. The man you've agreed to testify against, in exchange for leniency in your child pornography case." He motioned for Stoller to get out.

Stoller didn't move. "The police turned me over to defense attorneys?"

"Not exactly."

Stoller stared up at him. He looked at Gordon. "Oh, God," he whispered. "Oh, God, no. Please, no. Please—"

"Relax," said Crenshaw. "If we meant to kill you, we wouldn't be talking. Shea doesn't want you testifying, but he doesn't want you dead, either. Says there are still business opportunities you and he can exploit. He wants you to join him in Andorra. Skiing, fine cuisine, and no extradition treaty with the US." He took a handcuff key from his pocket. "Let's get those off you."

Stoller shook his head. "It's a trick. You want me to try and escape so you can charge me."

"That'd be unprosecutable entrapment," said Crenshaw. "Trust me—I work for a law firm."

Stoller's eyes narrowed. Running the numbers, like an accountant. Looked at Gordon. At Crenshaw. At the cuff key.

"Okay." Stoller held out his hands.

Crenshaw took the shackles off. Tossed them into the Spark. Led Stoller around the pickup truck, past where Gordon was rummaging in the rollout cargo drawer. Crenshaw opened the rear passenger door of the crew cab. A tracksuit was folded on the seat, with cheap sneakers and a winter coat.

"Get changed," Crenshaw said. He gestured at the field. "Piss first, if you want."

"Won't they know I was here?" Stoller asked. "From DNA?"

"There's no DNA in urine."

"You're sure?"

"Hold it if you want. Either way, hurry up."

Gordon slammed the cargo drawer and tailgate. He shuffled to the Spark, lugging two milk jugs taped together, heavy with thick liquid. A cell phone, hooked to wires running through the jug caps, was tucked under the tape.

Stoller finished urinating and changed clothes. His body, pasty and freckled, shivered in the chill. Crenshaw tossed the jail scrubs into the Spark, near the jugs on the passenger seat. The three of them piled into the truck, Crenshaw and Stoller in the back, Gordon driving. The Green Monster sat forlorn in the snow as they drove away.

Crenshaw didn't bother shutting the gate behind them. At the end of the driveway, Gordon waited for a lone car to whoosh past. He turned north and gunned it, muffler rattling.

"Where are we going now?" Stoller asked.

"We'll split up," Crenshaw said. "They'll be looking for three guys traveling together."

"How am I getting to Andorra?"

"It's all arranged."

Gordon took a cellphone from the cup holder. He dialed and hit *Send*. Behind them, a flash lit the low clouds, and birds erupted from trees. A dull thunderclap rolled.

"*Adios*, Green Monster," said Gordon. He passed the phone back to Crenshaw, who yanked the battery and SIM card.

Stoller had found the wool hat with the Giants logo on it in the coat. "Thanks for this," he said. He tried a smile. "I'm more of a Bills fan, though."

"We won't hold that against you," said Gordon. Stoller laughed a bit loud. Releasing tension, or bonhomie with the hired help. Crenshaw would've preferred silence.

"How did you know I'd be at that diner today?" Stoller asked.

"He's the mastermind," Gordon said. "I just work here." Stoller looked at Crenshaw, expectant.

"Our lawyers know your lawyer," Crenshaw finally said. "That diner was where they did the handoff last time, when they brought you to Manhattan to make the cooperation offer. Once you agreed, it made sense they'd do the jail transfer the same way."

"Emmett's lawyers talked to mine? Isn't that unethical?"

"File a complaint with the bar, if you want."

Stoller laughed again. "I'll let it slide. I think I'll prefer Andorra to Brooklyn."

Gordon wound along back roads, turning a twenty-minute trip into almost an hour. On the truck's police scanner, they listened to the Fightin' 29th respond to a fire at the Campbell Inn. Then the State Police and an ambulance were dispatched to the Roscoe Diner, for two victims of an assault and robbery.

Eventually, they left paved roads for dirt tracks that threaded into the Cherry Ridge Wild Forest. They stopped at another gate, with another previously defeated padlock. Beyond that were slumping bungalows, rotting in the snow. It had been a campground once and might be again if the foreclosure got sorted out.

# THE FRENCH TOAST SPECIAL

A Jeep Wrangler, square edges rounded by piled snow, sat beside a cabin. The truck's brakes squealed as Gordon parked near it. Crenshaw took a phone from his pocket. Powered it up and dialed.

"So long, gents," Gordon said. "Nice working with you."

Crenshaw put his phone away. "You, too." He rattled his door handle. "The safety locks are on."

"Shouldn't be." Gordon looked at his door panel. "No, they're—"

Crenshaw pulled an N95 from his pocket. He clamped it over Gordon's face, hauling his skull back against the headrest. Gordon thrashed, bellowing.

"Oh, my God!" Stoller cried.

Gordon yanked a Marine Corps Ka-Bar from his belt. The knife slipped from his fingers and tumbled into a footwell. He strained, hauling on Crenshaw's arm. Strong, then weaker. He slumped. Crenshaw held on for another half-minute. Stoller stared, mouth agape.

"Get out," Crenshaw said.

Stoller fumbled with his door. Shoved it open and scrambled out. Crenshaw slid across behind him. He grabbed a handful of Stoller's coat and pushed him toward the Jeep.

"Listen to me," said Crenshaw. "Our orders are to kill you. I'm willing not to, but that guy loves revoking birth certificates. So you need to do what I say."

"Where—where are we going?"

"Canada. I can get you a new passport. After that, you're on your own. I know you have assets stashed away."

"Okay. All right." Stoller's voice shook from more than the cold. "Thank you." He pulled on the Jeep's door handle. It was locked.

Crenshaw said, "We need to take care of something first."

"What?"

"I need the login and both transfer authentication challenges for the Mauritius account."

"The—the what?"

"The bank account where you dumped the money you skimmed from Shea." Crenshaw looked back at Gordon. "Don't waste time. That stuff wears off."

"Why do you need the money? For my trip?"

"No," said Crenshaw. "For not killing you myself."

Stoller looked at him. At Gordon. Narrowed his eyes. Running the numbers.

"I don't...have them memorized," said Stoller. "I mean, I have lots of accounts. I had the passwords on my computers, or on my phone." He tried a smile, teeth chattering. "But I can get you money. Once we're in Canada, I can reach out to places. I'll pay you. I swear."

Crenshaw stood still, thinking.

"I'm telling you the truth," Stoller said.

Crenshaw nodded. "Okay." He reached into his coat. "I guess it was a long shot."

"As soon as we're safe, I can—"

Crenshaw pulled his Ruger from his shoulder holster. He took the suppressor from his coat pocket. Screwed it onto the threaded barrel. Stoller stared.

"You can run if you want to," Crenshaw said. "But if you don't move, it won't hurt." He raised the gun.

"Jesus Christ!" Stoller cried. "Okay, okay! The login is 'persimmon,' with a three for the E and a zero instead of the O. The challenges are 'Unicorn,' all caps with a number one for the I, and 'Buffalo Bills,' one word, lowercase."

Crenshaw kept the pistol aimed.

"Please!" Stoller said. "I'm sorry, okay? Please, just don't."

Crenshaw reached into his coat. Drew out the cellphone. "Did you get that?"

"Good morning to you, too," said Nicole. His assistant's voice was tinny over the cheap burner's speaker. "I sure did. The login's legit, and the first transfer challenge looks good, too." A pause. "The second challenge also worked. Wow! Some balance.

## THE FRENCH TOAST SPECIAL

That's the biggest one I've ever seen up close, sailor."

"You're on speaker, young lady," said Crenshaw. "Try to sound professional."

"Sorry. Hi, Mister Stoller. Thanks for the donation." Another pause, longer. "The transfer's going through."

"Outstanding. Spend your share wisely."

"Maybe I'll just scram with all of it. Go live on an island someplace."

"Please don't," said Crenshaw. "The world would be a sadder place without you."

"You know I'm kidding, right?"

"Goodbye to you, too." Crenshaw hung up.

Stoller stared at him, fighting to get his breathing back under control. "So, we...we're okay?"

Crenshaw put his phone away. Twisted the suppressor off the Ruger. Dropped it in his coat, and reholstered the pistol. He nodded. "We're fine."

"Then can we please get the hell out of here?" Stoller yanked the handle. "Right now? Before that other asshole wakes up?"

"Be polite," Crenshaw said. "Or I'll ask about the Samoa account."

He reached into his pocket, rattling keys, and stepped toward the Jeep. When Stoller moved aside, Crenshaw punched him in the solar plexus, slamming him against the door. As the smaller man wheezed and groaned, Crenshaw pulled another mask from his coat and slapped it over Stoller's face. The accountant's struggles were much weaker than Gordon's. He wailed like a trapped fox.

"Relax," Crenshaw said. "It won't kill you." Sevoflurane had a good safety record. When Stoller subsided, Crenshaw lowered him to the ground. He secured the mask straps over his ears.

Behind him, the pickup truck's door creaked open. Gordon clambered out, knife in hand.

"How was my performance?" Gordon asked, sheathing the Ka-Bar.

"Masterful. You looked exactly like a guy falling asleep."

"Masterful enough to get a cut of that bank account?"

Crenshaw stood. "Your client's not paying you enough? That list you showed me will be labor-intensive and require special equipment. Don't tell me you're not gouging him."

Gordon snorted. "Believe that shit? Guy thinks he's Caligula." He grabbed Stoller under the arms, and Crenshaw took his feet. They carried him to the truck.

"Oh, get this," Gordon said. "On the way up, he texts me—now he wants a recording. *'Hey, while you're torturing that guy to death, be sure to film the whole thing, okay? Thanks.'*" They set Stoller down by the tailgate.

"Will you?" Crenshaw asked.

"Hell, yeah," said Gordon. "For an extra fifty percent." He snapped his neck gaiter. "I'll wear a mask." He dropped the tailgate and rolled out the drawer. It was padded with thick eggshell foam—once Stoller woke up, he could scream all he liked. They lifted the accountant and set him inside.

"Why's he want a recording?" Crenshaw asked, as Gordon taped Stoller's ankles and wrists. "To show at parties?"

Gordon shrugged. "What would you do if it were your kid? That girl was nine years old." He leaned over the snoring Stoller. "You're a sick little prick, Dale." He and Crenshaw rolled the drawer shut.

Gordon slammed the tailgate and locked it. "Want to help? Like you said, it's a lot of work. I'll cut you in."

"No, thanks. I just ate."

They stood quietly for a moment.

"Well, so long," said Gordon. "Nice working with you."

"I'm sure we will again."

The pickup rumbled off, spewing diesel smoke. Crenshaw unlocked the Jeep and took folded clothes off the seat. Once he'd changed, the old stuff went into a rusting trashcan. It burned merrily as Crenshaw drove away.

Driving down Route 17, he used an electric razor to get rid of the itchy goatee. Traffic was humming right along. No roadblocks yet—the State Police were probably still putting the puzzle together. As he passed the Roscoe exit, he looked toward the Campbell Inn. No smoke. The Fightin' 29th had triumphed.

The Roscoe Diner's lot was crowded with haphazardly parked police cars. The Northern District SUV was back, recalled so Marsh and his partner could have a long day explaining themselves. The kid would get to say *I told you so.*

Crenshaw figured he'd have to go back there someday, once the heat died down. That really had been some damn good French toast.

# BURNED
## Hugh Lessig

Henry tried to run away last week, and Jenna found him sleeping on a bench in the park downtown, a cardboard sign on his chest asking for money to find his father. Now they're back at the apartment complex, mother and son huddled around a fire pit, the flames fed by cheap grocery-store wood. A two-dollar packet of chemicals turns the flames into tiny rainbows. Jenna hugs herself against the November chill and looks across a dark courtyard about half the size of a football field.

"Henry, can't you put down that phone for a minute?" The fear in her voice is palpable. Her words hang in the night with nowhere to go.

Henry ignores his mother and thumbs a message. An hour ago, she caught him texting with his gamer friends about a utility tunnel that runs underneath this apartment complex. Jenna didn't call him out. If he's exploring underground, at least he's not running away.

"Someone's coming," Henry says, looking at his phone.

He's listening with one earbud. He turns sixteen next year and has been studying photos of Hank, his father and Jenna's ex, an over-the-road trucker who hauled mysterious loads and last year decided not to come home. Hank remains in the wind, a stubblecheeked ghost that haunts mother and son, but for different reasons. The son remembers that smile. The mother still smells the bourbon on his breath.

"Someone's coming," Henry says again.

"Hon, it's rude to talk to your friends when I'm right here. Talk to your mother."

"I'm trying. Look."

A shifting shadow moves across the courtyard toward them. It morphs into a heavyset man with a box under his arm and a ballcap on his head. Jenna has lived here for six months and knows many residents in this complex on sight. This guy is new. As he makes a beeline for the fire, Jenna pushes up from her camp chair.

"Can I help you?" The darkness seems to swallow her words. She plants her feet and puts a protective hand on Henry's shoulder. He shrugs it away.

"Hello, hello. Sorry to bother. I come in peace." In the firelight, the man looks about fifty years old. He wears a flannel shirt, jeans, and work shoes. His cap advertises a trucking company. With an exaggerated groan, he puts down a banker's box full of documents.

"I moved in this morning." He points to the far side of courtyard, the buildings barely outlined in the gloom. "I've got a bunch of papers that need burning. These first-floor units don't have much storage."

He appears calm and calculating. In Jenna's mind, that means he's either at peace or about to be a mass shooter. Since Hank's disappearance, she has stopped taking things for granted. "What kind of documents?" she asks.

"Old stuff with personal information. Social Security numbers and whatever. I was a packrat in my old place."

"You should buy a shredder."

The man grins. "You can only do a few pages at a time. Your fire is quicker."

Jenna had wanted to spend the night alone with her son. Ever since Hank left a note on the kitchen counter—*won't come home for a while after this trip, dealing with things, H*—their lives have been uprooted and tossed to the wind. Jenna sold the house after six months, unable to make the payments. She quit her job as a counselor for troubled kids in search of a new career with more work-life balance and better pay. She ended up at a financial planning firm downtown. The CEO hired her as his administrative assistant with the understanding she would train to become a financial planner in her own right. She spent five grand to learn about investments, taxes, estates, and other mysteries. The online courses take up her available headspace, and the CEO now says she must stay as "my admin" to keep his calendar, order office supplies, and organize after-work happy hours. She wants to throat punch him at least three times a day. It takes all her willpower not to stare at the soft, vulnerable skin under his Adam's apple.

Without asking for permission, the man tosses a sheaf of papers into the flames. "See? It burns right up."

In the financial planning course, Jenna was asked to name her biggest fault. She wrote down "endorsing the unwanted by my silence." Disappearing husband, asshole boss, morose kid. Now the strange neighbor. Orange embers rise and disappear. For some reason, it reminds her that hope is not a plan, and right now, all she has is hope.

"I'm Brooks, by the way. Brooks Badger. That sounds like a cartoon character, but it really is my name."

"I'm Jenna. This is Henry, my son."

"Pleased to make your acquaintance." His glasses reflect the rising flames. He tosses in a plastic binder, held together by a black spine. It melts and covers the rainbow-colored flames. "One other thing now that I know you. I'm only halfway moved in. I'd like to employ a strong young man like your son to carry a few boxes up the stairs. I'll pay well, but you'd need to start tomorrow. Good way to spend a Saturday, yeah?"

"I'm in," Henry says.

Jenna can see the wheels turning in her son's head: *Dad, I'm getting money. Here I come.*

The next morning, Henry is gone by the time Jenna wakes up. Her heart skips when she sees a note on the kitchen counter: *Went to help that neighbor dude.* She checks his room and breathes easier after seeing his empty backpack and a pile of dirty clothes. After her second cup of coffee, she goes to her third-floor balcony. A pickup sits across the courtyard near the open door of a first-floor unit. Henry emerges moments later and drags a box from the truck. He walks inside, ignoring his mother's wave.

She retreats into her apartment.

Around eleven o'clock, her phone dings with a text message. Only Henry sends her texts. Jenna has a few friends from college, but most are married and remember her and Hank as a couple. They've stayed away since the divorce.

*Brook Badger here, on your son's phone. Wanted you to know Henry is working out great.*

Her son treats his phone as if it's crusted with diamonds. No one touches it. Handing it to a stranger is nothing short of amazing. Jenna responds with a thumbs-up emoji and resists the urge to call. Around five o'clock, Henry returns and immediately takes a shower. Jenna finds him in his bedroom with one arm draped across his eyes, surrounded by blank walls. In their old house, his room was covered in posters of various apocalyptic games and novels. Now he's settled for apartment complex white, as if this is temporary.

"I guess someone worked hard today," she says.

"No big deal."

"You let that man send a message on your phone. I almost fainted." She means it as a joke, smiling from ear to ear, but it comes out as an accusation.

"He's not 'that man.' His name is Brooks."

"Right. Brooks. What does he do for a living?"

Henry thinks for a moment. "Security? Something at a warehouse."

"Here in Hampton?"

"I just helped him move."

"Did he say why he wanted to burn those documents?"

"Jesus Christ, always with the twenty questions. Can I get some sleep? I'm going back tomorrow. Should be gone all day."

The boy learned from his father how to end conversations. In the final years of their destructive marriage, Jenna wondered why Hank needed a week to complete a three-day haul. She always imagined him in the sleeper cab with a stringy prostitute, her teeth rotting from meth. When she asked what he hauled, the answer was always the same. Dry goods. Years ago, when Henry was eight or nine years old, he would accompany his father on short trips. The boy would come home, wide-eyed, as if he'd spent the day blowing up planets from the Death Star.

Jenna spends Saturday night curled up with an old detective movie and a tumbler of vodka from the bottle she hides inside the freezer, behind a stack of pizzas. After a while, the fake hand-to-hand fighting on-screen lulls her to sleep. Actors have no idea what real fighting is like. She wakes up at one in the morning with a gasp, dreaming of her scraps in juvie, ending up on the floor, handfuls of hair and bitten earlobes. Henry is not in his room, and his bed is made. His backpack and suitcase are here, as are his clothes, but Jenna goes from room to room and doesn't find him. She opens the door and scans the open stairway that runs up the middle of the building, a favorite place for people to talk and smoke.

He's there, hunched over her laptop.

From a distance, she sees her work calendar on the screen. All her appointments. When she goes to the gym. Everywhere she needs to be.

Henry is taking notes on a pad on all the places his mother can be found.

\*\*\*

Sunday is a repeat of Saturday. Henry leaves a note and is gone when Jenna wakes up. Across the courtyard, the same pickup is parked near the same open door. Henry carries boxes inside and comes out empty-handed. He and Brooks leave in the truck and return half an hour later with another load. Using a two-wheeled dolly, they wrestle a portable generator through the front door, Henry steering and Brooks steadying the load. Around ten o'clock, she texts him.

*He's got lots of stuff. You're working so hard. Looking good.*

He doesn't respond, but that's fine. Weekends are now the danger, when Henry has free time to plan an escape and Jenna runs errands. During the week, he's trapped in school. If he wants to hang out with the new neighbor on Sunday within sight of her balcony, so be it. Explore underground tunnels? Fine.

Later that morning, Brooks Badger walks across the courtyard with a metal bucket and begins cleaning out Jenna's fire pit. She rushes downstairs without a jacket, hugging herself against the chill.

"You don't have to do that," she says.

"The least I can do is clean up my mess," he says, scooping out debris with a large dustpan. "That paper makes so much ash. Besides, your son has things under control. I thought I made a mistake not hiring movers, but he saved my bacon."

"Where are you moving from?" She waves a cloud of ash away from her face.

"North of Williamsburg. A place out in the country. More of a cabin, really."

"You left this morning with my son and came back in thirty minutes. That's not enough time to get to Williamsburg and back."

"I have a self-storage unit here in Hampton." He tips the fire pit on its side and bangs the bottom.

"What brings you to Hampton, Mr. Badger?"

He grins, but his eyes turn hard. "It's closer to where I want to be."

"Do you work around here?"

"Henry said you used to be some kind of youth counselor. I feel like I'm on the couch. Yes, I work at London Industries. Not in the foundry itself. They make all kinds of castings and valves. I do security in the warehouse. How about you? Henry says you're now at some fancy financial planning outfit." He draws out the last three words, as if her company is a front for Russian spies.

"Foxworthy Solutions," she says. "I'm an administrative assistant to the boss. I fetch doughnuts and make coffee." She looks across the courtyard as Henry carries in another box. The stock of a rifle protrudes from the top. Brooks follows her gaze, sees the hint of recognition. "I have a couple of guns," he says, "but they have trigger locks and aren't loaded. No need for concern."

What condescending bullshit. *Don't worry your little head.*

"I have a gun myself," she says. "A forty-four magnum with a two-inch barrel. It blows a big hole coming out the other side."

"Okay then."

Talking about the gun makes her hands tingle. An old anger rises. "I got it after my husband left. Did Henry say anything about that?"

Brooks seems to ponder the question. Then he says, "I'll clean up this fire pit and be out of your hair."

"I also have boxing gloves. Back when I had money, I'd go to the gym and hit the heavy bag." As he turns to leave, she holds up a finger. "Could you wait a minute, Mr. Badger? I'd like to make a call."

"I guess so."

She finds the website for London Industries. Since it's Sunday, she calls the after-hours number. With her new neighbor standing there, she says: "Excuse me, hello? I'm trying to reach a Brooks Badger. He works in the warehouse. In security. Yes, I'll hold."

Brooks shakes his head in disappointment, as if to say, *you really shouldn't have done that.* Jenna stares him down because she's tired of it all: a husband who disappears, a boss who doesn't care, and a son who is a stranger in her own house. Tired of trying to be a good person and abandoning violent solutions. The woman from London Industries says no one named Brooks Badger works at the company.

Jenna cuts the connection. Her white-knuckled fist squeezes the phone. "That company has never heard of you."

"They outsource security. Technically, I'm a contractor."

"Cut the bullshit. Last night, my son was spying on my work calendar. He's never shown an interest in my job. Did you pay him to stalk me? Maybe you saw my fire and thought you'd get your hooks in my family. My son is looking for money. He wants to find his good-for-nothing father."

"Henry doesn't need to find his father. He knows where he is."

The words echo in her head. So nonchalant. Of course, her son knows Hank's location. Of course, Brooks Badger, this cartoon character, would have such information. Questions pile into one another. She opens her mouth, and nothing comes out. Brooks raises his hands in mock surrender.

"I don't want to get in the middle of a family situation," he says. "Henry talks a lot. And yes, he was spying, but not on you, Jenna. It's about your boss. *The* Mr. Carlton Foxworthy of Foxworthy Solutions. He's been avoiding me."

She pictures Mr. Foxworthy in his usual pinstriped suit, a gold collar pin over a red power tie, sitting in a conference room with Brooks Badger and his wardrobe of flannel shirts. She asks, "What do you want with Mr. Foxworthy?"

"That's between him and me, if you don't mind. I hadn't planned to recruit Henry to spy on your calendar. If you must know, my plan was to move here, make your acquaintance, and find out where Mr. Foxworthy goes to lunch or hangs out after work, so I could talk to him."

She rewinds the past twenty-four hours. "Hold on. You move here, to this apartment complex, specifically to be my neighbor? How did you even know I was here?" Then she catches herself. Moving in six months ago, she posted photos of her new apartment and tagged the location. Her bio on the Foxworthy Solutions website touts her as Mr. Foxworthy's assistant. Someone who is stalking Mr. Foxworthy might have concluded that knowing Jenna was the key to tracking his movements.

"I know it seems like overthinking," he says, "but I like preparing. It's half the fun." Brooks turns and looks around the courtyard. "To be fair, I needed a new place to live anyway because my cabin wasn't working out. I might have moved to this complex even if you weren't here, but I like the unit and the rent is reasonable."

"And your job?"

"London Industries was doing pay cuts, so I left. I'm currently between jobs, but security positions are easy to come by. I even paid my rent a year in advance."

"And my ex-husband?"

He holds out his arms as if to push her away. "All I know is what I just said. The rest is between you and Henry. He talks a lot, and there are things I shouldn't know."

"Tell me."

His shoulders sag, and he rubs a calloused hand across his face. He's thinking on the fly now. "Tell you what," he says. "Let me know when your boss leaves the building tomorrow, where he has appointments and such. After he and I conclude our business, I'll fill you in on what Henry knows about your husband's location."

"You should already know Mr. Foxworthy's appointments. Henry saw my calendar."

"It's filled with abbreviations he didn't understand." Brooks looks at the sky and appears to study the clouds. "It's better you don't know anything else."

She rattles off his Monday routine from memory, and Brooks Badger smiles. As the words spill out, it feels like she's lighting a fuse.

\*\*\*

That night, Jenna makes Sunday tacos. Henry takes a plate to his room and closes his door, insisting he has homework for the coming week. Jenna spends a minute or two at his bedroom door, hoping to hear whispers of conversation. There is only silence. She wants to ask about Hank but ends up falling asleep on the couch. For some reason, it feels better to hear news of her ex-husband from a stranger.

But is Brooks Badger a stranger? He feels more like an accomplice.

Monday comes in a rush. Henry is off to school early, and she gets to the office around seven-thirty. Mr. Foxworthy rolls in around nine, his suit jacket buttoned, shoes shined like a gym floor on prom night. Jenna's desk is just outside his office door, and he stops to ask about her weekend.

"Fairly boring," she says.

"Good. Good," he says, his mind elsewhere. "Listen, hold my calls for an hour. I need to clean up a few loose ends."

Mr. Foxworthy has a rotating set of girlfriends and sometimes takes long lunches to points unknown. He is close to Jenna's age, early forties, and once called her Miss Moneypenny, as if she was the handsome secretary with a hopeless crush and he was James Fucking Bond. The company employs five other financial planners who handle taxes, estate planning, and the like. Mr. Foxworthy dabbles in crypto currency and precious metals. His first name is really Carlton, and he corrects anyone who calls him Carl. As he closes his office door, her heart races.

Will Brooks Badger will show up here? Foxworthy Solutions occupies a suite of offices on the second floor of a three-story building. Several other businesses are tenants, and a security officer on the first floor makes visitors sign in. Jenna will get a call if someone wants to come up, so for now she dives into the office routine. Mr. Foxworthy has a late morning conference call with a Chamber of Commerce business development group, lunch with a regional precious metals broker, and tonight he'll teach a personal finance course at George Wythe Community

College, where he also picks up girls. The "loose ends" from this morning probably involve a weekend conquest.

At noon, Mr. Foxworthy emerges from his office, still buttoned up and freshly scrubbed. He asks Jenna to print two copies of his lunchtime briefing for the precious metals broker. She stands at the copier as paper falls into two separate slots. She puts his presentation in a clear plastic binder with a black plastic spine.

"Here you go, sir."

"Thanks."

She returns to her desk and jiggles her computer mouse. The screen comes to life. A new email has arrived.

SECURITY ALERT

Security is monitoring a suspicious individual in the parking lot. At this time, there is no reason to be alarmed. This individual has been told to leave the lot. He is in the process of relocating to the street. Out of an abundance of caution, please avoid this individual if you are outside.

A photo is attached to the email. She opens it and sees Brooks Badger's pickup. He is partially visible in the driver's seat. She looks at the presentation in her hand and remembers the clear plastic binder with the black plastic spine that burned up in her fire pit. Mr. Foxworthy takes his copy and walks out the door, whistling a nameless tune.

She freezes.

Rationalizes.

Security says there is no reason to be alarmed.

*When this is over, I'll know where Hank is. That is what matters.*

Twenty minutes pass. Jenna allows herself to think that Brooks Badger met Mr. Foxworthy on the sidewalk and had a tense but productive conversation. Mr. Foxworthy will return with a sheepish grin and a story about a strange man who wanted to resolve a misunderstanding. *A tempest in a teapot, Moneypenny.* Security never sent a follow-up email about a suspicious person, so nothing must have happened. She walks to the break room for coffee, wanting to know if others have been outside. But the room is vacant. Everyone is busy.

She returns to her desk and finds two police officers standing there, a tall man and a woman with black hair tied into a bun. The woman fires a series of questions, asking if this is Carl Foxworthy's office, if any clients had been angry with him, if he expressed any concern for her safety. Finally, Jenna puts on her most innocent face and asks what happened.

"You're scaring me," she says. Which is true, but not how they're thinking.

"There was an incident about ten minutes ago," the woman says. "Mr. Foxworthy was shot a few blocks from here."

Jenna plows ahead, finding that switch she used in an earlier life, allowing her to go on automatic pilot. "Oh my God, no. Security sent us an alert about a suspicious individual, but they said not to be concerned about it."

The guy frowns and shakes his head. "Yeah, that's what they said."

"Is Mr. Foxworthy okay?"

"I'm afraid he's deceased, ma'am. We don't believe the shooter is in the area. The incident occurred outside a nearby restaurant where Mr. Foxworthy intended to eat lunch."

Jenna sits down. She wants to act shocked, but she's more pissed than anything. Her son might have exchanged emails with Brooks Badger. The police always find those trails.

"We're trying to figure out why this happened," the woman says.

Jenna shrugs. "He had a lot of girlfriends."

The cops look at each other. Then the woman says, "Let's start with that."

***

Everyone gathers in the conference room, hollowed-eyed and hushed. There is general agreement to close the office until further notice. The police say everyone can leave, but first they want to question each employee. Jenna volunteers to go first, still role-playing the shocked assistant. As a girl, she polished her routine before social workers and court officers as someone forced into violence as a last resort. When she applied for her old job as a counselor for troubled youths, she wrote on the application: *I can see right through these kids. I used to be one.*

She plays the game with the two police officers. No, she's not aware of a suspicious person trying to see her boss. Financial planning is a boring business. Everyone is friendly. The police describe a man who could be Brooks Badger and Jenna says, no, that doesn't sound familiar.

"I keep Mr. Foxworthy's calendar on my computer," she says, calling it up on her screen. "I just looked at it Sunday night. That was last night, wasn't it? My gosh, I'm all mixed up."

The male detective thanks her. He has a heavy, hound dog face and seems to have lost the ability to smile.

It is close to noon before she returns to the apartment. She finds Henry sitting on the couch. He's hunkered forward, staring at the floor. "I didn't go to school today."

She grabs his bony shoulders. "Hey. Look at me."

His cheeks shine with tears. Jenna tries to hold his gaze and shakes him. He goes limp, and she imagines Mr. Foxworthy falling like a puppet with cut strings, dead on the sidewalk. "We need to have an adult conversation," she says. "I know you looked at my calendar. I know Mr. Badger wanted to see my boss."

"The dude's in my bedroom."

Henry's door is half open. Brooks Badger sits on the edge of the bed, hands in his lap, head down like a scolded child. Without looking up, he begins to speak. "You wondered why I took the time to move here. I'm what they call a prepper. Some say survivalist, but I don't like that term. I like to plan things out. I'm very interested in acquiring gold for when the economy collapses. It will happen, even if people don't believe it. Your boss deals in gold, but he swindled me. I wasted a lot of money, and he never came through. This happened to my friends, too. He's a shyster, that man."

"I'll concede the point."

"I shot him from a distance and got away clean. The police won't come here." He looks up and smiles. "Henry says that man denied you a promotion. He says you mumble about how you want to slap him around."

She didn't realize the words leaked out.

"Henry should come with me for the time being," Brooks says. "Friends and I have land in North Carolina along the water. It's an old site with coastal defense artillery installations. I avoid saying bunker because it perpetuates the stereotype of people like me, who prepare for the worst that we know is coming. But yeah, it's a bunker."

An old strength rises. Jenna resists the urge to grab that turkey neck and shake it. "Henry will go nowhere. I am his mother."

"He wants to run away, and he'll do it sooner or later. This way, he's with adults and not hitchhiking or some fool thing."

"Do not tell me how to handle my son."

"He's growing up, Jen."

The voice inside her head no longer screams. It's her old voice now. Calm and cold. The voice that came with punching kids in the dark, squaring off in a restroom, being fast with her fists. Throat punching bullies. Brooks Badger presents her with two clear options. The police have a photo of his truck, so he'll get arrested, and she and Henry will get caught up in it. Or he will escape and bide his time before returning to kill Henry and her. Or he'll have someone else kill them. They both know too much.

"Your gun," she says. "Where is it?"

He points to the floor. A rifle sits on the carpet with the bolt open. She steps forward and picks it up.

"No one touches my gun," he says with a gentle smile. "Don't do something you'll regret."

She smashes the butt of the gun into his face and feels the satisfying crack of cartilage. Blood pours from his nose. He gasps, falls back, and fumbles in his pocket. He pulls out a small black object and presses a button. Electricity crackles.

She torques his wrist, and the stun gun falls to the floor. Brooks launches himself off the bed, but he goes for his gun instead of her. Men and their guns. As he grabs the stock, she rams a knee into his groin. He mumbles "bitch" as she throws him across the room. His head knocks against the corner of the dresser, and he falls in a heap. The screaming inside her head won't stop. She once killed a girl in juvie. A girl who thought Jenna was small and quiet. A girl who died in a restroom stall and whose murder remains unsolved to this day. Even Hank never knew that. Her son sure as hell doesn't.

She plants a foot on Brooks's throat and presses. His face turns red. His hands slap at her leg, but she doesn't move. As his body goes limp, a gasp comes from behind her. Henry stands in the doorway, his face drained of color.

"Mom?"

"Fuck. Tell me where your father is."

"He's—Shit, mom. He's in jail in New Mexico. I found out on Google. I just wanted to see him."

The stench of shit fills the bedroom. Henry ducks his head outside the room and retches. Then he swings back inside to finish the job. A foul, brown batter spills onto the carpet.

"Get it together, Henry. You know of a utility tunnel that runs under this complex, right? I saw you messaging with your friends. Tell me you know of the tunnel. Tell me."

"Yeah, but..."

"Wipe your mouth. Listen up." She rummages in the dead man's pockets and finds his keys. The stench nearly knocks her over. "This asshole just moved in, right? He must have big boxes. I saw you using a hand truck. Go through the tunnel and get up to his apartment. Make sure no one sees you. Bring back the hand truck and the biggest box you can find. Return through the tunnel, not across the courtyard."

Henry turns to go, then stops. "You didn't even bother to look for dad. You didn't want to find him."

"I'm aware. Now get going."

Four days later, Jenna splurges for white birch wood at the hardware store and gathers dead branches in the courtyard for kindling. Across the way, yellow police tape is still stretched across Brooks Badger's door. It is unusually warm for November, and one of Jenna's neighbors has fired up a gas grill. He's barrel-chested with a lumberjack beard. She waves while Henry strikes a match.

She settles into a camp chair as her son feeds the fire, poking and prodding. "That's enough," she says. "Sit still. I'm not done."

"There is more to the story?"

"There is."

"Are there pictures?"

"I'd have to sort through boxes."

Henry smiles. "You and your gang. Women from cell block H who terrorized the other girls."

"Terrorized is a five-dollar word. I went to a tough school. I understand that cyber-bullying is a thing these days, but it doesn't compare to getting shoved up against a locker. Those vents cut into your head. We were scared, and we fought back."

"You got shoved up against a locker?"

She stirs the fire. "A few times, then it stopped."

"When the black T-shirt girls intervened on your behalf?"

"Yes. They became my friends, my protectors. And I protected them. Then it got out of hand, which is why a few of us ended up in juvenile court on assault charges, which is why I lost a couple of years of my life eating institutional food and watching my back when I should have been going to proms and football games. I wouldn't recommend the path." She isn't ready to tell Henry how she killed that girl in the bathroom stall. They found her with a Philips-head screwdriver stuck halfway into her ear.

"And you really went to the gym and hit a heavy bag with boxing gloves?" Henry asks.

"That was much later, when you were young. Your father thought I was into Pilates."

"Why did you stop?"

"I can't afford the gym. I can barely afford you."

Henry stirs the fire. "I could get a part-time job. Ever since COVID, restaurants need the help." He holds a breath, exhales. "Do you ever want to visit dad?"

It turns out that Hank was hauling drugs from Mexico, towing a trailer with otherwise conventional loads of dry goods. His lawyer says he was set up. The charges went to federal court because Hank crossed state lines, and she was able to download the affidavit that described the charges. The court papers said Hank had been monitored on previous hauls and "had realized significant financial gain." He never spent that money on his family.

"Visiting your father is not high on my list," she says. "But if we go, we go together. You run away to visit him on your own, don't bother coming back." Henry sinks back into his chair. His phone is on the ground. Jenna grabs a branch and stirs the fire.

Sparks fly.

# THE BOXER
## Bill W. Morgan

His right hand is a useless club, and his front teeth feel as though only sheer will holds them in. He stares across the ring. His opponent looks just as bad as he does, one eye swollen, the other trying to focus. There is a stabbing pain at the base of his skull when Chop runs the ice bag across his shoulders. He takes another sip of water, and it tastes like acid going down.

"What in the holy fuck are you doing, Ray!" the voice comes at him from somewhere off in a train tunnel and he tries to focus.

"He's eating too many punches. I'll let it go another round, but if he doesn't show movement, I'm stopping it."

Chop turns to yell at the referee, which gives Ray another second to force his eyes to see true. No good, the squinting makes him ill.

"Throw a fucking punch out there. You don't, and I'll get in the ring and do it for you!"

He hears the bell, and then Chop pulls him off the stool. Two steps out and he was already eating punches. How did the kid get over here so fast? *Punch.* Was that a right or a left? *Punch, punch.*

He falls back into the corner and covers up. Chop is yelling at him. The referee is so close he can smell his knockoff cologne.

"Duck the fucking hook!" he hears and does. The kid's open.

His entire left side is an open door waiting for a fist to fill it. Ray throws a lazy jab, then an uppercut that kisses the tender spot of his opponent's flank. Something in his left hand cracks, pain shoots up his arm, wakes him up. He throws a stiff jab, then another, backs the kid off enough to think. He ducks a jab, swings, misses, throws a left cross. He catches the kid coming in, the force knocks them both back. He sees the kid wobble, smells blood. The kid takes another step back, then one forward, then he's doing the dance.

Ray drops his left shoulder, digs in, and throws a punch low to the kid's stomach, hears him belch out air. He pushes off and throws a jab, then a left cross. The kid fights back. He swings and hits air, then a one two and Ray sees little pinpricks of light dancing in his vision. Bloody nose, blurred vision, but Ray is running on instinct. He moves forward, sets the trap with a weak jab that has the kid flicking his head to the right, then Ray throws the surprise party, an uppercut from somewhere south of hell. He waits for the connection, the abrupt halt of momentum, but it doesn't come. His arm is now in an awkward place, and that same instinct tells him he's fucked. He steps back and pulls his arms in close, but midway through someone flicks the light switch, and a split second later shuts them off completely.

Ray opens his eyes and lets the sudden wave of pain wash over him. It settles at the base of his skull and digs in deep, like an ice pick probing all the tender spots of his brain. He hears the count, eight, nine, too late. He rolls to his side and looks between the ropes at the front row, trying to focus on any of the faces.

He doesn't remember the journey to the locker room or Chop taking off his gloves. At the door, someone collects the wraps Chop cut off. His hands feel like hams taped to his wrists. He can't even make a fist. Chop is pacing the room. Ray sees him, and the phantoms that follow him.

"Stop." Ray begs, but Chop continues to pace the room.

Someone knocks at the door, and Chop jumps. Ray tries to stand, but his legs have gone out for the evening. He leans back against the row of lockers, ignoring the latch digging into his shoulder. Chop opens the door and leans out, not letting whomever into the room. Ray sees the man briefly, well dressed in a black-on-black suit with a gold and diamond tiepin. He gives Ray a nod, but it's not friendly. Ray thinks he knows him, has seen him before, but exhaustion stops the thought from going beyond vague recognition. Reporter maybe, maybe not considering the fight was a tune up on a non-televised Sunday card. Gone are the days of media frenzy over Ray "Tick Tick" Boomer. Ten years ago, he was at the top of the food chain. Now he can't even get a decent meal with what they pay.

Chop slams the door. He's more agitated than before. He walks toward Ray as if he's going to hit him.

Go ahead, Ray thinks, I won't feel it.

"Hit the shower, Champ," Chop says instead.

It feels like he's being sandblasted. Say what you want, the showers at The Provincial Hall are no joke. With each minute under the water, Ray feels more like himself. By the end, the knots in his back have loosened, and the sharp pain in his head has retreated to a dull ache.

There is no media waiting for them when they exit the locker room. The long hallway, much shorter now that the fight is the over, is empty. Ray takes his bag from Chop as he hustles forward toward the exit. Ray waits, leaned up against the wall a few feet from the exit, pacing his breathing, trying to get his head straight. He wants to see the kid and the beating he put on him. Wants reassurance that he's not the only one feeling like hammered shit. Wants to size him up for a possible rematch, even though he knows it's a long shot.

Two people stop him as he finally moves toward the exit. A man in his mid-twenties asks for an autograph while his friend pulls his phone out for a picture. Ray watches Chop push through the exit doors into the parking lot at the rear of the building. He's reaching for the pen when he hears the steady *pop pop* of gunshots. He's at the door when he sees a car speed by. Two men, driver ducked low, but the passenger still has the gun out the window. Something on his chest glints off the overhead marquee as they pass.

Outside, a small crowd has gathered around Chop, who leans up against the building nursing his own war wound.

Five days later, Ray steps outside of Chilton's Funeral Home with the remains of his best friend in a plastic box. He spends the day carrying his friend around to all the spots that he could remember he liked. Doing the things they used to do. A quick drink at the One and Done, sitting at the park watching the pickup games while eating a steak sandwich from Slaps Barbeque, finally an ice from the vendor on Elm Avenue.

When the sun finally dips low over the buildings, Ray tips the open box into the Tallyho River and watches Chop take his last ride. Chop had no family, father walked out, mother gone, a wife who found something better, and no kids that Ray knew of. All Chop had in this world was a room at a hotel and a few boxes of memories. Ray did his best to memorialize his friend, but in the end, even that felt cheap.

Cops say they got spotty accounts. One witness says a blue sports car, another claims it was a black sedan. The crowd was too busy looking at their phones to pay mind to an old man as he took a bullet. Ray's own memories are hazy, but he remembers something flashing off the man with the gun as they drove by, thinks he knows the man, but can't remember his name or prove he pulled the trigger. He tells the detectives what he can, and they nod. No way the case can be built on the hazy memories of a punchy fighter less than an hour after he took a world-class ass beating. In the end, they tell him, unless a suspect comes gift wrapped to the station, the odds are nil he'll be caught, but they'll keep trying, they always keep trying.

He spends two weeks swimming in booze before Eddie the promoter knocks on his door. Eddie steps back when Ray opens the door and asks if he could speak to him in the hallway. Ray throws on a shirt, winces at the stink of himself, and steps out of the room.

"How's going?" Eddie asks in his choppy, nervous way.

Ray shrugs.

Eddie stokes a cigar and flicks the match down the hallway. Ray feels the bile in his stomach creeping up his throat.

"So you know, gotta a fight if ya want," Eddie says.

Ray leans against the wall, lets the coolness of the drafty hallway tickle his neck. He uses his tongue to press on his teeth, feeling the loose ones and the soreness of his jaw. Chop would have told him it was too soon to take another fight, if he should ever fight again. You have to let the wounds heal naturally, else they come back twice as bad, but Ray needs the money. He has maybe a week before he's homeless. His landlord is already circling his room like a vulture around fresh kill.

"Who is it?" Ray asks, pressing his tongue against the sorest tooth until it stops hurting.

"Same kid wants a rematch. Says he went soft on you. He wants to break your spirit this time. Good money," Eddie answers with a twitchy smile.

"Never got paid for the last one."

"Chop got the money, not much though, not after Sims and Harris."

Ray pushes off the wall. For weeks, he's tried to remember the names.

"Who?" Ray asks, trying to keep the malice in his tone minimal. Eddie flinches slightly, enough to send the gray ash from his cigar tumbling down his shirtfront to the floor.

"Sims Barker, Harris what's his name."

Ray flashes back to the night of the fight and the two men in the car. He didn't know the man with the gun, but the driver he knew was Sims. He had seen Chop talking to him on a few occasions while Ray worked the bag, but he never got a straight answer from Chop when he asked why.

"And?"

"And what? They split before Chop got, you know. Says they'd catch up."

Ray looks past Eddie to the stairwell. He's thinking, but the thoughts come in and go out too fast for him to settle on just one. It's like the flicker pics of an old film, one image then another, with a bit of blackness between. His head begins to hurt.

"I'll take the fight soon, though. No three months to prepare. I'm ready now," Ray says.

"Gonna have to be at least a couple weeks. You got medical suspension still, both you do."

"Fine. How much?"

"Don't know, but the purse will be good."

"I need money now."

Eddie sucks in a deep breath then stuffs the wet end of his cigar into his mouth, tucking it into his cheek like chaw. He looks around as though what they are discussing is suddenly illegal, then reaches into his pocket and pulls out a roll of bills.

"Look, I'll float ya three, good enough? You pay me back first thing, though."

Ray nods agreement. Eddie peels three bills off the roll and hands them to Ray. It was enough, enough to pay his room rent, enough for some food.

"I will." He says with genuine gratitude.

Eddie puts the bankroll back into his pocket and turns, then turns back. He looks nervous, as if bad news had crossed his mind.

"Ah, hate to ask Ray, but who's going to be your corner man?"

Ray thinks for a moment. He needed a corner man, no doubt. The state athletic commission requires at least one. It might be a local fight, but they still had rules.

"Don't know."

"Pay me back my three and five percent of your purse and I'll do it."

"You've cornered a fight before?" Rays asks.

"Two brothers and a couple of prospects before I wised up and went to the business side."

"That'd be fine then."

Ray watches him go, then walks to the other end of the hall and pays his rent for the next three weeks, at fifty per. He spends another fifty on food that requires actual cooking, not just popping the lid off the can. Several times, he takes and puts back a bottle of whiskey, every time saying there'd be enough time for that after the fight.

His first run felt like a hammer hitting him in every sore spot he had. Three blocks in, he begs off and walks home defeated. The next day, he pushes until he gets three miles, spitting bile and vomit the whole way. He doesn't worry so much about bag work or the science, that stuff is the last to leave you, but stamina needs to be bribed and threatened before it comes around, and every bit of the journey is a walk through hell.

Eddie comes back a week after his first visit and gives him the date and has him sign a contract. It would be at the same location, same locker room, only piece missing would be Chop. Ray asks about Sims Barker, whether he'll be in the crowd and Eddie tells him Sims Barker is co-promoting the fight. Ray hides his anger well enough that Eddie doesn't catch on.

They plan to meet up a few nights before the fight to talk strategy. Eddie gives Ray his number and only laughs when Ray tells him he doesn't have a phone to call it with.

Ray spends the next weeks beating his body into shape. He goes heavy on the bag. With every punch, he hears Chop's voice in his head, the gravel of it. He hears disappointment and encouragement and relishes the sting he feels when a punch hits solid and sends the bag swinging. Few bother him at the gym. He's not used to working alone, but he's unable to trust anyone else.

Three nights before the fight, someone knocks at his door. He thinks it's going to be Eddie, come to talk about his role in the corner, but instead he opens the door and Sims Barker and the other man are standing there. Sims makes as if he's going to walk in, but Ray steps out into the hallway instead.

"Look at this guy, can't hardly tell he took a beating not two months ago." Sims smiles at his friend, who nods. Ray plays dumb to it all.

"Can I help you?"

"Sure can, Ray." Sims pulls a handkerchief from his pocket and dabs at the sweat on his brow. "I think you know who I am. I just wanted to come by and make sure you're ready for Saturday."

"Ready as I'll ever be." Ray says and looks past Sims to the other man, sees the tiepin, sees the sunlight from the hall window dancing off the large diamond. He wonders if he only wears his gun with the black-on-black suit.

"Good, good. We want this to be an amazing fight, like the last one." Sims says.

"Only a few more rounds." The man says with a laugh.

"I didn't catch your name?" Ray asks.

"Didn't offer it, but since you asked, it's Randal."

Ray nods. He wants to ask the man if it's hard to shoot at someone from a moving car, but decides he'll wait until the night of the fight to ask.

"Ray, that last fight was, well, less lucrative than we had hoped, and we really can't have that happen again. I was hoping we could have a private conversation and work out a bit of business beforehand." Sims steps forward to put a hand on Ray's shoulder but stops short when he notices the look in Ray's eyes. The look that says, I'll rip that arm off if it touches me.

"What, you want me to play the heavy bag?"

"No, nothing like that." Sims replies, shock in his voice.

"Then what?"

"Merely a good show and, at the end of the fight, your hand gets raised in victory. Think of it, best two out of three, a trilogy, not many fighters have a good trilogy."

"The kid's gonna take a dive?" Rays says, letting the disgust come heavy in his tone.

"Jesus no, I said no dives."

"Good thing this punchy dipshit's a fighter and not a fireman. Half the city'd be burning. Either you win the fight, or you never fight again, understand."

"Calm down Randal. Ray, I hate to continue bringing it up because I know it was a rough time, but before that last fight, certain assurances were promised but never fulfilled, and that cost me a lot of money. More importantly, it cost me respect and trust. I don't expect you to do anything about that now. After all, what's in the past cannot be changed. We can only look to the future now."

"And that is?"

"You win this fight. You win, understand, or what my associate put so bluntly will indeed happen."

"I plan on winning," Ray says coldly.

"Fine, fine. Look, we'll catch up the night of, before the fight. Hash out any changes that might come up, okay?"

It was a statement more than a question, and they let the words hang until the silence became unbearable. Sims finally walks away but Randal lingers, sizing Ray up the way any opponent would, enough to make Ray want to hit him.

Eddie shows up the next day. This time, Ray moves aside and lets him in. They talk strategy, what little there will be. Eddie knows how Ray works, has seen enough of his fights. The sweet part of the science was never in Ray's toolbox. He wasn't a textbook fighter, just a hammer Chop pointed in the right direction.

His head is hurting, so most of what Eddie says gets lost in the steady thrum deep in his skull. Every move carries with it a bit of nausea, like a chaser after a shot of whiskey. In the end, he agrees with whatever Eddie says just to get him out of the room so he can take a handful of aspirin and lay down.

Ray doesn't see him again until fight night. Eddie's already there in the locker room when Ray shows. Ray drops his duffel on the floor next to a row of lockers and sits heavily on the bench.

"You all right?" Eddie asks, eyeing Ray suspiciously from the corner of the room as he packs his supplies in the blue bucket at his feet.

"Yeah, little sore, that's all."

Ray cranes his neck, feels tendons stretch and pop. It gives him some relief from the steady headache. Eddie lifts the bucket and comes over to sit with Ray.

"We need to get your hands wrapped. We got about ninety minutes before the first round, so..."

"Not yet. I'm going to change out. Catch up in thirty, cool?"

"Sounds good. I gotta bag up some ice, anyway."

Ray watches him walk out, blue bucket banging against his knee. He wonders if anyone else will use the locker room. He scans the other lockers and sees they are all empty, like last time. Main event fighters always got the private rooms at the back of the Provincial, while the openers and mid-card fighters had to stake claim to the open locker room right off the main floor. Down the hall in a room just like this one, his opponent is getting ready. Ray wonders if he is nervous. Ray's had thirty pro fights and double that in amateurs and still he gets nervous, or maybe it's something else. Maybe it's that for all those fights only one person was ever in his corner, ever took the time to tell him he was good enough. Maybe he's missing his friend like an amputee misses a limb.

Before he can finish the thought, someone knocks at the door. He sees two shadows moving around behind the frosted glass and already knows who's going to walk in only milliseconds before they do.

Sims comes in, all smiles followed by Randal. Sims is dressed in a gray suit that makes him look like a banker. Randal is wearing the same suit he wore the night of the first fight, black on black, the diamond tiepin catching the overhead light in just the right way.

"Ready champ?" Sims asks.

Ray watches Randal as he shuts the door and flips the lock. Ray wonders if he still has the gun he used to shoot Chop, or if it found its way into the Tallyho River.

"Sure." Ray replies, leaning down to unzip the duffel.

"Excellent, good to know. I want to make sure we don't have a repeat of last time."

"Maybe you'll last longer than it takes to cook a steak," Randal says.

"It's just that we had some friends of ours betting you'd win that last fight handily. I mean, the kid's a soup can, nothing more than a club fighter. Christ, he looks out of shape when he's in shape, so we figured you'd at least show up."

"Is that what Chop told you, that I would drop the kid. How many rounds did he say it would take?" Ray asks. He reaches into the bag and pulls out his trunks, black to hide the blood, always black. His head is throbbing again, steady with the beat of his heart. He remembers where he had seen Randal now, days before the fight. When he walked in on him talking to Chop, but he wasn't wearing his black-on-black suit then, only a pullover sweater and jeans, like every other hoodlum hustling for money.

Sims smiles, a sly smile that barely hides his hatred.

"That was unfortunate," he says.

Ray reaches back into the bag and notices every time he does that, Randal's hand dips slightly to his right hip. He also notices that his suit jacket is still buttoned. He's smart, he doesn't want to advertise he's carrying a gun.

"Yes, it was," Randal replies in a cold monotone.

Ray pulls his shoes out and drops them at his feet and then reaches into the bag again. He wonders if Chop was slick enough to game these two that easily. Get them believing Ray could hold his own, knowing he didn't stand a chance. Chop wasn't a genius by any stretch, but he was smart enough to catch on when Ray's gears started slipping. Chop told him he needed to stop the fight game because no one was going to be there if he went punch dumb, but Ray had nothing but boxing, so he begged Chop to let it be. Told him he needed a break and then after six months, when nothing had changed—only gotten worse—he begged Chop to set up one more fight. Maybe for the first time ever, Chop had bet against him.

"But that's in the past. Today is a new day," Sims says with all the bravado of a used car salesman lying his way through selling a lemon. He's turned toward Randal, so he doesn't see the blow coming.

It lands at the base of his neck, and Ray hears something crunch. Sims falls fast, hitting the bench with his chest, then falling to the floor. The force knocks the wind from him with a throaty *huh* sound, and Ray knows he won't ever get it back. Randal is already reaching for his gun, one hand expertly popping the button on his jacket. Ray has to step over Sims's outstretched legs, but he drops the hammer in time and catches Randal's hand before he can clear the gun from the holster, then throws a left hook. His left hand was never as strong as his right, but it didn't much matter when you punch like a freight train and catch the chin. Randal buckles, forgetting about the gun, and Ray follows him down. He grabs at Randal, who is conscious enough to know something bad is happening but not enough to stop it. Ray leans down hard, a hand on each side of Randal's head, and cranks his neck to the left until it breaks.

He's sure he's broken something in his left hand. He can feel it swelling already, but he ignores the pain and starts pulling Randal away from the wall and into the little bathroom at the rear of the locker room. From his hip, he pulls the pistol, carries it back into the locker room, and drops it into his duffel bag along with the old hammer. Next is Sims, who watches the ceiling blankly as he's pulled into the bathroom.

Someone is knocking at the door, and from the look of the shadow on the other side, it's Eddie. He works fast, crowding the bodies into a heap on the tile floor of the shower stall and locking the bathroom door before he closes it. Eddie is now calling for him.

He takes a moment to center his thoughts. Flexing his hands open and closed, feeling the knuckles and bones in his left-hand protest. He continues to flex until the pain lessens.

He hopes he dies in the ring, goes out on his shield as Chop used to say. There is no way to guarantee it, but he thinks he can hedge the bet in his favor. He hopes the kid is ready for a fight because Ray wants a battle. A war that will have everybody on their feet. He wants to give them something to remember, something legendary. And if he does survive the fight he's got Randal's pistol as an exit strategy, another way to go out on his shield.

He rounds his shoulders and cranes his neck left and right until the pain in his head goes away, then confidently walks to the door and flips the lock.

# RED DUST EXPRESS
## K.L. Abrahamson

The train pulled out of Arusha at four o'clock or near enough to make the tourists sit up at the fact they were almost on time. Red dust swirled through Guy Radner's open compartment window, obscuring the view of Mount Kilimanjaro as the town's red dirt streets fell behind. Ahead were only the tracks and the long red road like a scar eastward to Moshi and the blue-white bulk of the mountain and then south-east to Dar es Salaam on the coast. Stick-figure women carried water and market goods on their heads along the road toward distant villages. Some herded children before them. Men rode upright bicycles carrying huge burlap bags of coal balanced precariously behind them as the train picked up speed. The hypnotic clickity-clack rumble seeped deep into Guy's marrow, reverberating like troubling memories.

Or guilt.

Guy settled back on the uncomfortable red vinyl bench seat meant to fold down to become a bed and let the dust-tinged wind blow into his face. The dust itched in his day's growth of beard and tasted of iron, but the wind smelled ancient—carrying reminders of the acacia, cattle dung, and coal fires the earliest humans had smelled. Arusha and its ramshackle wooden buildings fell behind and small villages of mud and thatch boma sprang like warts on the landscape. A trio of giraffes silhouetted their long necks against the sky and the sunset painted red streaks down the mountain. The sun fell quickly this close to the equator, racing to escape the day. The train did its part, thankfully picking up speed and sending the plain's red dust swirling so the sun was blood red and the villages and their livestock barely black smudges on the unforgiving landscape that so many in the world romanticized.

Africa was just another place that could bite you in the ass if you didn't have a plan and a good one.

Guy shifted in his seat, wishing the damned train could go faster.

The red dust quickly layered the seat across from him. He shoved his bag under the seat and praised whatever god ruled this forsaken land that he had the compartment to himself. That, at least, *was* part of the plan.

If it could be pulled off.

He'd been in Tanzania for two weeks now, secretly providing security to the archaeological dig at Olduvai Gorge. The head of the dig, Doc Jack Springer, had called him in from New York when, as he said, "things got interesting."

But two weeks was two weeks too long in this drought-stricken landscape of blood red rock, scorpions, and thorn bushes. He'd done the tourist safari thing as part of his cover, but before he'd ever arrived, he'd learned more about the old bones of Olduvai than he'd ever wanted. The two weeks had been spent feeling trapped between the old stone and the weight of the sky, like a butterfly some kid pressed in the leaves of a book.

He'd met Springer nine years ago in 1995 at an art auction reception in New York when he was still working for Brinks. Not long afterward, he'd left the company to form his own small, exclusive security team, specializing in personal protection for the elite and security for items of great value. Think artwork, precious jewelry, and antiquities that the great museums of the world loaned to lesser institutions. He had established a good team of tried-and-true men and women, but Springer made his unusual request to have Guy provide direct service.

So, this was the first time in years that Guy had been in the field. He planned on it being the last.

Springer was in the compartment next to Guy's, carrying a carefully prepared box of bones. Accompanying him was young Richard McPhee, a burly youngster who was one of Springer's grad students. The two of them together should provide protection against all but the most heavily armed robbers. Guy was here as backup—Springer's last line of defense known only to him—seemingly disconnected from the archaeologists.

The sky turned blood red, and the voices of the tourists oohing and aahing in the next compartment were picked up by the wind and carried through Guy's open window. He leaned back and closed his eyes, the weight of his bag pressing comfortably against his heels. Soon he'd be on a flight home, and this would all be over. The murmur of Springer and McPhee's voices carried through the wall behind Guy, so all was well.


After the brief stop at Moshi and the bustle of men in dusty long pants and short-sleeved white shirts and women in colorful sarongs disembarking or climbing aboard with burdens of produce and bleating and clucking animals, he heard Springer's compartment door open. The two men's voices came through the wall, and Guy got up to check whether things were all right. In the dimly lit passage, McPhee had just closed the door behind him. The interior lamps of the train glowed green on his blond hair. His khaki clothes were dull with dust. He glanced once down the passage in Guy's direction but didn't see him behind the curtain on his compartment door window. McPhee headed away from Guy, toward the toilet at the end of the car, swaying to the train's motion and trying not to stagger against the compartment doors that lined the passage.

Guy sat next to the door, listening to McPhee's footsteps retreat over the omnipresent metal-on-metal clack and rumble of the tracks. The red dust filtered through the window and covered where he'd been sitting. The evening wind was cooler, but still scented with charcoal and manure.

Finally, footsteps returned, and Springer's compartment door opened. Guy glimpsed McPhee step inside. Settling back near the window, Guy stretched his legs across the aisle and rested his eyes.

A shout through the wall brought him staggering upright. The door of Springer's compartment slammed open.

"Help!" McPhee yelled. "A man's been killed."

Guy kicked his bag further under his seat and yanked open his door. McPhee swayed in his doorway, the whites of his eyes catching the light. His tanned skin had gone pale, and for a young man who liked to show off for the girls on the archaeology team, he was shaking.

"What is it, man?" Guy demanded.

"It's Jack—Doctor Springer! Someone's killed him!"

Guy shoved past McPhee into his compartment.

Same vinyl bench seating that doubled as bunks for sleeping as Guy had in his compartment except here someone had rolled out a sleeping bag on one bunk. On the other sprawled a man in bloody clothes.

Jack Springer wasn't a big man physically, but his vivid blue gaze and his energy had always left Guy amazed at the way he seemed much larger than his slim five-foot-eight. It was that charisma that had allowed him to attract and hold his crack team of paleoanthropologists at the dig. The same charisma had led Guy to agree to Springer's crazy scheme.

It was the skills of that team that had led to the discovery of a lifetime at Olduvai, the birthplace of humanity. That same discovery had led to Guy's recruitment to protect it.

Now Jack Springer was reduced to...this. A skin bag of flesh and bones and blood. All the energy had drained from the blue gaze that stared blankly at the metal compartment ceiling. A raw, wet cut stretched from ear to ear under his chin. Guy didn't need to check his pulse to know he was dead. The blood soaking Springer's clothes was clearly his own.

For a moment Guy allowed himself the luxury of sadness at the loss of a good man. Then he straightened and stepped up to the corpse.

No sign of defensive injury on the hands, though they were covered in blood. The walls had been caught in arterial spray. Clearly, his assailant had been deadly efficient, though Springer had lived long enough to try to stop his own bleeding. Blood on the floor—lots of it—but no footprints other than a boot print or two that likely belonged to Springer or McPhee.

It had been fast, and he'd been standing when he was cut. Any investigator worth his salt would know a cut like that would most likely have come from someone striking from behind, surprising him. Otherwise, surely there would be defensive wounds.

A stir came from the hallway and a murmur of voices. "What are you doing, Sir?"

Guy glanced over his shoulder. Through the open door, the passageway had filled with other passengers—locals and tourists roused by McPhee's yells. He still stood clutching the door as if he needed it to stand, but in minutes he'd composed himself and not allowed anyone else to enter. Beside him stood a porter—the slim, dark woman dressed in her maroon uniform.

"What has happened?" she asked.

"This man is dead. He's been murdered," Guy said as he examined the scene for evidence of the perpetrator. "How long until we reach the next large town where there are police detectives?"

The porter cocked her head. "Many hours, Sir. The last large police station was in Moshi. Now we must wait until Dar es Salaam for an investigation team. There *is* a railway police officer on board the train, Sir. I will get him."

She disappeared through the crowd.

"H—how could this happen?" McPhee asked. "He was fine

when I left. He said he'd get the bunks ready while I went to the toilet. I didn't even realize what had happened when I stepped back in because the lights were out…"

It was a good question. Guy hadn't heard their compartment door open until McPhee returned. "I'll go back into my compartment. I want you to try opening and closing the door as quietly as you can."

In his empty compartment, Guy sat down where he had been. "Whenever you're ready."

When he heard nothing other than the steel rails' roar, he finally went to the door. "You opened and closed the door?"

McPhee nodded. "Several times."

People still pressed around him.

"So someone could have gone in while you were in the toilet." That would widen the field of suspects considerably.

McPhee shrugged. Beyond him, the compartment's open window allowed wind and dust to invade the scene, placing a red-pink pall across the body. Guy stepped over the blood and tugged the window up.

Unlike the cloudy, smeared glass in his compartment, the window here was remarkably clear—as if someone had recently cleaned it. No fingerprints that Guy could see, but there was a bit of red on the edge of the sill that chipped off under his fingernail. "Was the window open when you went to the toilet?"

"I—I think so. Maybe. Maybe—I can't be sure." McPhee shook his head as if to shake the memory loose. "God, what's wrong with me?"

As useless as most witnesses.

The red was blood, Guy was certain. As if Springer had died next to the window. As if someone reached through when Springer least suspected it and cut his throat. The slow-moving African trains were once known to have people ride illegally on the roof. The culprit had likely done so and then entered the cabin and shifted Springer's body to the bed. In the brief time he'd had, had the culprit stolen the bones?

Guy glanced back at McPhee as the railway policeman arrived.

The officer was a tall, thin young man whose khaki uniform hung on him. Only the pulled-tight utility belt seemed to hold his trousers up. Close-cropped black hair fuzzed his narrow skull. Deep sockets hid his eyes and gaunt cheeks gave him a hungry look. The nameplate on his chest read A. Juma.

"What is wrong here?" he asked, puffing out his chest and drawing himself up to his full height—about the same as Guy's six feet. He stepped into the room.

"This man is dead—his throat cut. I think perhaps someone has moved the body," Guy said.

The officer spun around to the crowd. "Who was in this compartment?"

"Just me." McPhee raised his hand. "I'd just stepped out to the toilet. When I returned, I found him like this."

The officer pulled out a notebook. "And you are, Sir?"

When he'd gotten McPhee's particulars, the officer swung back to Guy. "And you? How are you involved?"

The agreement with Springer was that Guy would not disclose their connection. "I responded to the young man's call for help. Is there anything missing? Surely there must be a reason for the attack..."

McPhee stilled, and his face further paled, so his five-o'clock beard was a stark shadow on his face. "Fuck me, I forgot to check." He shoved into the room and Guy stepped outside. Juma—a constable by the lack of epaulettes on his shoulders, squeezed to one side as McPhee gingerly went down on his knees to check under the bunks. Careful of the blood pool, he shoved around a suitcase and valise, then poked his head under the bunks and sat up.

"It's not here. It's not here!" His voice rose three octaves. "The box. It's gone."

The twelve-by-twelve padded box carrying what amounted to Olduvai gold. The skull remains of what could be the missing link in human evolution—at least Springer had thought so. So had his team of paleoanthropologists and the people at SoCal Berkley after seeing the photos Springer faxed them. The contents Springer had engaged Guy to protect on the train.

He scrubbed his face. It didn't make the situation any better. No matter how many times it happened, the death of someone you knew was never good. But it wasn't part of the plan for Guy to disclose what he knew. Far better to keep his involvement a secret, as he had planned with Springer.

"Will someone please tell me what is going on?" the young constable asked. "What has gone missing?"

For a moment, it looked as if McPhee wasn't going to answer, but then he turned to the officer. "There was a box containing some valuable bone fragments. We were moving them to the museum in Dar es Salaam."

Which wasn't quite the truth, but it was the official story. Sure, a few bones were destined for Tanzania's national museum, but the truly ground-breaking bones were planned for elsewhere—leaving the country in Springer's carry-on bags.

"Bones?" the young female porter asked from beside Guy.

McPhee shook his head and sank down on his bunk. "Hominid bones. *Homo Habilis* from Olduvai, but earlier—unique. I'm part of the dig team. He..." He glanced at Springer's body and back to us. "He was the team leader. Doctor Jack Springer, paleoanthropologist." Olduvai, synonymous with the discovery of some of humans' earliest evolutionary ancestors.

Constable Juma at least knew enough to take the information down, though he didn't seem to know enough to clear the scene and keep his witnesses separate. But that was Africa, from what Guy had seen. Who knew how much training young Juma had?

"You boarded the train in Arusha?" Juma asked.

Guy edged back from the door, resuming the part of the bystander that he and Springer had planned.

"You!" The voice of young Juma stopped Guy short. "Where are you going? What have you to say for yourself?"

Guy turned back.

Not part of the plan.

Juma's dark brown gaze unexpectedly had zeroed in on Guy like a set of rifle sights.

"I was returning to my compartment. I don't want to be in your way." Guy went to turn away again.

"Where were you during the killing?"

Mentally about a million miles from here, but the youngster was proving he was better trained than Guy had expected. "I was in my compartment next door and had been since I climbed on the train. Until I heard this gentleman's yell for help."

He jotted this down in his notebook. "Your name?"

"Guy Radner."

"Identification, please."

With misgivings, he dug his passport out of his shirt pocket. Juma took the information down but didn't return the documents.

"What brings you to Tanzania?"

The train swayed under Guy as he considered the best answer. "The wildlife, of course. Ngorongoro Crater. I did visit Olduvai, as well, and met Mr. Springer. He showed me around the dig site." It was more or less the truth, for Guy had made a point of visiting the crater and had kept his time as brief as possible at the dig site. He'd posed as a tourist and Springer had shown him around. During that time, they had come up with the plan—a plan that was currently under assault.

He nodded and jotted down Guy's statement. "You may return to your compartment, but I will have more questions. Wait for me there."

The passage was still crowded, dark faces trying to catch a glimpse of the foreigner's death. Guy returned to his seat and closed the curtains on the compartment door's window. Then he went to the train window and peered out into the night—dust and wind be damned. The dust peppered his skin. The wind shoved him back. It would not be easy for someone to crawl along the roof and let themselves down into a compartment. Not impossible, but dangerous and difficult.

A man had died, and Guy was of mixed feelings. For all the death he'd seen in Vietnam, this one was a little closer to home. He might not have known Springer as well as he'd known his troop mates, but this death felt more intimate—and troubling. Guilt wasn't something new to him—those who returned stateside carried the guilt of surviving—but he had been retained to help Jack Springer.

The second time Guy met Springer, Guy's team was providing security for a religious icon that they had been hired to escort from an undisclosed location in Ukraine to New York for auction. Guy had built his company on discretion so that those who retained Guy's company could be confident that their shipments reached their destinations, no matter the shipment's provenance. That was why Springer had hired Guy. Hominid bones of human ancestors were the property of the Tanzanian government, as per the Tanzanian Antiquities Act of 1964, but Springer had other ideas.

And now the box of bones had disappeared.

The night wind blew, and the red dust continued to flow. The white, short-sleeved shirt Guy wore gradually absorbed a tinge of pink. From out in the passage, the voices of the passengers faded as people grew tired and returned to their berths. From Springer's compartment, the voices of Juma and McPhee rose and fell. At first there were simply questions, but then Juma surprised Guy again, by the thumps and bumps that suggested he searched the compartment. Then their conversation changed—Juma became accusatory while McPhee choked out his denial.

There were the sounds of a scuffle, and then a knock came at Guy's door. Juma entered without invitation, just as the sky began to lighten. The wind had changed—the cool of night replaced by a sultry breeze off the Indian Ocean. Sweat stood out on Guy's skin as he stood to meet the constable and wondered what McPhee had said.

"Yes, officer?"

Juma took off his cap, leaving a line across his smooth forehead. "Thank you for waiting."

As if Guy had anywhere else to go.

Juma rubbed his face as if he was almost relieved. "I realize this is most difficult for all involved, but the matter is resolved. The culprit caught."

"Really?" Guy asked, sinking down onto his seat. Juma perched on the other seat.

"At first, the type of wound made me think Rwandan Hutus had begun killing again, but the young man had the bones hidden in his bags. A bloody knife was found as well. It is most troubling."

Guy digested his words. "That is—most troubling, indeed. To think a man would kill his employer. Are you sure?"

Juma nodded. "There can be no doubt. Not when he was in possession of the goods and the weapon. I believe the victim was killed before you saw Mr. McPhee go to the toilet. He must have cleaned himself and his clothing then. Or perhaps he threw his bloody clothes and the box out the window after he had done the deed. I will ensure the tracks are searched today. What I can't understand is why he kept the knife..." He studied Guy as if awaiting an answer, but then reached into his shirt pocket and pulled out Guy's passport. "I return this to you, Sir. Please have a good day."

He stood and left the compartment as the train slowed. Outside the window, the landscape changed from miles of dry plains to the verdant green of the coast and thick clots of houses as they neared Dar es Salaam.

An hour later, Guy climbed off the train with his bag. On the siding waited three khaki-uniformed police officers who eyed him as he passed. He lost no time in catching a taxi to the airport, where his flight was already booked. So was one in Jack Springer's name.

The interior of his lone carry-on bag was mostly padding. It cradled the precious remains of the missing link. Springer had been a conflicted man when he decided to spirit the bones out of Tanzania. It went against everything he believed in. But a diagnosis of stage 4 pancreatic cancer had changed all that. He wanted to leave a legacy for his family. Between his life insurance and the proceeds of the bones' sale, they would be able to live a comfortable life.

So, he and Guy had planned this whole thing, from Guy taking custody of the bones before he left Olduvai, to Springer's murder on the train.

On the plane, a young black man settled into the seat beside Guy and nodded as their gazes met. He had the broad shoulders and strong athletic build of someone who could climb along the roof of a train, and yet he was slim enough he could easily fit through a train window. Originally from Kenya, he had settled in America. Guy had found him ridiculously unscrupulous but useful because he always seemed to need money. He'd worked for Guy for three years and his performance had always been stellar.

"Well done," Guy murmured. "No fingerprints and there was only a spot of blood that I dealt with."

The cabin staff closed the doors and made their announcements before the aircraft began to taxi onto the runway. Chances of the police stopping them diminished with every minute. The plan had worked, as Springer had hoped, and Guy was on his way back home. On the runway, he clenched the seat arms as the engines roared. He pressed back in his seat, considering his final decision. And then the aircraft roared down the runway and into the air.

With Springer's death, there was no one who knew what had been planned except for Guy and his man, who would be compensated far better than his usual work warranted.

Guy focused on the proceeds of the sale of the bones and how those proceeds would look far better in his bank account than paid out to Springer's widow. Besides, she would never expect anything beyond the insurance, while Guy had expenses and

Caribbean bank accounts ready to receive the funds for the sale. He even had a private collector primed and ready. Springer would never know there'd been a change of plans, or that Guy had incriminated Springer's star student. It was just how things had to be.

The sharp prick on the back of his hand brought Guy out of his reverie in time to see his man shove something back in his pocket. He looked sideways at Guy as a hot flush rushed through Guy's body and he struggled to breathe. With the heat came the iron taste of African dust. He went to stand, but his man easily shoved Guy back in his seat.

"Change of plans, boss. I've got a few money problems to deal with," his man said softly, just as the seatbelt sign turned off and everything around Guy faded to red dust and darkness. Absolutely not according to plan…

# SISTER

## Eddie Generous

The buzz from the intercom had Markus Bellows on his feet immediately. Total dark beyond the drapes when he pulled them aside. "Huh?" he said and hurried out of his bedroom, down the long hallway lined with photographs of himself and all he'd accomplished, past the entries into the dining room and parlor, and to the foyer to reach the little beige box on the wall by the door. Even before he hit the button, he knew it was Mercedes. She hadn't come around in nearly two years, but he knew, because it had to be her.

"Yeah?" he said as he held the button.

"Markus," she said.

Her voice took on a little more gravel every year, the wear and tear of making mistakes. Her only way out had come too late, had come too simply. Easy come, easy go was particularly true when it came to money and people not used to having it.

"Mercedes."

"I need help."

Of course, she did. She always did. Help was the only excuse strong enough for her to swallow her shame, only excuse strong enough to face him in her various states of distress.

"Okay," Markus said before lifting his finger and pressing it to the button that opened the gate. He shifted the sheer curtain over the window next to the door to watch a single yellowy headlight flare to life, then play up the driveway to his home.

Not quite, but it had almost been a surprise when she didn't show for her mother's funeral a month prior. Mercedes only had room for one need at a time, her mind not equipped to juggle all that life might toss into the mix. She didn't seem to consider that other people, like Markus, had their own woes to wade.

The one-eyed car pulled up next to his brand-new Porsche 911. Markus flipped the garage light switch to see Mercedes, belly big with pregnancy, climb out of a Buick Skyhawk with a smashed grill and waves of rust creeping up the fenders and hood. That she was pregnant was a surprise, but not. He'd come to expect it, ever since the time she appeared back in his life some six years ago, a week after he'd knocked off the fourth ranked contender and cashed his first real payday in the ring.

Markus spun the deadbolt and opened the door. As she drew closer, the swollen eye and purple cheek came into view, the split lip and the fresh bend to her nose. He didn't say anything, just let her come to him. She didn't clear the threshold before her arms were around him and her face pressed against his barrel chest.

"Hey," she said.

"Hey, yourself."

She pulled her face back and Markus saw something else: she was high. Her pupils filled almost to the whites, even coming into the bright yard light of the home.

"I did something," she said.

"How far along are you?"

Mercedes ignored his question. She shook against him as he turned her, directed her into the foyer. Markus kicked the door closed.

"I think I killed them. I don't know. I think I did."

"What? Who?"

Mercedes reached into the front pocket of her baggy jeans and withdrew a small Ruger 9mm. "Darcy and Oates. I didn't want to.

It's not my fault."

Markus considered the scene. For years he'd been accused of not keeping it real, of faking who he was because he refused to be dragged back into the sewer he'd crawled from. All his buddies growing up who popped in and out of jail, the old heads on the block talking endless bullshit about tougher characters, the strung-out mommies who were furious it was he and not them who got to live in a home with a foundation, a yard, a gate, and whatever else they thought he'd lucked or cheated his way into. All but Mercedes, because he couldn't tell her no.

And now she was standing there, about to drag his good life down the drain with an accessory charge.

Markus pushed Mercedes back to arm's length. "Why?"

"I kicked, for the baby. But I needed some money. They'd paid before, just mouth stuff, so I went to them. They gave me a beer, but it had something in it. When I woke up, I panicked, I was on a bed, naked, so were they...I started shouting."

Markus shook his head gently.

"They hit me, telling me to shut up. I did so good for the whole time I knew I was pregnant. She's my fresh start, you know?" Mercedes pressed the side of the gun to her belly. "All I could think about was their dirty dicks being near my baby."

A ball of fury dropped into his guts. "Go on."

"They were smoking up. The room was yellow, and I felt it, you know, like poisoning her. The gun was on the coffee table right by my head. So, I don't know, I guess I freaked out."

Markus was four when he and his dad moved in with Precious Gorman. Two years later, Precious was pregnant with Mercedes. A month before she was born, Markus's father was fatally shot by a cop who was in the middle of disrupting an armed robbery. The thieves were already on their way out the back door when the cop fired on two men who'd come to buy beer after a long day painting houses. By the time Markus was twelve, he was the only person in the world really looking out for Mercedes—Precious had a revolving door of boyfriends and dealers, who, as often as not, were interchangeable in those roles. But one boyfriend—on his way out the door, unable to deal with Precious' shit—took a frustrated boy, only a few wrong moves from a life in and out of incarceration, to the heavy bags hanging in Kingman's Gym.

"Where?" Markus said.

"Field Road, you know? There's that—"

"I know." Markus clenched his meaty fists. "That one of their cars?"

Mercedes nodded.

"Show me. We have to take the car back. And the gun. If this comes back to you...they'll take that baby."

Mercedes's chin quivered and Markus saw for the first time in the woman's miserable life she cared about something more than she cared about herself.

"Once this is through, we're going to give that kid a real future, okay?"

Tears streamed down Mercedes' puffy face as she nodded.

"Give me the gun."

She did.


Everybody from the rough side of the city knew about Field Road. Beginning about three minutes from suburbia, Beagle Street became Field Road and stretched for ten miles of nothing but trees and dilapidated bungalows until reaching the sewage treatment plant. The city never grew in that direction because so far, they hadn't been able to cap the stink that wafted free any day there was a westward wind. The homes were rented out and rarely kept up. Being beyond the city limits, Field Road fell to the jurisdiction of the RCMP rather than the city cops. The nearest RCMP station was more than twenty miles away, and busy with their own problems.

Markus had been out on this stretch of stinking and desperate road only twice. Once with one of Precious's dealer boyfriends, and once with some older buddies he hung with before Gus

Kingman gave him the ultimatum: in and clean or out and dirty. Now, as he listened to the gravel ping against the undercarriage of his car, he wondered if a Porsche had ever been down this road. He guessed some had; wealth offered no immunity from bad decisions.

They passed a burned-out house; its frame was a blackened skeleton, rising like sunflower stalks from an overgrown yard. The next house featured two cars riding cinderblocks, a shiny motorcycle, and a single light lit in a small, detached garage. The brake lights ahead of Markus glowed in the heavy darkness as Mercedes pulled the Buick onto a gravelly lawn in front of a bungalow with fuzzy vinyl siding and a mossy roof.

Markus followed her in and parked tight on her bumper. From the center console, he pulled out leather gloves. Gloves on, he handled the weapon. With the tail of the T-shirt he'd worn to bed, he wiped his prints from the gun. He took his keys when he climbed from his car.

Mercedes remained behind the wheel of the Skyhawk. Markus knocked on the driver's window. She rolled it down.

"Hand me the keys," he whispered.

There was no way to know if the dealers were truly dead.

Mercedes did. "Should I wait in your car?"

"Stay put," he said. "I have a plan, but we have to be careful. Okay?"

Mercedes nodded.

Quickly, but with the light steps he'd used to dance around the ring until he was forced from the sport, he stepped up to the side door. It was open a crack, and he pushed it wide. There were lights on inside and the blood was immediately visible. One of the dealers was dead on the kitchen floor. There were great Rorschach splatter marks on the fridge and wall. Avoiding the pooling blood on the linoleum, Markus moved to the dining area and the threadbare rug.

"Is somebody out there?" a weak voice said from beyond view.

There was a telephone on the wall just inside the living room. He lifted the receiver and heard the dial tone. Good, that was necessary. He dialed his own number, listening until the answering machine picked up. The lines would stay connected until the tape ran out, assumedly, if he let it. Didn't matter. He left the receiver dangling from its coiled cord.

"Help. Is somebody there?" The words sounded wet as well as weak.

That there were words at all was not ideal. A lamp on the nightstand glowed. Next to it was a small man with fiery orange hair, his mouth shiny red with blood. This was Oates, Karl Oates. Markus had known his older siblings, that hair a dead giveaway.

"Please," he said upon seeing Markus.

Blood had streaked, saturating the carpet from where the man had pulled himself along. Markus avoided stepping in any blood.

"Did you call for help?" Markus said.

Oates vibrated with shivers. "I woke up...wanted a smoke." There was a yellowy glass tube and a charred piece of tinfoil on the floor next to him. "You called, right?"

"What happened? Why did Mercedes shoot you?"

Oates clued into who Markus was then. "Oh, shit...man, she's crazy. She tripped hard. Been trying to ween her off, but she sneaks it."

Markus exhaled a heavy breath. That sounded a lot more plausible than Mercedes trying to kick. "She snuck in to rob you? How'd she get out here?"

A tendril of bloody drool played from Oates' mouth. "She lives here. Been living here."

"You the father?"

"Maybe. Could be any of us," Oates said, his words weakening with each syllable.

"Where's your stash?"

"You call the ambulance, if I tell?"

Markus shook his head. "No. You can die riding high, though."

Oates let out a single bark of humorless laughter, a blood bubble ballooning from his left nostril. "Fair enough."

Markus had had to do most of the work: loaded the foil, put the glass tube in Oates' mouth, and burn the powder until it liquified. Oates only had to breathe as deeply as he could. Markus pressed a pillow over his face for three minutes.

Once out, Markus took a deep, deep breath of cleanish air. He hung up the phone on his way by. He continued through until finding the room he had to assume belonged to Mercedes. There were a dozen bags of diapers, boxes of formula, and several little outfits strewn on the floor amid the woman's dirty clothes. Probably they'd been a team of junkie bandits, thinking they were doing right by the impending child.

That settled the final piece of the plan.

Mercedes was standing next to the Buick, smoking a cigarette. "What happened?"

"Hold tight. We're almost through," Markus said and sat in his car, closing the door behind him.

From the backseat, he grabbed the bag phone. He plucked the lighter from its port and powered up the phone. He dialed the operator and the moment it connected, he shouted in a breathy voice, "Oh my God, my sister's in trouble! Please, I need an ambulance! Endhoven!"

"I'll connect you," a woman said on the far end of the line, her voice scratchy and distant.

The line rang once before connecting. Mercedes stood outside the Porsche, frowning as she looked through the window at Markus.

"EU Hospital, is this a—?"

Markus cut off the woman working the line. "It's my sister. She called me. Something happened on Field Road. I'm on my way there. She sounds crazy. She's pregnant!"

"Sir, is—"

"I'm driving. She said the third house! I don't trust her, she's saying she's—" Markus hit end before inserting his key into the car's ignition.

"What was that about?" Mercedes said, her face a mask of despair. "I'll go to jail! I'll lose the baby!"

Markus pulled the 9mm from his pocket. "You know, when your mom was in the hospital, dying, she confessed to me that she'd lied all these years."

"Markus, I can't be here!"

"She told me how my dad thought you were a miracle because he'd had a vasectomy, how she got the doctor to go along with the lie because she said he'd beat her if he knew you belonged to someone else."

Mercedes scrunched her face. "What?"

"Think about all the times I've protected you, tried to pull you out of a jam, and here we are again, and I'm of no relation to you."

"Markus? She was lying."

"Why would she?"

The night was quiet but for the rumble of the Porsche's engine and the river flowing beyond the tree line.

"Because she lies."

Markus tilted his head. "Lied. Skipping her funeral doesn't make her any less dead."

Mercedes shook her head. "I couldn't. I just—"

Her words meant nothing, never had, never would; Markus interrupted her. "For a while, I dated a paramedic. He sometimes worked as a cut man. He told me about this call he went on where his partner pulled a baby from a dead mother's womb, saving its life."

"What?"

"You have to be quick though, he said within ten minutes, or the baby dies."

Mercedes put her hand to her tummy. "Markus, either we go, or I tell them you did this."

Markus closed his eyes and tilted his head back. "I'm giving you a final chance to fully consider someone else."

"AIDS drugs rotting your brain? I can't be here!"

Markus let out a huff. "HIV, and no. One of us is thinking clearly, and the other is a junkie who has to make a choice."

"Fuck you, I'm—"

Markus raised the gun. "You get one chance to do the most righteous thing you can for that baby inside you."

"What, you gonna shoot me?"

Distantly, a siren sang on the night.

"Quickly, now. You can acknowledge who you are and what you'd do to that child. I don't want to have to do it for you. You've never done a thing for anybody else. Do this one thing."

"Shut your fucking mouth, you faggot piece of shit! What do you know anyway? Just 'cause you learned to fight good? You think that makes you better than me?"

The lights flitted through the trees as the siren gained strength.

"You're just some fucking loser. Mom told me years ago we weren't real sister and brother. You fucking loser. You don't know shit about any—"

Markus popped to Mercedes's side in a flash, like he'd done to so many opponents on his way to the top. The gun pressed against her temple and fired in a single motion. She pitched sideways, flopping over the nose of the Porsche. Markus knelt and wrapped her hand on the gun, affixing new prints, before tossing it next to her. The keys to the Buick went into her pocket. He then slipped out of his gloves, tossing them into the Porsche after he killed the engine—the warm engine.

The lights and siren felt almost on top of him when he ran out to the road, waving his arms.

\*\*\*

"What exactly is wrong with her?" Markus said, looking through the window at the tiny pink baby beneath the clear dome.

"Neonatal abstinence syndrome, for sure. The long-term effects, we don't know those yet. This is the worst I've seen of any NAS baby who'd survived their first night," the doctor said.

The scandal was massive, but the silver lining seemed blindingly perfect. Of course, the news didn't get in-depth concerning the baby after it survived the initial night. The fact it was an addict and needed weaned off dope was far from palatable and tarnished the amazing thing the paramedics had done on the scene, so it was ignored.

The police accepted the story. Everything Markus said was taken as truth; little was questioned. He was the former lightweight champion of the world, and unlike so many others who'd found success in the ring, he'd never been in trouble outside the ring—even if rumblings of his sexual orientation lent plausibility to the rumor that he'd been pushed from boxing after testing positive for HIV. He was beloved, mild, a paragon who'd reached inspiring heights.

"Will she make it?" Markus said.

The doctor pursed her lips a moment before saying, "Probably be a blessing if she didn't."

Markus felt like laughing, felt like crying. Mercedes was Mercedes in life and in death, trouble through and through, and trouble was the only thing she had to pass on.

# QUACKERS
## Nils Gilbertson

Phil checked the contents of his JanSport. Flashlights, pry bar, gloves, needle-nose pliers, hacksaw. He wasn't sure what half the items were for, but Ricky had insisted. After checking, he tossed the backpack between the rungs of the folding ladder in the trunk of the old station wagon and shut the door.

Ricky's uncle, who lived in a single wide in the back corner of his parents' yard, drove them. He stopped at the 7-Eleven to pick up a Big Gulp of Mountain Dew, a box of Sour Patch Kids, and a tin of Skoal. He offered sour candies to the boys before tilting his head back and guzzling them. At a deserted red light in the center of the sleeping town, he realized he didn't have a spitter for the dip and settled on the empty candy box. Phil watched from the backseat as dip spit seeped through the corners of the box, tinted red, melting a forgotten gelatin soul stuck to the bottom.

"So what's the mission this week, boys?" Ricky's uncle asked.

Before any of us could answer, he added, "I envy you kids. Growing up, me and my buddies used to get into all sorts of shit, same as you. This one time, me and a couple of the fellas were drunk down at the quarry—"

"Shut up, Uncle Pete," Ricky said.

He spat in the box. "I get it. Gotta keep focused."

Phil could hear Henry's breathing in the seat beside him. He was a nervous ginger kid who got a hard-on whenever a girl smiled at him. "Hey Ricky," he said. "You sure they haven't caught wind of the plan? You don't think they'll be there, do you?"

"That's bullshit," Ricky said. "They have no idea. Besides, it's—" he checked the clock on the dash. "Three in the morning. Those idiots are either sleeping or jerkin' it."

Uncle Pete chuckled. "Take charge same as your mama, don't you, boy?"

"Shut up."

Uncle Pete parked the car in the school's side lot. Phil felt something cold inside him as he surveyed the vacant darkness. Conclusions needled his mind—conclusions which, on instinct, he rejected. But ones which, as he grew older and paid more attention, started to make sense. *Nothing is as it appears. Everything can so easily turn to nothing. Existence is the exception to the rule.* He shook them off and grabbed the backpack from the trunk.

The boys shuffled through the halls—caverns in the darkness—murals replaced by crooked shadows.

"Remember," Ricky whispered. "We set up the ladder by the dumpster on the side of the gym. Me and Henry hold it in place while Phil climbs up and grabs the duck. Henry, you keep holding it and I'll follow Phil up."

"You guys gonna saw its head off right there?" Henry asked. "Leave it for everyone to see?"

The other boys didn't answer.

It took some doing to get the ladder set up, and Phil felt it shake as he climbed. From the second-highest rung, he could reach the edge of the roof of the gymnasium. Gravel stung his fingers as he yanked himself up.

The duck was taped to the corner of the rooftop. By day, it oversaw the sun-browned field. By night, only small-town blackness. A few brightened windows in the distance punctured the night sky. As he brushed gravel from his knees, Phil wondered who was still up at this hour. *You are*, something inside him said. Even though his old man was gone, he felt remnants of judgment—the blood flowing through his veins laced with congenital shame.

Alongside the duck was a figure surrounded by beer bottles. Phil shined the flashlight on it.

"The fuck?" The figure stumbled. Phil tilted the light toward the bottles at its feet. He recognized Cade Abbott, a boy in his class. Ricky was wrong; someone was there keeping watch. Alone. Even if it meant downing beers and passing out on the roof of the gym.

"Shit," Cade said, shielding his eyes. "That you, Phil?"

"I...I..." A voice deep within him—one he loathed but suspected knew more than the rest of him combined—stole the words and rendered him one with the night. "I'm here for the duck," he mustered. Distracting him were thoughts of the two of them as young boys, playing while their mothers worked the same shift at the laundromat. Friends by force. Was there any other sort of friend?

Cade started howling, stumbling, waving at the flashlight's gleam. "Fuck, man," he slurred. "You can kiss my ass you think you're getting your hands on him."

Phil started forward and Cade retreated until he was at the rooftop's corner—inches from the duck.

If there were words, neither of the boys noticed. Only a scuffle and wayward feet slipping on beer bottles. Then a wail and a crack and silence.

Phil scanned the darkness. His blotchy sight settled on Ricky, standing on the ladder, peeking over the edge of the rooftop.

"The duck!" he hollered. "Get the duck!"

Phil spun around, kicking gravel, confirming he was now alone. He went to the corner of the building and tugged, wrestling with night itself. Once he'd ripped it loose, he ran. Slowing him was a weighty pit that swallowed the rest of him, numbing the burn in his chest.

As they scampered through distorted halls, he heard Ricky. "We got him! We got Quackers!"

Night clouds masqueraded as bruises on the gibbous moon. The man sipped his drink as though, had he not spoiled its sting with one extra ice cube, his life might have turned out all right. There was a voicemail from his mother on his phone. He'd missed the call earlier that evening, too busy wooing potential investors at a sushi restaurant that charged a small fortune for a California roll. He didn't enjoy these outings, but he was damn good at them. The clients always stumbled out full of sake, laughing, shaking hands, ready to deal on Monday. He knew how to become who they wanted him to be. Besides, he thought, there was no use answering his mother's calls from that world; it would only be bad news. Good news didn't exist there, and anything between good and bad didn't warrant a phone call.

Even at night, it was still warm and humid enough to dampen the ridge of his brow. His backyard was silent but for the rustles in the bushes as his old pointer hunted rabbits and toads and any other creatures that emerged under cover of darkness. He finished the drink and played the voicemail.

*Phil, it's your mother. Too busy to answer the damn phone? I swear, sometimes you won't shut up and other times I gotta pull teeth to get a hold of ya. Anyhow, I'm calling to give you the latest 'round here, not that you care much. Remember Cade Abbott? Died the other night. Cancer. Bladder or pancreas or something down in his guts. Word has it he was sick for months, but didn't want to go to the doc for it. By the time they wheeled him in against his will, it was too late—gave him a couple weeks. Only took five days. I thought you might want to know. Funeral's next Thursday if you want to come, but I bet you don't. It might be best you stay away, what with the accident the two of you had all those years ago. If you go and his parents have to see the fella who put their boy in a chair, you know who's going to take the flak for it 'round here, don't ya?*

She coughed and wheezed and cleared her throat, as though choking on the thought.

*Thought you might want to know, is all.*

He walked from the patio to the back door of the sprawling brick home and felt the dog at his heels, licking sweat from his legs. Her warm tongue on his skin nearly brought a smile, but his mother's message chased it away. It was his fault Cade had succumbed to cancer; he was sure of it. Had it not been for the weeks and months and years of surgery and grueling recovery, only to end up in a chair, maybe ol' Cade wouldn't have been so loath to go to the doctor while the cancer was curdling his guts. He chuckled at the self-centeredness of his shame. As he checked the locks and alarms, he felt relief quarrel with guilt. Cade was dead now. He couldn't cause the crippled man any more pain because there was no one to suffer it. The crack of bone on pavement that lingered at the outskirts of his memory was rendered as immaterial as it was before he or Cade or any conscious being had ever come into existence. It was over. It *ought* to be over. But even the forgiving warmth of the dog curled up at his side couldn't turn *ought* into truth.

The smoke from his mother's cigarette stung his eyes. Across the desk sat Principal Rhodes and Officer Biggs, whom his mother had grown up down the block from. The way she told it, he had the spine of a jellyfish and balls like raisins.

"That Abbott boy probably tripped on his shoelaces," she said to them. "I saw his old lady at the supermarket the other day, damn near lost her footing in the frozen food aisle. More left feet in that family than the good Lord intended, you ask me. Besides, I'd bet a month's pay I smelled bourbon on her breath. Apple don't fall far."

"Thanks, Arlene," said Officer Biggs. He turned to Phil. "Tell me again why you and your friends were trying to get on the gym rooftop that time of night?"

"To get Quackers," Phil mumbled, eyes on the desk.

"Look at the officer when you talk to him," his mother instructed.

"To get Quackers."

"And who is Quackers?"

"He's the mascot for the Ducks basketball team, Cade's team."

The officer looked to the principal, confused.

Principal Rhodes cleared his throat and pushed his glasses up the bridge of his nose. "It's the basketball league we have here at the school. There aren't many schools with teams nearby, so we have two teams in each class. That way, they can play each other if we can't schedule anyone else."

"They're the Ducks and we're the Wildcats," Phil said. "Cade and those guys were all talking smack last game, and then they got a duck and taped it to the top of the gym, you know, like they owned the place. We went up to get it down. But Cade was up there, he was..."

"Was what?" the officer asked.

"Was keeping watch."

Principal Rhodes leaned on his desk. "We found the beer bottles on the roof after Ricky's uncle called the police. Were you drinking alcohol up there, Phil?"

"No, sir. Like I said before, we weren't drinking. Only went up for the duck."

"The *plastic* duck," Officer Biggs said.

"Uh-huh."

"And where's the duck now?"

Phil didn't say anything.

"He told you already," his mother said. "He don't remember. And how could he remember in a moment like that? Those boys ran and told an adult, who called the cops. Ain't a thing my boy did wrong."

The principal and officer exchanged glances.

"All right. We'll call if we need anything else."

## QUACKERS

\*\*\*

His headphones couldn't drown the shouting. It was his mother's boyfriend, Harvey. Phil lay in bed and closed his eyes and didn't open them until he felt a hand on his shoulder. His mother looked down at him, bleary-eyed and swaying.

"Officer Biggs called," she slurred. "Said there won't be any problem for the bullshit with Cade Abbott. School will have to punish you for going on the roof at night. Detention or something. Nothing new for you."

"He staying the night?" Phil asked, signaling to the shouts beyond the door.

His mother snorted with amusement. "He'll pass out soon enough. Just a loud asshole when he's drunk. Want to join us? Celebrate the good news?"

"I think I'll go to sleep."

"Suit yourself."

Phil woke to the squeal of his bedroom door's rusted hinges. He rolled over and saw a dark figure approaching. It staggered toward him and made a noise as though its esophagus was trying to crawl up its throat. As it leaned over his bed, hot breath stung his eyes. More than cigarettes, a cocktail of sin.

It groaned. He felt large, sticky hands on his neck and face. An index finger pinched his lips, and he tried to keep his teeth clenched but it pried them open, and he tasted a salty finger exploring the corners of his mouth. He tried to scream but was frozen. The finger tested the back of his throat, then started down his body. It was boiling, but he shivered as it explored him.

Then his mother's voice. "Harvey? The fuck are you?"

The hand pulled away, and he inhaled a sour breath, inches from his mouth.

"The fuck?" the figure said. "Jesus, this ain't the shitter." It coughed and swallowed hard and stumbled to the door, bumping into a dresser on the way out. He heard his mother's drunken laughter.

Phil stayed still for hours. Silent tears did their best to wash away the sting, but it wasn't enough. As blackness through the blinds turned to morning gray, Phil crept through the house to the garage and grabbed the hacksaw. Back in his room, he reached underneath his bed and retrieved the plastic duck. He wiped the snot from his nose and the tears from his cheeks and started to saw.

The man's dreams were clearer than his waking hours. In them, he knew he was dreaming, but held no agency. It wasn't like how he'd read about some people who know they're dreaming and the whole thing turns into their mental playground with no consequences. Awareness burdened him without the accompanying freedom. As though his consciousness was bottled and paraded through the musty caverns of his psyche. A reluctant passenger, it witnessed grisly scenes—scenes he prayed were confined to the isolated corners of his dream state. But the familiarity of the muffled howls and the feeble attempts to claw his hands from bruised necks warned that the vicious cravings no longer lay dormant within him. They had seeped into reality. Only when he dreamed did the partitions in his mind crumble. Only then did he recognize himself. As the bloodthirsty segment of his mind lay waste to its neighboring gray matter, it mocked him with boyhood memories of those who had tried to warn him. Tried to warn her.

That night, as he slept, his mind found its way into Cade Abbott's body. He observed himself, as a boy, climbing onto the rooftop of the gym and hesitating before shoving Cade's drunken body off the edge. His mind, trapped inside of Cade, plunged toward the pavement. But instead of the crack that reverberated through his memories, the concrete caved in, and they fell together through Earth's crust and mantle, and, at its core, Hell awaited. Once they arrived, he tried in vain to explain that it was him—Phil Bradley—inside Cade's mangled body. Hideous, fire-scorched goat-men, skin melting from their limbs like wax, explained that it couldn't be; his soul had already arrived.

He woke to the overwhelming emptiness of the house. The dog had moved to the foot of the king-sized bed. His phone read three a.m. He took a long breath and listened to his mother's voicemail again, then rose to dress, brush his teeth, and piss. The jeans in the hamper were stained with dirt and other dark blotches, but he couldn't remember from what. He pulled them on along with the muddy boots he couldn't remember stuffing into a trash bag in the corner of the walk-in closet. Back in the bedroom, the dog whined as he reached underneath the bed and retrieved an old Reebok shoebox, duct-taped shut. He snatched the boxcutter from the bedside drawer and sliced it open. Inside was Quackers and his decapitated head.

He drove compulsively toward a place he wasn't sure he'd ever been before. It beckoned, and he had no say in the matter, drawn to it by his own contradictions. It wasn't far from his suburban neighborhood to boundless miles of unspoiled earth. The dense pines assured him that, in the face of modernity and its lust for poison, purity still held the upper hand.

There was a rest stop about an hour out, burrowed into the forest's edge. It compelled him to pull off. He parked in the empty lot, a flickering bulb by the ramshackle bathrooms the only earthbound light. He grabbed the backpack, flashlight, and shovel from the trunk, and started into the woods, guided only by his fractured psyche and a yearning to sever the past. He knew the way, but couldn't figure why.

He buried Quackers's body and head in a shallow grave among the shrubbery at the base of a pine tree. As he did, he periodically flipped the flashlight back over his shoulder, suspicious of every chirp and rustle that cut through the burgeoning silence. As he tamped the soil and covered it with leaves, he considered saying a few words for the deceased. But muffled whimpers of the past distracted him—not yet ready to forgive. He closed his eyes and listened, as though he might hear something that would offer peace. But there was something else.

The sound drew him along a path deeper into the trees. He scanned the immediate ground in front of him with the flashlight, expecting to find a wounded animal, until he heard the sobs and fixed the light on a piece of small, braided rope in the dirt—a handle. He knelt beside it but grimaced as a prick of electricity burrowed through his head like an unsheathed wire. It did its best to drown the sobs and whimpers, which now grew to garbled calls for help. Too tired—words too far gone.

"Hold on!" He reached again toward the handle, but a light flashed, siphoning the brightness from the stars and infusing them into his corneas. Blinded, the calls for help grew louder, and he felt for the rope on the ground. Once he found it, he took hold and pulled as hard as he could. A clean cut of dirt separated from the ground. He felt concrete below—a bunker.

"Handle! There's a handle!"

He heard life in the voice now, nourished by the prospect of freedom. He felt for the handle and the blinding light began to fade, silhouettes of trees circling the boundaries of perception. Phantom limbs searched the slab of concrete, and at the opposite corner found a grip. Heavier this time, he yanked with his very soul, spurred on by the screech of concrete on concrete, until he'd heaved it off. Collapsing into a pile of leaves, it felt as though he'd moved the Earth from its axis.

A trembling, malnourished figure emerged. Peaking its head out toward him, he felt its dead eyes. Ones he'd seen before. Their gaze fell heavily on him, suffocating him with their familiarity. The figure screamed until his eardrums throbbed and ran until its movement was nothing but a speck in the darkness.

The counselor watched as Phil read a book of poetry in the chair across from his desk.

"Don't feel like talking today?"

"Nah," Phil said, flipping the page.

"You know, Phil, I don't know if you've been counting, but this is our tenth session. It's the last one you have to attend because of what happened with you and Cade Abbott."

"Who?"

The counselor removed his glasses and cleaned them on his sleeve. "What are you reading, then?"

Phil peeked up from behind the tattered library book. "Walt Whitman."

"Oh yes, the father of free verse. Do you have a favorite?"

The boy slid the book across the desk.

"Do I contradict myself?" the counselor read aloud. "Very well then I contradict myself, I am large, I contain multitudes." He looked at the boy. "What's your favorite subject these days, Phil?"

"English."

"Why the sudden change? What happened to biology?"

A knock on the door before the boy could answer. The counselor checked his watch and sighed. "Come in, Ms. Bradley."

She nearly took the door off the hinges, but the boy didn't turn his head. "Let's go, Phil," she said. "Last session, this damn school is making you go to. Grab your book and let's go."

"Ms. Bradley," the counselor said, "seeing as it's Phil's last session, do you mind if I have a word with you both?"

"Jesus," she said. "Haven't we heard enough? This whole damn school's been out to get my boy for months now. Putting him in detention, forcing him to come here to talk about his feelings, hoping he'll say something he doesn't mean. Didn't you hear when the cops said there was nothin' to it besides for that drunk Abbott boy tripping over his own feet?"

Phil took the book and held it to his chest.

"Please, Ms. Bradley. I assure you, I don't have it out for your son. I've enjoyed getting to know him over these last few months, and I have nothing but his best interest at heart."

She observed the meek smile on her son's face and said, "What is it?"

The counselor cleared his throat. "I'm concerned that Phil is, well, compartmentalizing his memories in a way that's not healthy."

"The hell does that mean?"

"It means, and Phil and I have spoken about this, that he has extreme feelings of guilt about what happened with Cade Abbott, and he's developing elaborate mental schemes to protect his psyche from that guilt."

She stared stone-cold at the counselor until she couldn't hold in the mocking laughter. "Guilt? Why in the hell would he feel guilty? He didn't do anything!" she said, emphasizing each word with a clap of her hands.

"And I'm not saying he did. But we are complex beings; experiencing the *emotion* of guilt is not an admission of wrongdoing."

"We're leaving." She grabbed her son's arm.

"*Please*," the counselor said, standing from his chair. "I'm afraid that, if left to fester, this subconscious effort to wall off certain parts of his past will only worsen. Who knows what damage it could cause him—cause others. I'm no doctor, but I've taken the liberty of reaching out to someone who would be a great deal of help—"

"And let me guess, this costs money?" she asked. "Another way for you people to make some easy bucks sitting us in a chair and telling us how screwed up we are, huh?"

"No, nothing at all," the counselor said. "It's a friend of mine and he's agreed to meet with Phil for free."

She scoffed. "So, we're a charity case, huh? To help you sleep better for all the shit *you've* done?"

"I wish you'd—"

"Let's go, Phil."

As she dragged her son toward the exit, the book fell to the floor.


The police arrived two days later. When the man saw the four patrol cars pull up out front, he thought of the commotion it must have caused at the front office of the gated community. Normally, Rodney, the man in charge at the gate, called in advance of letting visitors in. The thought of the exchange when they came—demanding he not make the customary call—made him cringe.

The officers banged on the door and presented documents and barked vaguely familiar phrases at him while he tried to quiet his dog. He couldn't imagine the feeling if something happened to his dog—he'd never get over it.

They started searching the sprawling brick home. He thought of calling his lawyer but didn't. They collected stained jeans from the hamper and muddy boots from a trash bag in the corner of the walk-in closet. They collected the backpack and flashlight and shovel, still in the trunk of his car. They collected toothbrushes and hairbrushes and any brushes they could find, bagging them carefully with gloves. Two officers stood with him while men with badges in shirts and ties conversed in the foyer. He wasn't sure if it was intentional that he could hear them.

*We got him. Clothes show he was out there in the woods. Positive ID by the vic. We got the son of a bitch.*

*Where's his lawyer?*

*Don't think he called anyone.*

*Show it to him.*

One of the officers went to the car and returned with an evidence bag.

"Mr. Bradley?"

"Yes?"

"Do you recognize this?" He raised the bag.

"Yes, sir."

"What is it?"

He smiled. "That's an old friend of mine. His name's Quackers."

# A ROSE FOR A ROSE
## Stacy Woodson

Waylon rolled down the window of his pickup truck. Even from the parking lot, he could smell the stale beer and the sawdust, hear the fiddles and steel guitars. The Wild Rose seemed like the perfect place—a real honky-tonk.

Not like the one in San Antonio.

He prayed his mama approved this time. Then, maybe they'd both find some peace.

He backed the beat-up Chevy into a parking spot next to a row of Harleys and struck a pothole. The shocks on the truck squeaked like rusty hinges, and the gas can in the back banged against the bed. Waylon smiled. The parking lot was certainly authentic enough.

He slid the box toward him, climbed out of the truck, and walked, eyes fixed on the worn building with the rusted tin roof, chipped paint, and smoky windows. Everything looked good until he got a closer look at the neon sign.

The Wild Rose—the name was right.

But the sign…

The colors were pink and bold. No flickering lights. No burned-out letters.

It was too perfect.

What if he'd failed again?

His insides twisted. His chest went tight.

He could feel himself already starting to slip.

He plunged his hand into his pocket and retrieved the Zippo, focused on the weight of the case, the way it felt in his palm. Then he flipped the lid, flicked the wheel, watched the flame—the tapering shape, the blue and red and orange hues—the mesmerizing way it danced in his hand. Until the pressure eased. Until his head was clear.

Until he could breathe again.

"Evening, son." An older man stood behind him. The woman on his arm nodded. The couple stared.

*Earth to Waylon.* His mama's voice needled inside his head.

He closed the Zippo, heat rising to his cheeks, wondering how long he'd been standing there. He ran up the stairs, pulled the door, and waited for the couple to pass.

"Such a sweet boy." The woman smiled. "Isn't he sweet, Clive?"

"Yes, Charlaine. Boy has some manners."

*Of course, he has manners. I may have raised a half-wit. But I didn't raise no heathen.*

Waylon's face flush again.

Sounds leaked onto the porch—glasses clinking, people shouting, and music.

*You gonna stand there all night, or are you gonna get on with it?*

From Arkansas, through Oklahoma, and now Texas, getting on with it was all he'd been doing. The Coyote Rose had been too country, according to his mama. The Thirsty Rose not country enough. And then there was Rose's Western World where she'd said there wasn't enough tonk in their honky—whatever that meant.

And the list of Roses went on and on.

Still, he kept trying to find the perfect Rose—trying and failing and trying again.

Waylon hoped that this was it. That he'd finally found it.

He shifted the box and walked inside.

Images of the Wild Rose, the ones he'd seen online, cycled through his head—the worn wagon wheels, the string lights, the Texas flag that hung from a water-stained ceiling. All pictures that belonged to a honky-tonk with an authentic vibe.

All things that *weren't* here.

Everything was lacquered and shiny—the walls, the floor, the wagon-wheel chandeliers that hung from the ceiling. The bar was lacquered, too. The liquor bottles were clean and perfectly organized. Everything matched—the dishes, the glasses, the barstools. Even the cocktail napkins were embossed.

*Place is prissy, Waylon.*

His heart sank. He looked at the door, but he couldn't bring himself to go back to the truck for another road trip, another Rose, another failure.

*Can't you do anything right?*

He couldn't. Not when it came to Mama.

Lord knows he tried.

He even came close, once.

It was Mother's Day. He made Mama pancakes with maple syrup and arranged everything on a tray. The fork to the left of the plate, the knife to the right, the napkin folded tip-to-tip like he'd seen in a real restaurant. He even picked a rose from Mrs. Dunnigan's yard. A rose for a Rose—he thought he was so clever.

When he walked into her bedroom, he'd placed the perfectly-put-together tray on her bed, and she smiled.

A real smile, genuine.

Not like the courtesy smile she gave the bagger at the Pack-and-Save or his second grade-teacher. He watched her cut through the pancakes and take a bite, excited she was so pleased.

Until her eyes narrowed.

"Wipe that stupid grin off your face. Pancakes ain't that good. Edges ain't even crispy. And this syrup tastes stale. Where the hell did you get it, anyway?"

The disappointment, her judgment, how helpless she'd made him feel—all washed over him again.

His insides twisted. His chest went tight. He plunged his hand into his pocket and pulled out the Zippo, heart jackhammering now—the *thud, thud, thud* thundering in his ears. And the pressure in his head—the godawful pressure. Staring at the flame this time wasn't enough. He needed to sit, he needed to breathe.

He needed something to burn.

He looked toward the bar, but it had disappeared behind a sea of cowboy hats, fringed shirts, and too-tight blue jeans.

*Thud. Thud. Thud.*

His eyes darted around the room—searching—hoping to find something small, something discrete, something to feed his need.

And then he found it, near the jukebox, an empty table with left-behind-drinks and discarded cocktail napkins.

He slung the box on top, fell into a chair, grabbed a cocktail napkin. He folded the napkin, tip-to-tip, lit the edge and watched it flame. Hues of yellow and orange and black crawled along the paper. And he stared, absorbing the energy from the heat. He loved how powerful it made him feel.

How he could finally breathe again.

He clung to the napkin. It singed his fingers. Still, he clung some more. Finally, he dropped the paper into the ashtray. And he watched.

Until it wilted.

Until it turned to ashes. Just like his mama.

It began when he was little—the obsession with fire.

He'd stand at the kitchen sink. Strike a match. Watch it burn. Strike another. He loved the friction beneath his finger, the smell of sulfur, the flame.

He was ten when he found the Zippo.

His daddy had left it behind—the day he left for good. Between pulls of gin and fits of rage, Mama told Waylon about her former life—how she was once a honky-tonk queen, a line-dancing champion, how she'd been destined for greatness.

Before he'd ruined it.

Waylon realized that night his mama loved three things: booze, roses, and honky-tonks. One day he'd take her to the perfect one—one that had all three.

Then maybe she'd love him, too.

Waylon looked at the box.

The flaps were bowed from a rainstorm in Norman, the bottom charred from a mishap in Lubbock. And the sides had dents and dings from sliding around in his truck and across countless tables and booths.

Would the Wild Rose leave its mark, too?

His chest went tight. He could feel himself already starting to cycle again.

*Place ain't that bad.*

Waylon's breath caught. He stared at the box, not sure he'd heard her right.

*Them wagon-wheel chandeliers are classy in a jeans and boots kind of way. Reminds me of that place where I met your daddy, may his soul burn in hell.*

He waited. For her to complain. For the other boot to drop.

But there was nothing.

Had he finally found the right place?

Seconds turned to minutes. And still only silence.

The joy, the relief he felt that Mother's Day filled him again.

He signaled for the waitress.

"What can I get you, Sugar?"

"C-c-c..."

The waitress flashed an encouraging smile.

"C-c-c-oors."

"Darlin', my sixteen-year-old looks older than you. I'm going to need some ID."

Waylon fumbled for his wallet, the nerve endings in his fingers gone. He managed to pull out his driver's license.

The woman's breath caught. "Oh honey, what happened to your hands?"

He looked at the thick, mangled skin, and heat rose to his cheeks.

The Ripped Rose, The Drunk Rose, the *Westfield trailer park*, and the countless other things he'd burned. They all had one thing in common.

Mama. She's what happened to his hands.

*You're such an embarrassment, Waylon.*

No. No. No.

He jumped to his feet. His legs hit the table. The box tumbled off the side and crashed against the floor. He watched in horror as Mama's urn rolled out, ashes trailing behind it.

The waitress gasped. "Oh. My. God. Is that—"

*Place was perfect. Until you ruined it.*

*You ruin everything.*

Blood rushed to his ears. And the pressure, the godawful pressure. His chest went tight. And the buzzing started now.

*Weeeeee.*

He scooped the ashes into the urn, shoved the urn into the box, and ran to the bathroom.

It was a single, just a toilet with a sink. He slung the box onto the counter, ash smeared against the sides. The room began to spin.

*Weeeeee.*

He grabbed a fistful of paper towels. Then, his Zippo. He angled the paper toward the flame. The fire died.

Someone banged against the door.

His stomach tumbled. "Nnnnneed a mmmminute."

More banging. "It's an emergency, man."

He shook the lighter, tried again. It didn't start.

The room continued to spin. *Weeeeee.*

*I was a honky-tonk queen until I got knocked up with you—a stuttering half-wit who can't even light a fire. No wonder your daddy walked out.*

He flicked the wheel, the paper finally flamed. But the buzzing didn't stop. The tension didn't ease.

He needed something more.

Desperate, he dropped the towels in the sink, opened the door, and went to the parking lot. When he reached his truck, he grabbed the gas can.

*Earth to Waylon.*

He blinked. He was inside the cab of his truck, hands on his steering wheel, box buckled into the passenger seat, engine running.

He wondered how long he'd been sitting there.

*You gonna sit there all night, or are you gonna get on with it?*

He pulled out of the parking lot, gas can banging in the back, eyes on his rearview mirror, the Wild Rose behind him, engulfed in flames. Even from the parking lot, he could feel the energy from the heat. He loved how powerful it made him feel.

How he could finally breathe again.

He followed the road to the interstate and continued driving toward Waco and The Country Rose. He'd seen pictures online. It seemed like the perfect place—a real honky-tonk.

Not like the one in Austin.

# ALL APPLES
## Andrew Welsh-Huggins

Jessica nervously zipped and unzipped the top of her Columbia autumn fleece jacket as she eyed the knot of people on the opposite sidewalk beside the dented white panel van. She did her best to ignore the graffiti covering the vacant church one building up from the van, and the shine of smashed glass on the street. Her heart was still hammering from braking for the hooded pedestrian who'd darted in front of her three blocks up. What had seemed like a good idea two days ago—an idea, anyway—was quickly shriveling into a foolhardy concept, like a letter applying for a dream job crumpled into a ball at the last moment. Jason was right. What the hell was she thinking?

"Mom?"

"Yes."

"What are we waiting for? Did you change your mind?"

"No." Annoyed at the note of hopefulness in Maddy's voice even as her own doubts crept in. "I just...No, let's go."

She took a breath and opened the Sienna's driver-side door. She waited for Maddy, hit the fob to lock the minivan, and crossed Sullivant. Reaching the small crowd, Jessica stood uncertainly. But not for long.

"Can I help you?"

"I'm here to volunteer?" Jessica said. "I sent an email? I was told seven o'clock?"

"Who told you?" The speaker was a thin, wiry man who hadn't shaved in a few days, wearing faded jeans, a green Army coat, and an olive watch cap.

"I'm not sure," Jessica said, uncomfortable with the man's tone as she felt her throat catch from the cigarette smoke infusing his clothes. She fumbled for her phone. "I've got it here someplace..."

"Have you volunteered before? Like this, I mean?" He stared at Jessica and Maddy with eyes as hard and dark as asphalt at midnight.

"I've volunteered, of course," Jessica said, growing flustered. "But not—"

"Where are you from?"

"Here. Columbus."

"You live in Columbus?"

"Well, Upper Arlington."

"So you don't live in Columbus. And in fact, like ten million light years from here. Not to be rude, but what are you hoping to accomplish?"

"We're just trying to help, is all."

"We?"

"Maddy—my daughter Maddy and me." Jessica pointed at Maddy, who couldn't have looked more mortified had Jessica removed all her clothes and begun dancing in the street.

"Why?"

"Why what?"

"Why is somebody from the suburbs trying to help down here?"

For a moment, Jessica's embarrassment turned to irritation at the reception she was receiving from, well, from a guy like this. Compounding her mixed feelings, she had to admit the drive here had seemed to encompass a distance that wasn't purely physical. A twenty-minute ride not helped in the least by Maddy's quips about "the ghetto" that started out snarky but grew increasingly

## ALL APPLES

apprehensive.

"It just seemed—I mean, these poor girls."

"You mean poor women."

"Yes. Women. Of course."

The speaker adjusted his cap and took a step toward Jessica, startling her enough that she reflexively backed up. "Did you know that eight of every ten men who buy sex in central Ohio live in the suburbs? Maybe you even know some of them. And maybe if they stayed home, you wouldn't have to crack a heel driving yourself down here to help these 'poor girls.'"

"I didn't—" she said, recoiling from his coffee breath on top of the cigarette smell.

"Chris—a second?"

A woman wearing a lightweight gold zip-up top and black leggings appeared before Jessica, arms crossed, frowning at the man.

"What."

"Something with the kits?" the woman said, pointing at the van.

"Like what?"

"Like I don't know. Somebody said they needed you."

"For God's sake." He shook his head and walked away.

The woman leaned toward Jessica with a secretive smile. "Diversion tactic," she whispered. "Sorry about that. Chris runs a little rough." She thrust out her hand. "Elaine Chatfield. I'm the volunteer coordinator. And for what it's worth, a proud Worthington resident."

Jessica, inordinately relieved at the mention of another suburb, shook Elaine's warm, firm hand as she introduced herself and Maddy.

"Of course—we exchanged emails. Thank you so much for coming. Both of you."

"I'm sorry he feels that way," Jessica managed, glancing at the van. "It's our—it's Maddy's first time doing something like this."

"Chris's bedside manner leaves room for improvement," Elaine said. "In fairness, there's a lot going on right now with the grant. He's feeling the pressure. He also lives down here and gets a little...proprietary about things."

"Grant?"

"Sorry. Safe Streets received five hundred thousand dollars from the Justice Department, renewable annually over three years. It's a game-changer. It's going to take things to a whole new level—more staff, an intake shelter, counseling services. The works. Chris is feeling the pressure as executive director. Target on his back and all that."

"That guy...he's the executive director?"

"That would be correct," Elaine said.

"Well, okay. That's great—about the grant, I mean."

"I should say so. It's about time these girls caught a break. I just hope—well, never mind that. Anyway, it's so nice to meet you. You can't imagine how happy I was to receive your email. And for the record, unlike Chris, I don't care where you live, how you vote, or who you root for. We can use all the help we can get."

"Thanks." Jessica felt herself relax in the presence of Elaine, with her Warby Parker cranberry red glasses and mass of shoulder-length gray curls. "As long as we're not in the way."

"With our numbers, that would take some doing. Step over here and I'll show you the drill."

With Elaine as their guide, Jessica and Maddy crossed the street and maneuvered themselves to the side of the van. Chris, his face etched with impatience, was handing out heavy-laden white vinyl string bags.

"Here's the deal," Elaine said. "We work in teams to be safe. Each bag"—she gestured at Chris—"contains soap, shampoo, tampons, condoms, a toothbrush, toothpaste, a hairbrush, two all-day COTA passes, a bottle of water, and three granola bars. The soap and shampoo are labeled with an 800 number that connects to social services. We don't identify the numbers because we don't want their daddies taking the stuff away first thing. Most of them figure it out anyway, unfortunately."

"Daddies?" Maddy said.

"Sorry," Elaine said. "The, ah, men who make the girls work for them." She looked at Jessica, who nodded her permission to continue. "Not their real daddies, of course. Well, for the most part."

"Rules, please," Chris said, looking up.

"I'm getting to that."

"Rules?" Jessica said.

"Rules," Elaine said, frowning at Chris. "Number One, no hard sells. We just offer the bags. If they take them, great. If not, or they react badly, we move on. If they want to talk, we listen. We suggest ways to get assistance, but that's not our primary job."

"Which is?"

"Helping them get through the week. Big picture stuff comes later. That takes me to Rule Number Two, which is don't engage the men down here. They might be johns, they might be, well, daddies. You can't predict what they're going to do. How they'll respond to you. Always assume a man down here wants to hurt you—that's why we work in teams. Understood?"

"Yes," Jessica and Maddy said simultaneously.

Then, after a moment of silence, Jessica said, "Is there a Rule Number Three?"

Elaine paused, almost as if she were waiting for something. Then, before she had a chance to reply, Chris said, "Never come here alone."

"Chris—" Elaine said.

"I'm serious," he said, ignoring Elaine, who was clearly annoyed at the interruption. "No freelancing. I know it's hard to believe tonight, but if you stick it out"—he ran his eyes up and down Jessica in a way that made her feel instantly uncomfortable—"you'll be tempted. Especially if you make a connection with a particular woman over time. 'Oh, what could it hurt? We're friends now,'" he said in a mocking voice. "No. You're not friends. And Elaine's right. It's dangerous down here. Understood?"

Maddy nodded her head several times.

"Thanks, Chris," Elaine said, drawing out each word a nanosecond longer than necessary. But then she turned to Jessica. "You understand, right?"

"Definitely."

"You sure?"

"Yes. Of course."


Jessica wasn't usually one to affix blame. But looking back, anyone could see that Natalie started the ball rolling.

Case in point: Jessica first saw the video clip via a text from her best and oldest friend. *Cool!* Natalie said in her accompanying message.

Then it showed up in Jessica's book club Facebook group, then in her Pilates text circle, then in an email blast from the high school.

A Channel 7 feature. Ava, daughter of their across-the-street neighbors. Same class as Maddy. A Six O'clock News profile of Ava's trip to Uganda over the summer, volunteering at an orphanage. Clips from an interview with Ava in her high-school jersey—obviously filmed before or after soccer practice—interspersed with iPhone video of Ugandan orphans in smart blue-and-white outfits sitting as Ava read to them, played soccer with them, helped them plant vegetables. A closing shot of Ava, deeply tanned but still pale by comparison, grinning in the middle of a pile of beaming children.

"What a gift to give on your summer vacation," the male anchor intoned in his familiar baritone, chit-chatting with his young female co-anchor after the segment ended.

"The kind of story we all need right now," the woman replied in a voice like warm honey.

Two nights later, propped on her pillows in bed, tablet in hand as she read the latest Colleen Hoover, Jessica said, "Hey—there's this thing, downtown. Well, near downtown."

"Thing?" Jason said, eyes glued to his fantasy NBA trades.

"It's a volunteer thing. You hand out toiletries and stuff to, well, to trafficked women."

Jason glanced at her. "You mean prostitutes?"

"I don't think we're supposed to say that anymore. Anyway, I'm thinking it would be good for Maddy. Volunteering there, I mean."

"Huh," Jason said. "What brought this on?"

"Nothing," Jessica said, peeved at her white lie. "It's something I've been considering. I did some research and found out about it."

"It wouldn't happen to be research involving that video about Ava, would it?"

Jessica sighed. "No. Well, not exactly. That story got me thinking."

"Yeah," Jason interrupted. "Thinking what a big sacrifice it was for Ava to give up her vacation at the lake house to fly to Kenya on her parents' dime to play with brown children. Oh, and by the way? You know damn well that's going to be at the top of her admission applications."

"Uganda. And wow, really? At least she's not complaining about working five hours a week at Graeter's."

"At least Maddy knows the value of work. Is she on board with this? Going down there?"

"She said she'd try it out."

"Amazing. Okay, then. When is this? The prostitutes—the victims, I mean."

"Friday night. Just an hour or so."

"You're going to take Maddy down *there* on a Friday night to hand out soap to, um, to these kinds of ladies?"

"That's what I said."

"I heard what you said. I'll believe it when I see it."


Of course, Jason was right. Maddy bailed after one night.

"Friday's like the only time I have with my friends, mom."

"Except for Saturday. And all the other times you see them. And you don't have to do it every week."

"I know, but..."

Jessica let it go. She was miffed at her daughter for not embracing the concept—Jessica herself had raised hundreds of dollars for cheer squad uniforms putting on car washes at Maddy's age. Yet she was also, truth be told, a little relieved that she could try out the volunteering on her own. Because to her surprise, she had liked it despite her initial encounter with Chris and the bad impression he left. She still couldn't get over the idea he was the actual executive director.

"You're going back?" Jason said in bed the following week after a predictably snarky comment about Maddy quitting.

Jessica haltingly explained that she found the work interesting. That she felt like she was making a difference. "Plus, I need something to do."

Jason looked at her. "You mean besides your full-time job? And Moms? And the kids and...*me*? No offense, but you seem pretty scheduled the way things are."

She shook her head in frustration. He wasn't getting it. She said, "I'm busy, sure. It's just—"

"Just what? Not busy enough? You're the one always complaining about feeling overbooked."

"That's not fair," she said, realizing it was entirely fair. "I just feel, I don't know, like I could be of value to people who really need what I have to offer."

"You seem valuable to me. Starting with Moms. You mean more than that?"

"Well, yes. I think."

"You think? Or you know?"

Two years ago, Jessica joined the board of Moms for Proms. At Natalie's urging, who told her she'd never regret the required $2,000 board donation. And she didn't, if she were being mostly honest with herself. It was a positive program. Moms wearing prom dresses put on a charity dance, with proceeds providing free trips to Disney World for cancer-stricken kids. Tickets for $250 and then cash donations for each dance with a mom made it a goodwill bargain. They'd raised nearly $24,000 last year.

In truth, Jessica had mixed feelings about it until she met her first class of trip recipients. Such sweethearts. And well, until her first event, when she realized every eye in the downtown Hilton ballroom was on her as she entered. On her and her low-cut, flounce skirt, rose-colored Sherri Hill. Not the same dress she'd worn for her own prom, of course. And a little more expensive this time, despite the sale price. But the same size, she reminded herself.

"Sorry. Seriously, it sounds…"

"Yes?" She turned to him. He was doing that thing where he bit his tongue by partially closing his eyes instead of finishing a sentence. It was annoying, though also, if she had to admit it, kind of cute.

"It sounds a little…different than what you usually do."

"Out of my comfort zone, you mean? Or my skill set?"

Jason set his tablet down and looked warmly at her. "Not your skill set, obviously. And I'm not here to judge your comfort zone."

"Really?"

"C'mon, hon. You're the most compassionate person I know. Like Mother Theresa in Lululemon. I'm only…I mean, it's not dangerous, is it?"

She relaxed a little, savoring the compliment despite herself.

"I don't think so," she said, wondering if that were really true. What was it Elaine said? *Always assume a man down here wants to hurt you.* She said, "It's all organized with an executive director and volunteer coordinator and everything. And a website."

"Well, if there's a website…"

"You know what I mean," she said, elbowing him.

"I'm teasing." But then his voice turned serious. "You're not going to leave Moms, though. Are you?"

"I'm not sure. I guess I haven't decided. Why?"

"Because you've done good things there. You make a difference in people's lives. And also, I mean…"

"What?"

"Well, Jesus, your dress."

"What about it?"

"Are you kidding me?" He pushed his hand under the white goose-down comforter, found the hem of her lacy, brushed flannel nightgown, and inched his hand up her thigh.

"Whoa, boy. The kids—"

"What about them?" he said, slowly moving his hand up and over. He leaned in and kissed her on the cheek and then her neck. "Ethan's out like a light from lacrosse and Maddy's on TikTok, which means she might as well be on the moon. We're fine."

"Just wait a minute…"

"I can't. That dress. The way you looked in it. Between that and these guns"—he gave her left bicep a gentle squeeze—"I mean, Holy Tent Pole, Batman." He kissed her on the lips. She hesitated, then kissed him back, warming to him. As she did, he slipped his hand under her panties.

"Hoo," Jessica breathed out, rolling toward him. "All this from a prom dress?"

"Guns and a Moms dress," Jason said, leaning back and switching off his light. "It doesn't get any better than that."

Despite Jason's skepticism and his frustration at losing so many of their Friday nights, Jessica kept at it. And each time, she felt better and better about her contribution. Every year, she and Jason made a point to volunteer at a Columbus Marathon water station down the street from them, and she increasingly found herself comparing the two experiences favorably. In each case, she was handing something useful to people in need, who didn't say much in return but whose tired eyes still suggested their gratitude.

She hadn't been able to make Safe Streets every Friday night, of course. Book club, for example, especially the time they read the new Princess Di biography. No choice, since it was her recommendation, and she was leading the discussion. A Moms board meeting another night. And then the evening of the Coldplay concert at the Schott—no backing out given what those tickets cost. But most Fridays, for sure.

And on one of those nights, she first met CeCe.

Following in Elaine's footsteps, Jessica came across her loitering in the front yard of an abandoned bungalow east of Central, eyes dully glancing at the cars driving past, measuring with her hollow gaze which vehicle might be slowing, who might be a driver on the prowl. Jessica, feeling bold, approached first, then backed up, barely suppressing a gasp when she spied the bruise on the girl's cheek, the injury's ripened banana mottling visible even at night. Wearing ripped sweatpants and an oversized gray hoodie, she could have been seventeen or twenty-seven or really almost any age.

"CeCe," Elaine said, intervening. "Jessica and I are going to look at the bruise from your...fall."

Jessica, a pit in her stomach, stepped into the yard, nearly tripping over a pile of old bricks in the process. She tried not to stare at the bruise, at the grime on CeCe's hands, at the glassy stare in her eyes.

"Hi there," she said. When CeCe didn't respond, Jessica cleared her throat and said, "Here's a few things for you." But before she could retrieve anything, Elaine said, "I think she's probably okay on that front."

"I'm fine," CeCe said, underscoring the point.

At Elaine's suggestion, Jessica spent the next few minutes trying her best to engage the girl, counting it a victory if CeCe's monosyllabic replies expanded into three or four words. Eventually, Elaine tapped her on the shoulder and gestured for her to follow.

"Should we call the police? I mean, that bruise. She didn't fall, right?"

Elaine didn't answer right away. While she waited for a reply,

Jessica snugged up the Aran Island lambswool checked scarf that Jason bought her on their trip to Scotland the previous summer. It felt good against the night's chill, which she was feeling literally and figuratively.

"We could call the police," Elaine said at last. "We could also fart into a hurricane, pardon my French."

"They wouldn't do anything?"

"They might take a report. They also might run her name, find an outstanding warrant, and haul her in. But we can't…"

"Can't what?"

"It's complicated, all right? I'll leave it at that."

"But what about—"

"What about what?"

"The man who did that to her?"

Elaine turned in the direction of the Safe Streets van. "What about him?"

"He just gets to walk away? There's no accountability?" Flushing, Jessica thought of Jason's initial skepticism, which hadn't really faded with time. The biting his tongue thing with his partially closed eyes. *It's not dangerous, is it?*

Jessica shook the thought away as Elaine stopped and faced her. "In this case, yes."

"This case? What's that supposed to mean?"

"It means nothing. Except that the streets are tough, which is why we're trying to help these girls. Listen, we need to get going. You did well tonight—it's great to have you along. Like I said, I can't tell you how happy I was when you first emailed."

"Thanks, I guess."

"No—I mean it."

And in truth, it had felt good, the conversation—if you could call it that—with CeCe. Like she was doing something real. Being of value to someone who needed what she had to offer. She recalled the clip of Ava amid the beaming scrum of Ugandan orphans. Jason's snide commentary. *What a big sacrifice it was for Ava to give up her vacation at the lakehouse.* Really?

"Thanks. I appreciate that. But—are you at least going to tell Chris?"

"Yes," Elaine said. "I'm definitely going to tell Chris."

Two Fridays later—the one after Coldplay—they saw CeCe again. The bruise had faded but had been replaced by ugly red marks on her neck.

"We have to do something," Jessica said, looking over her shoulder as she and Elaine left the girl behind.

"There's nothing to do. In this case."

Jessica grabbed Elaine's left elbow. "You said that before. What's it mean?"

"It's nothing. I shouldn't have said it."

"It doesn't sound like nothing."

Elaine stopped and sighed. "Listen. I shouldn't be telling you this."

"Telling me what?"

Elaine glanced up at the street at the Safe Streets van, her hammered silver earrings swinging with the movement of her head.

"There's something about CeCe you should know."

"Which is?"

Elaine took a breath. "She's Chris's girlfriend."

"What?" Jessica stared, not sure she'd heard correctly.

Elaine sighed again, a little louder this time. "Look. I probably shouldn't have told you. And, honestly, it's complicated. Maybe girlfriend doesn't fully capture it."

"What does then? I mean, she is, or she isn't?"

Elaine moved Jessica back down the sidewalk. "CeCe was one of the first girls Chris connected with down here. As far as I can tell, one thing led to another. He may have confused rescue with romance. Or something. It happens in these situations, unfortunately."

"But that's—I mean, it's unconscionable. And a huge conflict of interest, right?"

"I told you, it's complicated. And they're off and on—more off now, I think, if that matters."

"But is she, you know, turning tricks?" Jessica felt justifiably proud at how natural the lingo came to her now.

"Who knows? Where CeCe's concerned, it's not totally our business."

"If she's not, though, then who's beating her? Don't tell me that Chris—"

Elaine paused, and then said, "There's no evidence of that."

"You don't sound convinced."

"I'm just giving you my perspective. I haven't seen evidence that he's responsible. Hard evidence."

"That's comforting."

"Let me put it this way: I think he thinks he's trying to help. Chris definitely has a certain mindset about the world. Living down here, he sees things we don't. And being perfectly honest about it, we probably wouldn't have gotten the grant without him."

"But if she's on the streets, how can he justify any kind of relationship? Grant or not?"

"Maybe he sees it as protecting her? He can at least offer her a safe haven. Which is more than anyone else has."

"While he's beating her up?"

"I said there's no evidence of that."

"You said hard evidence."

"Yes, okay. That's what I said."

"We need to do something," Jessica said. "Say something."

"You need to calm down. I've thought about it. Trust me. But he's tight with the board. And once he got the grant—what could I do? It's not like I'm executive director. If it makes a difference, I don't think he's any more comfortable with the situation than you are. Like I said, he sees himself trying to help."

"You should be executive director. Not someone like him."

"That's nice of you to say. Maybe someday. But for now, this must remain between us. Things might change once the grant money comes in. But we can't do anything to jeopardize that. Do you understand? That money will go a long, long way down here. Including for girls like CeCe."

"It's not right."

"Maybe not. But we have to live with it. I only told you because I trust you. And admire you and everything you do. And for now, that's how it has to be."


"Leaving Moms?" Natalie said in disbelief.

"Thinking about leaving Moms," Jessica said, somehow angry at herself for the reaction of her friend.

"For God's sake, why?" Natalie picked up the remaining half of her croissant, then returned it to her plate.

Saturday morning. A girls' breakfast at Le Chatelaine on Lane, a restaurant Jessica and Natalie had been coming to for twenty years, since high school. Their weekly guilty pleasure after hot yoga down the street.

"I just feel like I'm making a difference for a change. Like I'm offering something of value to needy people."

Jessica explained, with a hint of pride in her voice, about persisting despite Chris's first-night jab—*You wouldn't have to crack a heel driving yourself down here.* She left out the whole Chris and CeCe thing to honor her promise to Elaine. It was their secret, for now.

Natalie wasn't having any of it. "*Down here*? Oh, so you can only do good if you live in the city? What a load of crap. Like a zip code makes your time and money special. You don't believe that nonsense, do you?"

"Of course not. But that's not the point of what I'm trying to say."

"What is the point, then?"

"Well, with the Moms kids, it feels like they'll always have someone. Maybe not taking them to Disney, but taking care of them. It's a good cause, sure, but is it enough?"

"Enough for who? For the kids? Or for you? Because I guarantee you it's enough for the kids. Trust me. I get the thank yous from their parents. Some of the cards? They're literally tear-stained—no lie."

"I don't know," Jessica pleaded, nibbling at a corner of her buttery croissant. "Maybe both. Or neither. The funny thing about all this is you're the one to blame in the first place."

"Me?"

"When you texted me Ava's TV thing. I thought you were trying to tell me something. I took it seriously." She frowned, thinking of Jason's dismissive comment about Ava.

"I was showing you something I thought was interesting," Natalie said. "Some kid doing something good for a change instead of making one more goddamn Instagram reel about bubble tea. I wasn't comparing anything. We're not talking apples and oranges, you know. Moms for Proms vs. Safe Streets vs. whatever else. It's all helping people. It's all apples."

"Calm down. You're overreacting."

"All apples," Natalie said. "Don't ever forget that."

*CeCe's missing. I thought you should know.*

Jessica stared at the text the following Tuesday, sitting in her home office on the second floor next to Maddy's bathroom.

*Oh God. Since when?*

*Call me,* Elaine texted.

Elaine filled Jessica in as best she could. She'd heard it from another volunteer and then went straight to Chris, who begrudgingly confirmed it.

"Do the police know?"

"Chris said he'd take care of it."

"Will he?"

"We have to assume he will."

Jessica stood and walked away from her desk. She was shaking. She'd grown close to Elaine in recent weeks, or as much as their Friday night work allowed, as they bonded over doing what they could to protect CeCe and the dysfunctional rot at the core of Safe Streets. At Elaine's suggestion, they'd made sure CeCe had both their cell phone numbers, just in case. One night, briefly, CeCe even rested her head on Jessica's shoulder like Maddy did once upon a long time ago.

"Do you trust him? Chris, I mean?"

"What do you mean?"

"Do you trust that he doesn't know what happened to CeCe?"

"Of course, I do," Elaine said, but even over the phone, Jessica could sense the skepticism in her tone like a brave smile belying a broken heart.

"Is there anything I can do?"

"Well…"

"What is it?"

"I was thinking of going down there. Me and a couple of others. Looking around. Off the books, so to speak."

"Not telling Chris, you mean."

Elaine didn't say anything.

"I'll be there."

Jason wasn't happy when she let him know he'd have to pick up dinner from Whole Foods's prepared meals aisle tonight. He especially wasn't pleased when she reminded him that Ethan was gaming at a friend's house until eight, and Maddy needed help with math if she had any hope of raising her ACTs. She told him she'd be back as soon as she could.

"I hope you know what you're doing," he said.

"Thanks for the vote of confidence."

Elaine shook her head when Jessica met her by the boarded-up church at six o'clock. "Welcome to my life. Looks like we're it."

They went block by block, showing CeCe's picture to the few women they found. The yard of the house where Elaine first introduced Jessica to CeCe sat empty and dark, the streetlamp's smashed bulb mixing with the lawn's discarded brick pile in a tableau of urban decay. Street by street—nothing.

Dispirited after an hour, they were headed back to their cars when Elaine looked up, hearing her name.

"What are you doing down here?" Chris, wearing the same outfit as the night Jessica met him. Brow furrowed with suspicion. Cigarette smell, if anything, even stronger.

"Looking for CeCe," Elaine said. "Like you should be."

"What the hell do you think I'm doing? I've been out here for hours."

"And no sign of her after all that?"

"What are you implying?"

"She's implying that you of all people should know how vulnerable she is," Jessica said, unable to help herself.

"Jessica."

Chris planted himself in front of her. "And what's that supposed to mean?"

"What do you think it means?"

Chris jerked his head at Elaine. "No—you didn't. Are you kidding me?"

Elaine pursed her lips and crossed her arms.

"For God's sake—she's a soccer mom from fucking Upper Scarsdale," Chris said, staring at Jessica. "This isn't any of her business."

"How dare you?" Jessica said, stepping toward him. She gasped a moment later as Chris reached out with both arms and lightly pushed her back.

"How dare you get involved in what's none of your business?"

"Chris—" Elaine said.

"Get out of here. Both of you," he said, his eyes shining, his face drawn in anger. "You're doing more harm than good."

"That's rich," Jessica said.

"Enough, both of you," Elaine said, grabbing Jessica's sleeve.

But even as she reluctantly followed her mentor, Jessica kept her eyes on Chris, who glared in their direction before turning, shoulders hunched, and walking slowly down the street.

## ALL APPLES

\*\*\*

The Moms for Proms board had convened in Natalie's basement for takeout Donato's and some California reds two nights later when Jessica's phone buzzed with a text.

*Please help me.*

Jessica rose and crossed the room, standing by the end of the pool table.

*Who is this?*
*CeCe.*
*Where are you?*
*Down here. Please help me.*
*Down where?*
No answer.

Jessica stepped into the laundry room and tried calling. No response. She tried again, and texted again, all to no avail. Then, two final texts from CeCe.

*I'm scared.*
*Chris.*

Jessica called Elaine, panic flooding her insides.

"Jesus," Elaine said after Jessica explained.

"What are we going to do?"

A long silence. "I'll call Chris. And then—shit."

"What?"

"If she's calling you, things are even more complicated. Now I'm worried. I hate to ask this…"

"I can leave right now."

"I'll be there as soon as I can. But remember the rules. Don't do anything alone. Wait for me, all right?"

Jessica checked her Apple watch. Seven fifteen.

"All right?"

"All right," Jessica said.

Jason was predictably furious when she texted him with her plan and called her right away.

"How is this your issue? This is why we have police."

"We can't call the police."

"Why in God's name not?"

"We just can't."

"You should not be doing this."

"How about backing me up for a change?"

"I am backing you up. I'm trying to protect you. You're not listening."

Jessica tried venting about Jason with Natalie as she took her aside and explained why she had to leave. But Natalie was, if anything, more upset.

"He's right. It's not your fight."

"And why not? All apples, right?"

"Helping people, sure. I stand by that. But you're not endangering yourself raising money for Disney World trips."

"Maybe I should be."

"You can't be serious."

Even Ava's mother, a founding Moms board member, weighed in.

"Are you sure you want to get this involved?"

Jessica went anyway, irked at their reactions. Ava's mom—well, that was predictable. But she had hoped for more from her husband and her best friend. Why couldn't they see the value of what she was trying to do?

Once there, parked opposite the church, Jessica waited thirty minutes. What felt like an eternity—alone in that part of town, sticking out in a two-year-old Toyota Sienna she'd just washed at Moo Moo, unwilling to let their monthly subscription go unused. A couple of men driving past leered at her. She texted Elaine, then called. Twice. Nothing. Finally, she gave up, climbed out of the van, and began a nervous canvass of the dark block.

*Never come here alone.*

Easy for Chris to say.

"You," she said, as she began her next grid pattern, one street over. He was standing in the yard of the abandoned bungalow where Elaine first pointed CeCe out to Jessica.

"What are you doing here?" Chris said, eyebrows rising in anger.

"I'm looking for CeCe. She texted me. She said she was scared. She mentioned you. But you probably know that already, don't you?"

"Know what?"

"Did you hurt her, you sonofabitch?"

"Hurt her?" he said, approaching Jessica. His face was red, his cheeks shiny, as if he'd been exerting himself. "I'm trying to help her. I'm really worried."

"Yeah. I can see that. Even though I'm only a soccer mom."

"Look, I'm sorry I—"

"You didn't answer my question. Did you hurt CeCe?"

"Hurt her? I love her," he said, taking another step forward. Jessica backed up and then gave a small cry as she tripped and fell.

"Shit. Are you all right?"

"Get back," Jessica said, rubbing her calf where she'd tripped on the pile of old bricks.

"For Chrissake—"

"Back," she gasped, as she glanced around in desperation before grabbing the nearest brick. It felt hard and solid; practically the size of the hand weights her trainer had her working with.

"Give me your hand—"

"I'm warning you."

"About what?" He extended his arms toward her, his hands appearing to Jessica like a pair of sausage-thick pincers reaching for her neck.

"Gad," he said, when she struck the first time, the brick hitting the left side of his head with a sharp smack. He staggered, staring at her with wild eyes. "What the—"

He didn't say anything after the second blow, which drew

blood and sent him to his knees, then over and onto his side. After the next several blows, Jessica atop him now, flinging her arm down over and over, he quivered like a fish on a dock that wouldn't give up. After the last blow, he grunted, sighed, and went still.

Behind Jessica, a voice said, "Oh my God."

Startled by the sound, Jessica lifted the brick and stared at it. Even in the dim light, she realized it was the wrong color. A deeper red than a normal brick. And shiny and wet, as if rain had fallen on it. Shiny, like Chris's cheeks. Which, she now realized, catching her breath, had been damp from tears, not sweat. She turned. Elaine. Appearing as if from nowhere.

"I waited for you," Jessica said in a daze.

"Waited for me? What are you talking about?"

She still hadn't seen Maddy or Ethan. Natalie tried coming, but Jessica wouldn't leave the pod when she found out who it was. After two days, she relented and approved Jason.

"What happened?" he said numbly.

"I waited for her."

"Waited for who?"

It was ironic how she heard the news. Or rather, who she heard it from. CeCe told her. They shared the same pod. CeCe a veteran of five days. Where she'd been the whole time, under a different name she used sometimes. One Chris didn't know about. Not knowing anything about messaging Jessica since Elaine had taken her phone last week, telling her she'd replace it. CeCe a little nervous about that, given the beating she'd taken in recent weeks from two different johns—the bruise on her cheek, the red marks on her neck—but acquiescing in the end.

CeCe had seen the announcement on the news. Elaine Chatfield reluctantly accepting the position of Safe Streets executive director under such tragic circumstances. Promising to honor Chris's legacy with her administration of the DOJ grant. Shaking her mass of curly gray hair at what she called the "act of a troubled woman clearly out of her element."

"I asked you not to go," Jason said.

"I waited," she whispered.

"Jesus, Jessica. I mean—there's footage. There're security cameras everywhere down there."

"Jason?"

"Yes?"

"The cameras? They show the truth, right? About what happened? About him attacking me?"

"They..." Jason began.

"Jason?"

He didn't reply. Instead, he did that thing again. Annoying, but kind of cute. Rather than finish his sentence, he slowly, reluctantly, partially closed his eyes.

# GONE FISHIN'
## James A. Hearn

Dressed in pajamas, Herb Middleton slipped into his office chair and switched on his work laptop. He checked the time and smiled to himself. At three minutes to nine, there should be plenty of time for entering his passwords and logging into Sunrise Bank & Trust's timekeeping software. He was proven right when his screen populated this message:

Employee: Herbert Q. Middleton
Department: Reverse Mortgages
Position: Compliance Specialist III
Log on time: 08:59:47 EST
Welcome, Herbert! Have a wonderful day.

"A new record, Lady Godiva," Herb said to a sleepy tabby cat curled at his feet. "I woke up thirty minutes ago, had a leisurely breakfast, and still had thirteen seconds to spare."

The old cat raised her head, her whiskers twitching in annoyance. Herb slipped his bare feet under her belly and said, "Remote work, where've you been all my life?"

When the pandemic struck in 2020, Herb exchanged a long, nail-biting commute to the heart of downtown Jacksonville,

Florida, for a twenty-step jaunt from his couch to the kitchen table. Rush hours and bumper-to-bumper traffic were replaced with morning coffee and crossword puzzles.

Herb missed his coworkers, a little, but he didn't miss company potlucks of vegetarian chili, bad coffee, and singing "Happy Birthday" to strangers. And he certainly didn't miss managers popping up unexpectedly to hassle him at ten minutes to five.

For the first time in years, the monotonous task of auditing the bank's reverse mortgages for regulatory compliance became *tolerable*. In fact, life itself became tolerable, even enjoyable. Freed from the office's chains, Herb had more time, money, and energy. He bought a home gym, cooked gourmet dinners, and watched entire movies without going to bed halfway through them.

On Saturday nights, as the pandemic loosened its grip on the world, Herb ventured forth beyond his humble home. He found an old-style English pub he liked, a place where the bartenders called him by name and served his favorite whiskey at a good price. As a fifty-six-year-old divorcé, Herb was a bit out of practice in the singles game, but at long last, he was back out there.

Felicity, his ex-wife, would be surprised to see him enjoying life again. *You'll die alone, Herb*, were the last words she'd spoken to him. In 2012, a nervous breakdown had cost Herb his real estate law practice and his marriage of twenty years. Rather than curtail her spending habits or help him forge a new path in life, Felicity asked for a divorce. *You'll die alone, Herb, and that stupid kitten will eat your face off before they find you.*

With those words, something snapped inside of meek, mild-mannered Herbert Middleton. He raised his hands to Felicity's throat, to...what? Choke her? When his vision cleared, Herb found himself sprawled on the living room floor, staring at the ceiling with the unnamed stray kitten perched on his chest. Outside, Felicity's Mercedes was roaring away to her lawyer.

In the lopsided divorce settlement, Felicity showcased the red marks on her throat like a trophy. It wasn't quite bruised, but Herb didn't deny what had happened. In genuine contrition, he acceded to her every demand, lost his shirt, and gained an expensive psychiatrist.

Herb's grown twin daughters took no sides. Perhaps they preferred to maintain good relations with both parents, but Herb suspected their husbands wanted to guarantee no daughter was cut out from either parent's will.

Flush with cash, Felicity and her latest boy-toy eloped to Europe. Herb kept the house and slid to Rock Bottom, Population Two, where he and his cat remained in the darkness of a premature burial like characters in an Edgar Allan Poe story.

Ten years later, the words from Felicity's Botoxed lips still burned. Before the pandemic, Herb knew his ex-wife's prophesy was coming true: he was a man caught in a dreary but safe job, destined to die alone. But now, thanks to a terrible virus and remote work, Herb was back among the living, better than ever.

"I'm going to finally buy a boat," Herb announced. "What could be better than real fish for your dinner, Lady Godiva?"

In answer, the cat jumped into Herb's lap and nestled herself against his shrinking-but-still-present paunch, as if to say, *Stroking me is better.*

Herb obliged her. Whistling "Whistle While You Work," he opened Microsoft Teams and clicked JOIN MEETING.

WELCOME TO THE SEPTEMBER 2022
TOWN HALL MEETING
WAITING ON HOST TO JOIN...

Herb sighed. Robèrt Baudelaire, the new CEO of Sunrise Bank & Trust, was once again late to his own meeting. These virtual town halls were Baudelaire's brainchild, where the new CEO encouraged participation from his "family" of remote employees.

But more like a spoiled child than the responsible parent he imagined himself to be, Baudelaire deflected criticism by ignoring it. The CEO pointedly *did not* acknowledge Herb's anonymous questions about cost-of-living adjustments and rising inflation. In fact, Baudelaire seemed to be under the impression he ran a morally *good* company doing *good* things for the world. Foreclosures, repossessions, and high interest rates were unfortunate but necessary parts of the banking business.

Once in the company chatroom, Herb scanned through hundreds of names for colleagues he hadn't seen since March 2020. There was his former cubemate, Albert Jackson, telling everyone *Top o' the mornin'!* Herb could almost hear Albert's attempt at an Irish brogue or the crunch of his cereal as he ate his daily breakfast of Lucky Charms.

*Hello all*, typed Cynthia Walls. She was a phone operator in the Reverse Mortgage Department and had a musical voice Herb enjoyed hearing...even if she was part of an infernal economic machine that preyed upon elderly people afraid of losing their homes.

Every day, new customers sold their homes back to banks, a month at a time, so they might die where they lived. It was all well and good, if they were lucky and died before the money ran out or some condition of the reverse mortgage triggered an immediate foreclosure. And if they were *un*lucky, Herb made sure the bank dotted the i's and crossed the t's on the foreclosures.

"It's the way of the world, Lady Godiva," Herb said.

After years of remote work, Herb talked to his cat. He told himself that was perfectly normal, and his psychiatrist said not to worry unless the cat started talking back.

"Cynthia answers the phones and signs up the customers. I audit the sales and foreclosures for compliance, while the Robèrt Baudelaires of the world rubberstamp my work and cruise through life to early retirements."

Lady Godiva purred in agreement.

As if speaking his name summoned him, Robèrt Baudelaire's enormous face flashed on the screen. He was sitting much too close to his camera again. "Rise and shine, everyone! It's another glorious month at Sunrise Bank & Trust."

Herb groaned. Robby, as Baudelaire insisted upon being called, was a young executive with ice-blue eyes and a head full of bright ideas itching to get out. Even on a computer screen, the CEO had an infectious energy Herb found unbearable without coffee.

Behind Robby, someone had tacked up a child's crayon drawings. Was that an elephant with wings or a fat pterodactyl? Whatever it was, it shouldn't have rainbows shooting out its ass. Beside these, gilded diplomas hung above a bookshelf lined with works on business management. *How to Win Friends and Influence People* by Dale Carnegie. Spencer Johnson's *Who Moved My Cheese?* And worst of all, *Chicken Soup for the Entrepreneur's Soul.*

Among these books Robby had probably never read, there were two with their spines turned to the back, one very thick. Herb frowned. What were these books, so triggering they should be hidden? Donald Trump's *The Art of the Deal* and Ayn Rand's *Atlas Shrugged*, perhaps?

Everything about Robby was a contrivance, including his name. The things behind his head of perfectly combed hair said, *I have children; I am one of you.* It also said, *I went to expensive colleges and own books on management; trust me.*

Herb double-checked that his microphone was muted and said, "Okay, Robby. Let's see if you ignore me again." Herb was crafting a message in the employee chat room: *We need a raise. We're stressed because we can't afford eggs for breakfast anymore, and your proposed online yoga classes aren't the answer.* But before he hit the Enter key, Robby made the first of two shocking announcements.

"After careful consideration, I'm pleased to announce everyone's coming back to the office." With a flash of his winning grin, Robby declared working remotely was a "tired strategy," as though a mutating virus were some trifling thing that could be disposed of by a carefully crafted memo.

"We're a team," Robby finished. "How can we work as a team if we aren't on the same field?"

Herb's finger, poised over the Enter key to send his criticisms, was suddenly clenched into a fist. Return to the office? That would be more money out of his pocket for gas, laundry, and lunch when the cost of living was skyrocketing out of control.

As Robby droned on about his brilliant decision, Herb sank into a black mood. No more quiet morning coffees. No sleeping in until eight thirty. Rush hour. Lost personal time. Nattering managers. Weak coffee. Herb's bass boat dream sank in a whirlpool of clichéd business-speak about synergy, leverage, and game-changers.

Robby's second announcement was more perplexing than his nonsensical return-to-work order. "My friends, we're adding an ancillary headquarters in Illinois to service our new Midwest accounts. Studies show a physical presence will bolster our standing on the national stage. We're playing with the big boys of the banking world."

*Big boys? That's sexist,* an anonymous user typed.

"And the big girls, too," Robby hastily amended. "Looks like someone needs a refresher on microaggressions, eh?" The CEO's boyish face beamed like the light of a locomotive barreling down the tracks to crush all opposition.

Herb's hand itched to slap that face. Any idiot could see it was vastly duplicative to have *another* call center to sign up new customers and to have *another* compliance division to monitor the transactions. The existing Reverse Mortgage Department—and the bank's many other business divisions—already had a national scope, with customers in all fifty states and the District of Columbia. So why was a second location necessary?

*In this economy, companies are contracting, not expanding. This doesn't make sense,* Herb typed.

Robby didn't respond. "I'm counting on our leaders in the Jacksonville office to train your counterparts in Evanston. You'll have daily training calls, and the compliance departments will write manuals detailing your various workflows."

"Train them *and* write manuals? How can I do all that and my job?" Herb demanded of his monitor.

Robby raised a palm. "I know it'll be challenging to maintain your current duties, but I have every confidence in you. You're the best, and I've recruited the best efficiency manager to help you succeed. Ladies and gentlemen, I give you Sabrina Goode, our new Vice President of Efficiency."

A new face appeared on the screen, a woman with blazing green eyes and over-permed reddish hair. Sabrina was thirty-five going on fifty, and her painted-on smile of red lipstick dripped with insincerity. Though Herb only saw her head and neck, he could picture the rest: at once fit and fleshy, a strange mixture of attractive and ordinary. The all-American girl next door had grown up and let herself go to seed.

When the Town Hall ended, Herb absently continued stroking the cat, his eyes fixed on the place formerly occupied by Sabrina Goode's face. What was she doing now? Packing her suitcases for Jacksonville?

Lady Godiva began struggling in his hands, a barely contained tempest with fur, but the old cat eventually ceased struggling as Herb caressed her. She needed love, just like Herb did, whether she knew it or not. Whether she wanted it or not.

"Vice President of Efficiency," Herb said. He didn't like the sound of that. "Do you think she looks like Felicity?"

In answer, Lady Godiva's claws raked through Herb's pajamas. With a yelp of dismay, he released her from his grasp. Later that day, Herb's constant companion of the last ten years did not return from her nightly excursion. Herb searched for weeks, but Lady Godiva was gone.

Three months later, on a bitter December morning, Herb was snug in his bed and dreaming. In the dream, he wasn't ordinary

Herb Middleton, divorced father of two indifferent children and a new psychotic cat, Fluffy, in whom indifference would be her finest quality. He wasn't Herbert "The Hammer" Middleton, the former real estate lawyer who'd had a nervous breakdown in court and left the law for good. He wasn't the man who visited his ex-wife's grave on the anniversary of her death to say, *Karma's a bitch.*

No. Herb-the-dreamer was an average man living an average life, but with people he cared about. And those people, in turn, cared about him. He had a doting wife, the 1965 version of Barbara Eden, her skin the comforting grays of a black-and-white television. She liked having sex, laughed at Herb's jokes, and was content to age gracefully beside her balding husband.

As for Herb's dream-children, they valued his advice, needed no money, and visited without overstaying their welcome. Instead of a cat, he had a golden retriever who thought his human hung the moon. Topping off this fantasy, dream-Herb owned a fishing boat and had time to fish.

When the alarm finally roused Herb, cold reality rushed in. There was no loving family in the empty house. No happy dog. And worst of all, no boat. Why that was worse, Herb didn't know. Maybe it was because fishing was the polar opposite of work, the leisure activity of a retiree without a care in the world.

Herb knew with certainty he'd never retire. His anemic retirement account loomed over him like the sword of Damocles, and a boat was a luxury he couldn't possibly afford. On the way home from the bank, he drove past Barry's Boat Emporium and never stopped. Never ran a finger along a boat's sleek lines, if only to say, "I'm just looking."

Herb stared into the darkness of his room, dreading the chill beyond his blanket, and thought, *I'm a compliance specialist at a bank. And I'm going to catch hell from Sabrina for being late again.*

Herb swung his legs over the side of the bed, then felt claws scratch his right foot; his heel had found Fluffy's tail again.

"Sorry," Herb said as he pulled on yesterday's clothes. He'd left them on a chair in a wrinkled heap, but they were close at hand. On the way out the door, he let out the cat without her breakfast. Maybe Fluffy could earn her keep and catch one of the rats he'd seen crawling around the rose bushes.

On the road, rush hour was in full swing. Herb drove like a madman through stop-and-go traffic, never finding the best lane or catching the stoplights before they turned red. The bank's parking garage was no better. He finally found a narrow space on the roof, sandwiched between two oversized trucks. He dented the truck on the left, despite his best efforts, and headed to the elevator.

It began to rain. Herb was drenched by the time he joined the crowd of stragglers jostling to get inside. In the lobby, the bored security officers scanning ID badges took their sweet time. His identity confirmed, Herb crammed himself into the world's slowest elevator.

One woman sniffed the air in disapproval, her nose inches from his own. With horror, Herb realized the whiff of body odor was his. After stopping at every floor on the way to the sixth, Herb barreled out of the elevator. It was 8:58 a.m. on the nose, and it would take a Christmas miracle to be logged in and ready to work. Like a middle-aged pinball, he caromed through an obstacle course of mail runners, coffee carts, and an army of people in Santa hats.

The Holiday Decorating Committee was back with a vengeance this year, seemingly in an effort to make up for two Christmases away from Sunrise's world headquarters. They were chattering like magpies as they over-decorated artificial trees, strung tinsel in places tinsel had no business being, and hung garish garlands everywhere. To Herb, it looked like a tornado had hit Hobby Lobby's Christmas section.

As Herb rushed past them, he came away with tinsel in his thinning brown hair and red glitter on his shirt. One of the decorators spilled her coffee on the carpet when he bumped into her. It was Cynthia Walls.

"Be more careful," she called after him.

Herb didn't stop, as much as he wanted to. Cynthia's eyes were a soft brown above a button nose, her smile framed by deep dimples before hot coffee sloshed on her hand. Cynthia, despite fifteen years of being a phone operator, had somehow maintained her *joie de vivre*.

Herb checked the time. *One minute and twenty-six seconds left. I might make it.*

With any luck, Sabrina Goode, the new Vice President of Efficiency, was in the break room indulging her donut addiction. Herb could picture her stuffing her face with one hand and clutching her chest with the other, then sinking to her knees, still chewing.

*Well, maybe she doesn't merit a full-blown heart attack,* Herb chided himself. Sabrina was a bad manager and a broomstick away from being a witch, but she didn't deserve death.

*Perhaps a near-death experience?* One that would convince Sabrina to move back to her native Chicago, since she sweated like a pig in Florida's heat. Or at least send her to the ER for a day. In any event, the Reverse Mortgage Department could use a break from her micromanagement and incessant pep talks.

*If we don't pull together, we'll pull apart.* Or: *Folks, we only use ten percent of our brains; let's strive for one hundred percent.* And Sabrina's favorite: *Today's dreams are the threshold of tomorrow's discoveries. Dream big today.*

Just what dreams and discoveries had to do with Herb's duties as a Compliance Specialist III in the bank's booming reverse mortgage business, he never dared to ask. As always, he bit back his comments, swallowed Sabrina's unique brand of passive-aggressive abuse masquerading as advice, and returned to his desk like the good worker bee he'd become.

"Dreams and discoveries," Herb scoffed. Sunrise Bank & Trust is where dreams went to wither and die. It was a sweatshop masquerading as a bank, wringing every ounce of work from its lowly serfs—the phone operators, junior analysts, administrative assistants, and virtual tellers who slaved away in endless, twisting corridors of cubicles from which there was no escape.

Sabrina Goode was the Minotaur loose in the labyrinth, gobbling up people at random. The pay was low, and the turnover rate was high, but what did that matter to executives like Robèrt Baudelaire on the seventh floor? They were modern-day robber barons, feudal lords who drank on the job, putted golf balls into coffee cups, and ducked out early on Fridays.

Or so Herb imagined as he increased his speed-walk to a run for the final stretch. He'd been late three times already since the end of remote work, and one more infraction would earn him a slew of emails from HR and a visit from Sabrina. When her diabetes claimed her—not *if*—Sabrina would manage some corner of Hell, making sure the fires were hot enough for her underlings. And on Fridays, there'd be stale donuts and coffee for all.

"Cold, decaf coffee," Herb said when he finally arrived at his six-foot-by-six-foot cubicle.

"That sounds like hell," a friendly voice said from behind the wall. "Top o' the mornin', Herb."

"It is hell, Albert," Herb agreed. "And good morning to you."

Herb flounced into his chair and switched on his computer. As he waited impatiently for the boot-up sequence, a friendly face rose over the gray edge of the cube like a full moon with a dark, bushy beard.

"Tick tock," Albert Jackson said with a good-natured grin. He was a fellow Compliance Specialist III, the lone bright spot in Herb's dull job. Sabrina could be flying her broom through one of her shit storms, but Albert didn't seem to care.

As Albert often said at lunch, he had a steady job, a wife who loved him, and a roof over his head that didn't leak...except when it rained. So, what was there to complain about?

When the computer's boot-up finished, Herb's hands flew over the keyboard to enter his credentials. He said to Albert,

"Why are we here?"

Albert scratched his beard. "For you, a series of unfortunate events brought down a high-priced lawyer." He lowered his voice and said, "For an ex-con like me, I'm lucky to have this job. With today's electronic screening methods, I'd never get a call back for an office job, especially at a bank."

"I mean, why are we in the office at all? We were doing fine at home, working remotely."

"I dunno, Herb. Ask Sabrina the next time you see her. She's only here to help, you know."

Herb grimaced. The first day back in the office, Sabrina Goode was there to oversee the effort to train the ancillary office, just as baby-faced Robby had promised. What Sabrina described benignly as "helping out" turned into a Reign of Terror. The new VP demanded daily progress reports and didn't care if there was literally nothing to report. She monitored the break rooms for "excessive" lounging, held impromptu meetings when Herb was in the bathroom, and instituted a new demerit system that kept everyone on edge. She even forbade smoking in the parking garage (though that did nothing to stop the executives on the top floor, who reeked of cigars when Herb encountered them in the elevator).

But these dreadful practices were nothing compared to the ax Sabrina wielded like a dwarf in a fantasy novel. Every so often, dejected people passed Herb's cube carrying a box of personal items, potted plants, and pictures of loved ones. These sad souls were escorted by grim-faced security guards like common criminals who might steal office supplies. Sabrina Goode, a.k.a. the Ax Lady, was cutting out the deadwood.

As for Herb, Albert, and others in quality control, Sabrina sang a constant refrain: *Write your manuals, people. Train your counterparts.* In addition to his regular workload, Herb spent half of his days being remotely shadowed by his Illinois colleagues and documenting his workflows. It was enough to make him scream bloody murder.

## GONE FISHIN'

WELCOME TO KRONOS, THE WORLD'S BEST TIMEKEEPING SYSTEM flashed on Herb's screen. He punched in his passwords, hit the Enter key, and held his breath.

Employee: Herbert Q. Middleton
Department: Reverse Mortgages
Position: Compliance Specialist III
Log on time: 9:01:01 EST
Welcome, Herbert! An email has been sent to your manager of your log time. Have a wonderful day.

"Crap in a can," Herb said.

"Tsk tsk," Albert called from behind the wall. "Now Sabrina's coming over for sure."

"Shut up and eat your Lucky Charms," Herb said. "You're on time."

"Sure, but I don't like her being over here. How can I play *Clash of Clans* with one eye, have one eye on my screens, and keep one eye peeled for her ass? I only have two eyes, Herb."

But the morning passed uneventfully, and Sabrina never materialized. Once settled with his coffee, Herb held his final training session with Maria, his counterpart in Illinois. Fortunately, she was a pleasant woman and a fast learner.

At the end of their time, Herb said, "Well, Maria, that's it. You've wrung every bit of information out of me."

"Thanks for everything, Herb." Her voice was strangely sad. "Your manual is really what made my job possible. Everyone in our Reverse Mortgage Department has practically memorized it. I can audit a California foreclosure in less than five minutes."

"You're a great student," Herb said, pleased. "Any final questions?"

A pause.

"Maria? Are you there?"

"I'm so sorry, Herb."

Herb's brow furrowed. "Sorry? I don't understand."

"My boss is coming over; I have to go. Have a great Christmas, Herb."

"You—"

Click.

"—too."

Herb cradled the phone. That was a strange way to end their call. Sorry for what? He was about to ask Albert's opinion when he felt the skin prickling on the back of his neck. He swiveled in his chair to see Sabrina looming over him. She was holding her customary pen and legal pad, always ready to jot down anything displeasing.

"Hi, Herb."

Herb felt his throat tighten. "Good morning."

Sabrina was dressed in green and red, a Christmas tree with legs. She reached out a mannish hand and brushed something from Herb's collar.

"Is that glitter? There now, that's better."

Herb didn't move. From the other side of the cubicle wall, the tap-tap of Albert's keyboard ceased. He was listening.

"About this morning," Herb began, "I can explain. You see, the alarm was going off, but I couldn't wake up for some reason. It won't happen again."

"Don't worry about it, Herb."

The area around Herb's cubicle went dead. No phone calls, no keyboards, no banal chatter. Everyone, from all corners, was listening to this strange interlude.

*Don't worry about it.* Herb couldn't process these words. Had some pod-person changed places with Sabrina Goode during the night? He didn't know what to say, so he said nothing.

Sabrina smiled with her too-red lips. "You've done a fantastic job with your manuals, Herb. Robby's noticed."

*Well, well. Maybe a boat's in my future, after all.* "Thank you," Herb said.

Sabrina leaned against the cubicle wall; it gave way a fraction beneath her frame. "In fact, everyone in Jacksonville has really stepped up to the plate. The ancillary office will hit the ground running on Monday."

"It was my pleasure."

Sabrina took Herb's hand and shook it. "Whatever happens today, *do not* leave before visiting my office. I know it's Friday and your vacation starts tomorrow, but promise me you won't forget."

"I won't."

And with that, Sabrina Goode flew away on her broom. Herb stared after her, wondering what the hell was going on.

"I don't like it, Albert." Herb swirled a bite of beef pad thai on his fork. It was their lunch hour, and Bamboo Bistro was packed with office workers. Some were getting an early start to the weekend, with mai tais and ribald jokes.

"What's there not to like?" Albert said. He dunked a spring roll in peanut sauce and popped the end in his mouth. "You did a great job on your manual. So did everyone, according to Sabrina, including yours truly."

Herb pushed his plate away. "Something's up. On the phone today, my trainee was sad. She apologized to me about something, but I didn't get the chance to ask her what for."

"The trainees were a pain," Albert said. "She was probably apologizing for taking up so much of your time."

"And what about Sabrina? She had me dead to rights, and she let me off the hook for being late."

Albert fished out his wallet and left a nice tip. "That one's easy. She's in love with you."

"Don't joke, Albert."

The big man laughed. "Let's just say she's not coming around visiting me all the time, or anyone else, for that matter. Nope, you're her favorite."

Herb leaned over the table and said quietly, "If she loves me so much, why does she chew my ass?"

"The line between love and hate is a thin one, my friend. It gets crossed all the time."

"It does indeed," Herb said quietly. Before Albert could ask him what he meant, he stood up. "Let's go. I doubt Sabrina will give me a second reprieve if we're late from lunch."

As Friday afternoon dragged on, Herb became convinced the Sunrise Building was a cosmic black hole sucking everything into itself, including all time. At his desk, he found himself checking and re-checking a particularly nasty foreclosure on a reverse mortgage in New Jersey. The borrower, one Gordon J. Peabody, had missed paying his property taxes and homeowners insurance premiums, in addition to filing several bankruptcies. If only Mr. Peabody had had the good sense to die when he expected, he wouldn't have outlived the value of his home. Now Sunrise was coming after him with the force of the law on its side.

All was in order. Herb marked the file as Ready to Foreclose and shoved the keyboard away. He told himself he was only a cog in an evil machine, a bullet in a gangster's Tommy gun with no control over the trigger or target. But that didn't make Herb feel any better. People like Robby and Sabrina ate the Mr. Peabodys of the world for breakfast and asked for seconds.

"Albert? Are you there?"

No answer.

Herb stretched and looked around the quiet office. The steady clacking of keyboards and the clicking of mice was gone, as was the drone of conversation. People should be chattering on the phone or gossiping by the water coolers, but he didn't hear anyone. Even the customer service department was eerily quiet, their phones not ringing. All across the floor, people huddled in twos and threes; it reminded Herb of homeless people warming their hands around burn barrels on a harsh winter's night.

Something was terribly wrong. Herb stood up and instinctively looked toward Sabrina's office. Her shut door and drawn blinds increased his alarm, though he could see her shadow moving about.

"I'm here, Herb."

Herb looked over the wall. Albert hunched over his desk, his face in his hands. When he raised his head, Herb was shocked to see tears streaming down his friend's face.

"Albert, did someone die? What's wrong?"

"Read your email, man."

"Albert—"

In answer, Albert slammed a fist onto his desk, cracking the particle board. "Read what that bastard wrote." Without another word, Albert stood up and walked away.

With a sense of dread, Herb opened his Outlook and read this message from Robèrt Baudelaire.

*My friends,*

*We are living in interesting times, as the philosophers say. My teams and I have tried our best to meet the challenges of rising inflation and massive defaults by borrowers head on. But despite our best efforts, our margins have shrunk, and some tough decisions had to be made for the good of the company.*

*Effective next Monday, December 19, the world headquarters of Sunrise Bank & Trust will be transferred to the Evanston, Illinois, office. Our building in Jacksonville, unfortunately, will be closed. Its sale will infuse needed capital into our depleted reserves and should give us time to bounce back better than ever.*

*Your managers will hold meetings this afternoon to go over your severance packages, COBRA health benefits, and how to apply for unemployment. These packages will be based on your position, seniority, and job performance.*

*Our people have always been our best assets, and we intend to leave you with the means to provide for your families as you prepare for life's next journey. I'm confident all of you will land on your feet.*

*These events have affected every position, at every level. To cut costs, the Board of Directors reduced our management teams by one-third. Including me. Like many of you, I will be hitting the bricks.*

The email went on for some paragraphs, but Herb stopped reading. He looked around again. People were openly weeping, while a few looked relieved. Near Sabrina's office, Cynthia Walls was sitting in front of a Christmas tree and meticulously unwrapping the presents. As Herb guessed, the gifts were nothing more than brightly colored empty boxes. What did she expect to find? A new job?

Herb sat back down, unsure what to do. He waited for Albert to come back, but his friend never returned to his desk, nor did he participate in the meeting Sabrina held about severance packages. When the meeting broke up, everyone took a box and returned to their desks to gather up their things.

Something broke inside Herb as he watched his colleagues. Their jobs may have been thankless acts of drudgery, especially for the phone operators handling customer complaints. But there was dignity in all work, and these people who were leaving their livelihoods behind them deserved so much better.

At that moment, Sabrina raised a hand and motioned for Herb to follow her. Once inside her plush office, she shut the door.

"Have a seat, Herb." Sabrina was behind her desk, a monstrosity that looked like it required a crane to be moved.

Herb remained standing. "Was this the plan all along? To have us train our replacements?"

"Not at first," Sabrina said. She tried to look empathetic, but her glittering eyes belied the attempt. "Robby wanted to expand, to show potential investors we were ready to play on the national stage. But the economy kept tanking, and more borrowers kept defaulting. We foreclose homes and repossess vehicles, of course, but we also need buyers with the means to purchase assets. Last month, a developer from New York made an offer on this building we couldn't refuse, as the saying goes."

Herb held up a hand. "I can guess the rest. You proposed to Robby that Evanston become the national office."

Sabrina cocked an eyebrow. "How'd you know it was me?"

"Robby isn't bright enough or ruthless enough. But you are, no offense."

Sabrina smiled wolfishly. "None taken. I saved the company, with your help."

Herb felt the blood drain from his face to hear Sabrina gush over his training manuals, of how this odious woman engineered the mass firings of hard-working people like Albert and Cynthia. He schooled his features to stillness, though his fingers ached to take hold of her throat and squeeze, if just to make her stop talking.

The moment passed. Herb said, "In the process of 'saving' this great company, good people like Albert Jackson and Cynthia Walls were tossed away like garbage."

Sabrina shrugged. "Cynthia who?"

"Cynthia Walls, the phone operator who worked right outside your door. She's been here since the building opened."

"A phone operator?" Sabrina said. "I did her a favor then. As for Albert Jackson, did you know he was a convicted felon? He was fired for cause earlier this afternoon for lying on his application."

Herb sagged into a chair. "He's not getting a severance package?"

Sabrina waved a hand dismissively. "Herb, I brought you here to talk about your future, not criminals."

*Albert paid his debt to society. He's not the criminal in this room.*

"There's an opening in the law department for Assistant General Counsel. I want you to come with me to Chicago, and so does Robby."

Herb scowled. "I thought Robby was fired."

Sabrina's laugh was without warmth. "Yes. He jumped from the plane with a golden parachute securely on his back. He was out of work for all of two minutes before the board voted to retain him as a special consultant until a new CEO is found, one who'll work for two-thirds of Robby's previous compensation. So, you see, Sunrise will save money in the long run, even with Robby's outlandish severance."

Herb nodded to himself. The golden parachute was a lucrative package designed to compensate top executives with large bonuses, stocks, ongoing insurance, and pension benefits if they were fired. Men like Robby insulated themselves from the chaos they created.

"How efficient," Herb said. "You must be proud."

Sabrina stood up from her chair and came around to Herb's side of the desk, standing uncomfortably close to him. She leaned against the desktop, folded her arms, and looked him squarely in the eyes. "I'm giving you the world on a platter, Herb. A six-figure salary with excellent benefits."

Herb recognized the look on Sabrina's face. He'd seen it on many lawyers and clients in his previous career; it was a mixture of contempt and greed, when people of power took advantage of their wealth, position, and strength. Others had seen it on him, in the days before his nervous breakdown.

"Can we discuss the details over dinner?" Herb asked. "I know a little, out-of-the-way Italian place south of the city."

Like a catfish, Sabrina snapped at the bait. "I'm listening."

"The Big Ragu. It's attached to the Landover Resort & Spa."

Sabrina brightened. "A spa sounds good right about now. How's the lasagna?"

Herb's toothsome grin matched hers. "It's to die for. Oh, and don't tell anyone we're meeting. I don't want HR breathing down our necks, do you?"

"It'll be our secret, Herb."

Before heading to dinner, Herb stopped by Barry's Boat Emporium and made a down payment on a fishing boat. He would have to cash out his IRA to pay for it, but that didn't matter. Retirement was an impossible dream, so why not go fishing every day?

In the sheeting rain of an evening rush hour, hundreds of former employees of Sunrise Bank & Trust drove home to their families in despair, their lives in tatters, their Christmases ruined.

"Are they biting this evening?"

Herb Middleton looked up from his fishing pole at the approaching boat. The stranger had the good sense to approach with his trolling motor rather than the main engine, as some boats did. Revved up speedboats scared the fish.

"Not really," Herb answered. He reached into a bucket for a bit of chum and baited his hook for catfish, hoping the man would go away. Chatty fishermen were almost as bad as speedboats. But in the vanishing rays of the dying sunset, Herb saw the uniformed man was no mere fisherman; this was a Law Enforcement Officer of the Florida Fish and Wildlife Conservation Commission.

Herb groaned. Out of dozens of night anglers on the 9,637 acres of Lake Monroe, he had the bad luck to run into the law. He gave the officer a friendly nod and cast his line into the water.

The man pulled alongside Herb's boat. "A day without fish biting beats being at the office."

"Those days are behind me," Herb said.

"Retired?"

"In a manner of speaking."

The man scratched his head at that, but let it drop. "I'm Jim Strong, with the FWC," he said with a casual flip of his badge, as if his uniform and the boat's logos weren't proof enough. "Let me see your fishing license, sir."

"Certainly." Herb set his pole between his legs, rinsed his hands with a water bottle, and got out his fishing license.

The officer was looking at Herb's reddish hands as much as

the license. He wrinkled his pug nose and asked, "Fishing for catfish?"

Herb nodded. "Bottom feeders prefer dead bait. Gets a little smelly."

"And messy, eh?" Strong said as he handed back the fishing license. "I can't stand them myself. Any scavengers. People don't eat buzzards, so why do they eat catfish?"

"Buzzards don't pair well with hush puppies and coleslaw," Herb countered.

"I'll take your word for it, Mr. Middleton. When you see what they pull out of these lakes, you might change your mind. Garbage. Dead animals. Drowning victims. It's enough to turn you vegetarian."

"Not me," Herb said. "Humans are omnivorous, Officer."

"Predators, you mean. No argument there." The Officer looked dubiously at Herb's chum bucket and said, "What do you call that bait?"

"*Sabrina*."

"Sabrina?" Strong repeated. "Your bait's named Sabrina?"

Herb laughed so hard he cried. "Bait? I thought you said boat. The boat is called *Sabrina*, for an old friend. The bait is liver."

# RONNIE MERCER IS BACK IN TOWN
## Joseph S. Walker

Bailey first heard the news from Pinky, an aging homeless man who always wore the brightest pink clothes he could find in the charity bins. Most cops didn't pay any attention to Pinky unless they were rousting him or making jokes about him. Bailey knew that a man walking every street in the city, accepted as part of the background, sees things nobody else does. Which crews are on which corners. Who's hanging around schoolyards. Security cameras pointed the wrong direction. Every few weeks, when he happened to spot Pinky near a fast-food place, Bailey bought him lunch and let him talk, just to see what might surface.

Today, there didn't seem to be much. As he ate, the old man chatted about a gang of kids in a northern suburb stealing catalytic converters. Bailey would pass the tip to the appropriate precinct, but they'd probably ignore it. Most of what Bailey said to other cops got ignored.

After he finished his burger, Pinky had a new thought. "I saw your old partner the other day."

For a second, Bailey didn't understand. "Old partner. You mean Mercer? Officer Ronald Mercer?"

"Wasn't wearing blues."

"I don't think so, Pinky. Mercer went to prison five years back."

"He looks older." Pinky ran a hand through his own tangled mane. "Hair is just gray stubble. He's thinner."

"This can't be right."

"He went into that saloon downtown. Ivy's. With a couple of Flynn soldiers." Pinky put his bag on his shoulder and stood. "I see him again, I'll tell him you said hello."

In his cruiser, Bailey checked the state database. His onetime partner had been released early. Good behavior. Bailey wasn't going to have another three years to think about how to handle this.

Ronnie Mercer was back in town.

Mercer was already a star when Bailey graduated the academy. He was the department's boxing champ, the best shot on the range, and the cop with the most busts and the widest network of tipsters and stoolies. It was Mercer going out on ledges after possible jumpers, Mercer diving into the river when a drunk drove off a pier, Mercer the first through every door. Some people said he had a death wish. Everybody said he should have been a detective long ago, but he wouldn't leave the streets. For Bailey, being assigned Mercer as his first partner was both exhilarating and terrifying.

He was in such awe that it took him months to really register all the little things that should have stood out from the start. An envelope changing hands that he shouldn't have seen. An impulsive change in patrol route, leaving them out of pocket for an alarm. A piece of evidence mishandled. Ronnie Mercer was dirty. Before Bailey could decide what to do about it, the decision was taken out of his hands.

It was almost midnight on an overnight shift. Mercer called in for an hour break, then killed the radio. Bailey opened his mouth to ask what was happening, and Mercer raised his hand. "Don't. Keep your fucking mouth shut, rookie."

Bailey kept his mouth shut.

Mercer drove to a big downtown parking garage. The gate was raised. They headed up the ramp, spiraling higher into the structure. Above the first couple of floors, there were few cars.

Mercer stopped on the eleventh floor, next to a stairwell door. He killed the engine and lights and got out of the car. After a moment, Bailey followed.

Mercer was standing at the trunk. He held his gun, examining the slide closely. "You're not an idiot, kid," he said, "so you've noticed that I sometimes do favors for people."

Bailey stood still, carefully keeping his hand far away from his own holster.

Mercer ejected the gun's magazine, weighed it in his hand, and pushed it back in. "Not being an idiot, you also know what happens to cops who snitch. Especially on their partners."

"Yeah," Bailey said. "I know."

Mercer holstered his weapon. "Here's the situation, rookie. Colm Flynn and some of his guys are on the next floor up. You know who Colm Flynn is, yeah?"

The Flynns had run crime in this city since before Prohibition. "Yeah."

"Good. In ten minutes, he's meeting some Russians who've been dealing weight in Flynn territory. Nasty guys. So, we're here to do a favor for Mr. Flynn and provide some added security. And we're here in uniform so Colm can show he's got guys with shields on his team."

"You keep saying *we*. I didn't sign on for this shit."

"Hand you're dealt is the only hand you can play, rookie. I'm going upstairs. You can come up and try to arrest ten or twelve pissed-off, heavily armed guys all by yourself. Or you can sit down here and pray to fucking God you don't spend the rest of your career as the colossal prick who let your partner get shot while you sat in the car with your thumb up your ass. Or you can just come with me, keep your mouth shut for an hour, and get on with your life."

He turned to the stairs. "Whatever you're doing, do it now."

*This is how it starts*, Bailey thought. He would carry, for years, a crisp, distinct memory of watching his own hand grasp the stair rail as he started up after Mercer.

They didn't know that one of the Russians, taking offense at something Colm Flynn said and wired from sampling his own supply, would draw in the middle of the meet, and start blasting away, setting off a firefight with casualties on both sides. They didn't know that one of the other Russians was undercover DEA, or that, within thirty seconds of the first shot, federal agents would swarm the scene and clap cuffs on anything still breathing.

They found Mercer sprawled across Colm Flynn, having tackled him during the first volley. Right or wrong, Colm was convinced the bullet in Mercer's shoulder would have otherwise gone between Colm's own eyes.

Bailey was unhurt physically. Five years later, though, his mind was still branded with the image of the Russian who started the shooting. The man Bailey killed.

---

Mercer grabbed the ladder on the side of the small yacht and clambered out of the speedboat that brought him miles out into the lake. The city was a distant smudge, not much more than a thickening of the horizon. A barrel-chested man wearing a pair of shorts and a shoulder holster patted Mercer down, then pointed him to the stern.

Sitting in a canvas chair, Seamus Flynn was drinking a beer and watching the water. He stood as Mercer approached and extended a hand. "Officer Mercer," he said.

Mercer took the hand. "Not anymore."

Flynn laughed shortly. He looked like what Central Casting would send over if you asked for an amiable mayor of, say, Omaha. His hair was red, but not the blazing red of some of his cousins. He spent a lot of time going to the opera and hosting charity dinners, pretending not to be what the people around him pretended not to know he was.

He nodded Mercer into a chair. "Congratulations on the early release."

"I should be thanking you for that."

"I'm sorry it took so long. I didn't give up, though. You saved my son's life."

"How is Colm?"

"He's well, I'm told. Overseas, of course. I saw him briefly two years ago."

The night Mercer was shot, Colm Flynn slipped his watchers at the hospital and vanished. He was still a fugitive, the subject of multiple federal warrants.

"Give him my best."

"Sure." The smile never seemed insincere. It also never moved. "I'm told there's something else we can offer you. Aside from your freedom."

Mercer spread his hands. "All I want is a chance to make my living."

"Are you asking me for a job?"

"I'm asking permission to do a job on your territory. One job, then I'll relocate someplace with nice beaches, where people don't look at me like a leper."

"I'm listening."

"I know normally you take thirty percent tax. I think I can convince you to cut that in half. This job directly benefits you."

"I'm still listening."

"Okay." Mercer sat back and crossed his legs. "Once a month. a courier flies from Johannesburg to Marseilles to here, smuggling a pouch of uncut diamonds for a consortium of local jewelers. Your guys provide security from the airport until the pouch goes into a safe downtown. For that, you get three percent of the pouch's value. Right so far?"

Flynn's smile had changed a little. "How in the hell do you know that?"

"I'm guessing that number's been down in recent months."

"More like the last year."

"There's a second courier," Mercer said. "He flies on the same plane, with his own little pouch. While everybody's watching the guy in the sharp suit, three of your men are hustling to a limo. The second guy fades into the crowd. He takes a taxi to a cut-rate strip mall jeweler and puts his pouch in a safe, to be divvied later. You can probably guess which pouch is heavier."

"Son of a bitch." The smile was gone. "Mercer, you don't get off this boat without telling me where you got all this."

"One of the jewelers has a kid who's a firebug. Ended up on my cellblock, scared out of his mind of all the big bad convicts. I protected him." Mercer shrugged. "Protection costs."

"You want to hit the second courier."

"Think of it as a lesson about doing things behind your back."

Flynn stood and walked to the railing. When he turned to Mercer, the full smile was back in place. "I'll take twenty percent. And you'll use one of my guys."

"Done."

"All right, Mercer. Don't fuck it up."


The note taped to the front of Bailey's locker told him to see Captain Johnston before clocking out. It was the first time he'd been in her office or had a one-on-one conversation with her. He stood and waited while she did something on her computer. He could see, reflected in the glass over the framed diploma behind her desk, that she was playing a game of solitaire. At first, he assumed she didn't realize this.

Then he thought that she probably did.

At last, she looked up. "I hear Ronnie Mercer is back in town."

It wasn't a question, so Bailey didn't say anything.

"Has he contacted you?"

"No," Bailey said. "I just heard about it myself a few hours ago."

"He calls you, texts you, sends up a smoke signal, hell, if you see him on the damn street, you report it to me and IA that fucking day. Are we clear?"

"We're clear."

She started another game. "Good. Get out of my office."

Mercer sat on the low wall encircling a wide downtown plaza. Office workers from the surrounding buildings ate their lunches at metal tables under wide umbrellas. The woman he watched sat alone near the middle of the plaza, eating a salad and reading a paperback book. Mercer waited until the food was almost gone, then slid off the wall, walked over, and fell into the chair across from her.

"Lynn," he said. "Long time."

She looked at him blankly for a moment before realization came. She looked around, putting her hands on the table like she was going to stand up.

"There's a cop over there," Mercer said, pointing. "Must be new. I've never seen him before. Couple of private security assholes, too, but just between you and me they look like they couldn't find their dicks with both hands. I'd go with the cop, but I don't know what you're going to tell him. I've paid my debt to society, and you don't have a restraining order or anything."

"I'll tell him you're bothering me," she said. "I'll tell him I don't want to talk to you."

"So don't talk. Just listen. I need you to pass something along to your husband." Mercer paused. "You're still with Bailey, right?"

"Yes," Lynn said tightly. "I'm still with Kyle."

"That's great. I never found the right woman, you know. I was always a little jealous of what you guys had."

Lynn closed her book and put it in her bag. "Say what you want to say, then leave me alone."

"Just tell Bailey I've got no axe to grind. He stays away from me, I'll stay away from him. No hard feelings."

"No hard feelings." She stared at him. "Do you have any idea what you did to him?"

"Sounds like you're going to tell me."

"The clean cops think he's dirty. The dirty cops think he's a rat. Everybody thinks he was working with you, but they can't prove it. Nobody will partner with him. They won't even talk to him. The union just files his complaints. They stuck him on a terrible beat and ignore half his calls for backup. They're waiting for him to get killed or quit."

"He should quit. There are other ways to make a living."

"He's too proud. He doesn't think he should be punished for something he didn't do."

"That's cute. You'd think five years as a cop would cure him of that."

"So that's it? Just tell him to leave you alone? There's no threat?"

"Lynn," he said. "Having you tell him? That's the threat."

At a little past eleven that night, a silent alarm was triggered at Irion's, a small jewelry store on Bailey's beat. He didn't bother asking for backup. Unless dispatch heard shots, nobody was going to come running to help the department's pariah.

The strip mall housing Irion's was dark, a couple of cars seemingly abandoned in the parking lot. Bailey drove once, slowly, around the entire building, then got out of the unit and walked the same path, shining his flashlight into windows. All the doors were locked, all the windows whole. There was no sign of life in Irion's or any of its neighbors. Crossed wires, or kids playing pranks.

Mercer watched from the roof across the street as Bailey spoke briefly into his shoulder radio, then returned to the car. He made one more circuit of the building before he left. Thorough. He'd been that way even as a rookie. Some part of Mercer was proud that the kid still wasn't phoning it in.

However thorough he was, though, he was riding alone. He

didn't call for backup. If he did call, it wasn't certain anyone would come. If they did, they'd be far too late.

Mercer called Gerald, the big man who patted him down on Flynn's boat. He was going to be Flynn's man on this job. "It's tomorrow night," he said. "Be ready."

At eleven the next morning, Bailey walked into Ivy's. He should have been in bed, recovering from another night on patrol, but half an hour of trying had convinced him that rest wasn't happening. Bad enough always trying to sleep with the morning sun slipping around the edges of the shades. Now, eyes open or shut, all he could see was Ronnie Mercer going up to Lynn. The thought of him being so close to her was like something hairy crawling over every inch of his skin.

"I'm looking for Mercer," he said to the bartender.

There were only a handful of customers. The bartender was a heavyset woman engrossed in her phone. "Never heard of him," she said, without looking up.

"Ronnie Mercer. I know he's been in here."

"Never heard of him." Her eyes rolled up to him, then back to the phone. "Officer."

Three blocks away, Mercer sat at a kitchen table, cleaning and oiling a pair of Ruger LCPs. He was wearing only his boxers. The apartment was small and dingy and would never be anyone's home. It was a marginal place, a temporary haven for people on their way somewhere else. Mercer had it through the end of the month. He wasn't planning to ever need it again after today.

A woman in cut-off jeans and a T-shirt came out of the bedroom. She sat across from him to put on her shoes.

"I left the money on the dresser," Mercer said.

"I got it." She straightened up. "Ronnie Mercer paying for pussy. There was a time I wouldn't have believed it."

"You always had an attitude, Carissa." Mercer checked the action on the first gun. "I could take the money back if it's bothering you."

"I didn't say that." She eyed the guns. "Planning a big night out?"

"Most people in your profession learn to keep their mouths shut." Mercer finished reassembling the first gun. "You remember that last partner I had? Big blond kid, looked like a third-string Big Ten lineman?"

"A what?"

"He was a nice guy, wasn't he?"

"Damn, Mercer, I don't know. I barely remember me. You know what I mean?"

Mercer nodded. He started taking apart the second gun. "You'd better get out of here."

She had her hand on the doorknob when he said her name. She looked over her shoulder. Mercer stared down at the small parts in his hand.

"I always paid," he said. "One way or another."


Sheldon Shepherd was bone-weary as he got out of the cab in front of Irion's. Almost twenty-four hours in airports and planes. Terrible food, angry people shouting in angry languages, uncomfortable seats, filthy toilets, and just four weeks until he had to do the whole damn thing over again. Lately, he fantasized about getting on a different plane in Johannesburg. He could go to Fiji or Bali or Tahiti or some other place ending in *i*. He could rip out the lining of the suitcase and spend the rest of his life paying people to bring him drinks on the beach. They'd torture his wife to try to find him, but there were probably downsides, too.

He was putting a key in the front door of the jewelry shop

when he felt Mercer's gun against the back of his head. "Hello, Sheldon," Mercer said. "Don't let me stop you. Let's go right on in."

The front of the small store was a horseshoe of display cases. Behind the counter, the remaining space was divided into an open workshop and a closed-off office. Gerald took the briefcase from Sheldon's limp fingers. "Office, Sheldon," Mercer said. "Time to open the safe."

"I don't have the combination."

"Maybe you'll make an inspired guess. Take him back, big guy."

Gerald took Sheldon's elbow and steered him to a break in the counter. As he pushed the courier through, Mercer stepped up behind them, put his gun to the back of Gerald's head, and fired.

Sheldon screamed as the big body collapsed forward onto him. He scrambled away, falling to his side in panic. In the store's muted overnight lights, he could see the dark heap that was the bigger man, and the reddish black spray on the wall, and the glint off the smaller man's gun barrel.

"Office, Sheldon," Mercer said. "Never mind the safe, though. Let's just hit that silent alarm."

The alarm from Irion's came at nearly the exact time as the one the night before. Almost certainly some kind of computer glitch. Bailey thought about ignoring it, but if it kept going off, he'd have to go sooner or later.

"Do you want to request backup?" the dispatcher asked. She was new. She didn't know some cars didn't get that offer. He tried to sound grateful when he turned it down.

He did a slow roll around the building. Exactly the same as the night before, probably down to the cars in the lot. Except, no, something different—a light in an inner office in Irion's.

Bailey parked. He took his time walking up to the building, scanning the windows for any movement. Everything was still.

The front door was cracked open. Bailey drew his weapon and went through the door in a low crouch, gun pointed at the floor. He was all the way inside before he saw the dead man wedged into the gap in the counter.

"You call for backup, rookie?"

Bailey froze, shocked. The voice came from the office. The light inside was bright, and the door was only about a quarter of the way open. He couldn't really see anything in there.

"Don't stall, Officer Bailey. I've read the manual, too."

"Mercer?"

"Yeah. I've got a hostage, rookie. Say hello, Sheldon."

"Please help me," said a new voice. The speaker had trouble drawing enough breath to speak clearly. "This man is crazy."

Bailey sidled into the darkest corner of the store's front section and took a knee, his gun fixed on the light in the doorway. "Help is on the way, Sheldon."

"Sheldon's a smuggler," Mercer said. "See the stiff, rookie?"

"I see him," Bailey said. "And I'm not a rookie."

"That's Gerald. He works for the Flynns. He's got a suitcase there with—what, Sheldon? Million, million and a half in uncut ice?"

Bailey could barely hear the moaned answer. "They don't tell me."

"Well, a million, anyway. Tell you what, rookie. You take it. You and Lynn could be in Mexico in twelve hours and never think about any of this shit again."

"Don't say her name. You shouldn't have gone near her."

"Tell the truth, Bailey. You thought about it. Just for a second. Take the money and run. You wouldn't be human if you didn't."

"What do you want out of this?" Bailey said.

"My mother was sick," Mercer said. "They said they'd take care of her, for as long as it took, if I went to the academy. Became a cop."

Bailey shifted his weight and adjusted his grip on the gun. "You want to talk, Mercer, first you need to toss the gun and come out with your hands up. I'll talk all you want."

"You tell yourself you're still helping people. You're doing good. At first, they just want little things, a peek at a file, whatever. Who gives a shit? Then one day they tell you to lean on some people. Hurt them. And you think, this is where it really starts."

*His hand on the rail, going up after his partner.*

"Damn it, Mercer, what do you want from me?"

The light in the office went out.

"I killed the light, so I won't be silhouetted when I come out the door," Mercer said. "I'm coming out in just a minute. I'm going to point my gun at you and shoot. Remember all those marksmanship ribbons in my locker, rookie?"

"I am not a fucking rookie," Bailey said between his teeth.

"Some people are never anything else. Rookie. The good news for you is, I'm not using the gun I shot Gerald with. I'm using the one with the filed-down firing pin. I'll be charging you and pulling the trigger, and you'll have to put me down. It'll look great on the body cam. Your body cam is rolling, right?"

"Jesus Christ, Mercer."

"Doesn't matter. I've got the store's cameras going. You kill me, everybody sees we weren't working together, you get your life back. I'm *giving* you your life back. They'll kiss your fucking feet. You'll probably have a gold shield in two years."

"I won't do it, Mercer. I won't shoot."

"Yeah, you will." Mercer was talking faster. "'Cause here's the thing, rookie. Maybe I'm bullshitting you to get you off guard. Maybe I want to come out there and put a bullet between your eyes because you didn't back your partner."

"I never told them what you said in the garage, Mercer."

"Maybe you don't want to take a chance on making Lynn a widow."

"Don't say her fucking name."

"Gotta play the hand you're dealt. Here I come, rookie."

The door opened. There was a darker shape in the darkness, reaching out toward him. Bailey put four bullets square in the middle of it, and the shape staggered to the side, slammed against a counter, and fell to the floor.

Bailey straightened. Moving quickly, he rolled over the counter and around the corner. Through afterimages of the muzzle flashes, he made out that the shape on the floor wasn't moving. He knelt and felt the side of his former partner's neck.

Nothing.

Sheldon in the office, obviously crying, whispered over and over, "please help me, please help me, please help me."

"I'll be with you in a moment, sir," Bailey said. He picked up the gun by Mercer's hand, pointed it at a far corner, and pulled the trigger.

He could barely hear the click over the approaching sirens.

# THREE SORRY LANGERS
## Caleb Coy

The three of us were a riot. We sat in the back of the Jack of Knaves having a pint. It was me, Conall, and Brandon. We'd barely had our first taste of it when the news came on about a sudden explosion of cases in our area.

"Damned virus," said Conall.

"I'm not about to lose my freedom to some edict," said Brandon.

We had all tossed our masks in the corner when we sat down. We weren't keen on it at all, but Sean, the owner, insisted that he would have to close if he didn't enforce the rule. So we cursed him and compromised. No establishment said anything about the obscenities we wrote on our masks.

"They're lyin' about the death toll," I said. "I've not seen one person drop dead, have you?"

"Damn if they don't let us work," said Conall.

"They won't shut down the mill," I said.

"But there's talk of it," said Conall.

"There's talk of everything," said Brandon. "Say whatever you want. The day the union tells us we can't work on account of the virus is the day Hell freezes over."

We clinked our glasses to that truth.

"Would ya look at that?" Conall pointed at the wall TV. "Speak of the devil. There's been a death all right. Boys, is that Marsden? The foreman on the East Wing?"

"Damn," I said. "You knew him?"

"Not personally. But that's him. I swear that's him."

"I thought he was a healthy chap," said Conall.

"Not anymore." I took a long sip.

Brandon straightened up. "You know what I think?"

"Oh, here we go again," I said. Brandon and his theories.

"I think he was murdered."

Conall and I busted out in a laugh.

"I'd swear by it," said Brandon. "I knew the man. They're faking the numbers. The statistics. You go in their hospital and die of a gunshot wound, they'll write you got taken by the virus. It's been in the papers."

"He was shot then?" I reached for Brandon's glass. "I think you've had enough."

"It's only my first drink."

"What he means," said Conall, "is that sickness murdered him. Is that what you mean, Brandon? You getting philosophical? Metaphorical?"

"At this hour?" I said.

"I meant what I meant," said Conall. "Marsden was a healthy man."

"I beg your feckin' pardon," I said, "but were you his doctor? Perhaps he had something respiratory."

"Go to hell," said Conall.

"He's right, you know."

That was the voice of some fluthered little codger who had just butted in on our conversation. We thought we were alone in the back of the pub, and this young acne-faced header leans in like he's an underage yank five glasses in and in need of his dear mother's teat.

"Who invited you?" I said.

"Marsden was murdered," said the boy. "I knew him, too."

"That so?" said Conall. "Is he your daddy?"

We laughed.

"Come, tell us all about him, then." I gestured for him to pull up a chair. "Help us raise a glass to Marsden, the man only death could kill."

We killed a few glasses with the boy. We humored him because Brandon half believed him, and we were waiting for the punch line to his little joke. But I can tell when a man is shook, least of all a lad who looks barely old enough to quit nursing. Brandon was straight paranoid and known to speak his mind half in jest. This boy had a tale to tell. We were minutes into slagging him on when he filled us in on the murder theory.

"It was sudden, the doctor said. Not like how the virus works, coughing and having fits. No, this was the work of quick death. Purposeful. Marsden died sitting up, then fell down in the street dead. That's the end of it."

"I was right," said Brandon. "This proves my theory. They're writing off natural causes as the virus. Damn, they're even writing off murders."

I knew the boy was letting it on, so I played along. "By God, you're right. They're even out there killing people to bump up the toll. It's a conspiracy."

"Conspiracy!" Conall slammed the table with his fist and chuckled.

"And nobody saw who did it?" said Brandon.

The boy shook his head. "Some thief. Took his life."

"Thief's the right word," said Conall. "They're stealing our rights, one by one. I bet more are dying from the troubles from all this quarantine than from that damned virus."

"Straight through the heart," I said. "Damn it."

"They can get away with murder," said Brandon. "But if we so much as tried, we'd be behind bars without a fair feckin' trial."

"No justice," I said.

The boy knocked back the last of his pint. "It's like what my mom always says."

We stared at him. Blinking, we were met with silence.

"What does she say?" I asked.

"Be primed to meet death any minute. He's the best thief of all."

We raised a glass to the boy. Wisdom from the mouths of babes.

But our bitter joy was cut short when Sean bothered our table. "Boys, it's not looking good out there."

"Speak again?" I said.

"There's a protest in the streets. Haven't you been watching the news?"

"We know about the death toll," I said. "Did you know he's out there, picking us off, one by one?"

"There's about to be a riot," said Sean. "That means more than one."

"What about this time?" said Conall.

"It's another race riot," said Brandon. "Unrest about the blacks and the cops."

What did we care for it? We were the children of Irish expats, conservative Catholics and always with the union, but these hoodlums on the news never did a thing for a town if they ever loved it. The police could piss off, but so could these knockabouts. One man dies, and they give the city hell.

"I can pay for a window," said Sean. "But I'd rather close up before it goes to hell. You three need to scram. I'm kicking everyone out."

He was ignoring the boy at the end of the booth, who was now blacked out.

"That's the end of it," said Conall. He rose from his seat and bent over so as not to tilt himself and have a fall.

"Come on," said Sean. "I'll put it all on your tab for later."

"This won't be the end of it," said Brandon.

"Shut the hell up," I said, grabbing my coat.

***

We never made it home. It wasn't just that we were sloshed. We had walked home many times in a worse shape. We couldn't get around the protesters, so we kind of joined them, if only for a good time in mocking their demonstration. Whatever they shouted, we shouted. In the midst of it, two of the cops keeping the peace took off in their patrol vehicle on account of some robbery just up the road they'd heard wind of on their walkies.

"Great night for a holdup," said Brandon. "Chaos everywhere, everybody in masks."

Honestly, it was a fun ride, and we were so dowsed it was a pure carnival to us. It reminded us of the old days when the union stood up to the mill bosses. Or the days before the boys and I went straight, back when we did a job here and there for old Tommy—God rest his soul.

Robbing department stores was the old life, but I still remembered the sound of breaking glass and the feel of a good getaway. I always wondered what it would feel like to kill a man on a job. These crowds were about to get away with a heap of destruction. Chairs were flying. Tables were flipping. It was an opportunity, surely.

Some rowdy kids were trying to overturn a car up the road. So, what did I do? I took advantage of the situation. I don't even know what I'm doing before it's too late, and I've gone and chucked a rock at the hood of a parked Oldsmobile. It made a beautifully rotten cracking sound and left a mark to boot.

"What are you on about?" said Conall. "Are you feckin' crazy?"

"Come on, boys," I said. "Give it a shot. Hell, it's the one night you can get away with it."

They laughed along and the next thing we knew we were tossing whatever we could at whatever we could, three sorry langers looking for an excuse to break the world that done us in a hundred times over. We were a sorry lot, and it wasn't all our fault, with all the schemes out there to put us under.

"For Marsden!" I cried.

"For the thousand dead!" cried Conall.

Brandon wailed. "Death to the man that murdered Marsden!"

The city answered our cry with the sound of a gunshot blocks away. Our state was more hysterical than mad. We were kings already that night. I could see why anyone would want to lift a stone against society in the middle of such turmoil. We were so drunk it was right dreamy. The streets didn't look like our streets, but like some hellish copy. Every movement was suggestive. If we hung around, there was no telling what would influence us.

"I swear I'll kill the man who took Marsden," I muttered. "Look what they've done to these streets."

"We done some of it," said Conall.

"Damned dignity," said Brandon. "What is happening out here?"

I bent over, dizzy from ambling around and tossing bricks. "I'd do anything for you brothers," I said. "I swear to it. It brings me back, it does. The old jobs, working for Tommy. JC Penny's. Best Buy. The warehouse—"

"Shut it!" said Brandon. "The cops'll use it against you."

"They don't care about us," said Conall.

"I swear by God's body," I spat. "I would do one last job with you boys. Law or no law."

I stood back up and focused my eyes. Some poor raggedy old fool was stumbling down the avenue, as lost as we were.

"God bless you three," he said, all plaintive and senile. "Hard times. Can you spare any change?"

He looked the right opposite of the boy in the pub, too advanced in age to still be alive.

"Damn fool!" I said. "This is no place for a geezer."

The boys laughed.

Conall poked at him. "How—how have you lasted this long? Look around. This world's falling apart."

"He's not real," said Brandon.

"Have some respect for the old wanker," I said. "Look at him. His bones are held together in sawdust!"

We pelted him with our laughs. He modestly turned his head down toward the earth.

Conall was then stricken with some strange look of sobriety. "Wait a minute, wait a minute. I know this man."

"Do ya?" I said.

"Yes, yes. Can't you recognize him? A man of his age, out in the streets and no mask, and the virus didn't take him? He's part of it."

"Part of what?" said Brandon.

"The conspiracy!"

We could not contain ourselves. It was hilarious, and he stood still and ashamed in our midst. In our state, we couldn't tell if we were joyed or indignant. Both came across in the same breath.

"Saint Peter, you're right," I said. "He's working for the enemy. Do you know what happened to Marsden? Tell us. What took him? Who's next? What's the plan? Tell us, by God!"

The old vagrant, confused, lost in our accusations, pointed down the street away from the mad crowd. "In the park?"

We three turned. Up the road a few blocks was a park, more of a large grove really, full of hedges and bushes. Great for walking dogs and having a smoke in the shade.

Brandon pointed. "The park? Up there? Your partner? Your cohort?"

"That ain't far," said Conall. "We can make it."

We grinned at the funny prospect of the empty pursuit. More cops were on their way to face the chaos nearby, so we had best get out of there lively, we knew. We stomped on over to the park, for in this unreal dream of a night, who knew what lay ahead?

"God bless you," said the old fool, whom we left standing in the road, way behind the clamoring riot and into the shadows within shadows.


It wasn't as if he'd given us any specific directions. We half went along with his notion out of humor, lit up as we were. We ambled onward for a few solid minutes until we noticed a trail of spots on the ground that glistened like oil in the moonlight.

"Quick," I said. "You boys seein' this?"

"That's blood," said Brandon. "That fella was right."

We followed the string of spots to one of those evergreens that drape low to the ground. And speaking of green, there was a rectangle of a paler color sticking out of the shade of it.

"Grease me raw," said Conall. "That's a stack of twenties."

I reached down and parted the branches above it. There was more than a stack of twenties. A whole trash bag of banded money was spilling out of itself.

"What sort of feckin' lunatic do you suppose ditches all their money under a tree in the park?" said Brandon. "Bleedin' and all?"

I clicked my tongue. "What we have here is a simple case of finders keepers, my boys."

We forgot all about death in that minute. We searched through the bag and counted the wads, not caring how much like children we looked, huddling under a tree like that. On our first reckoning, the precious pile added up was a six-figure sum.

"Good God!" I exclaimed. "Who comes by this, and how?"

"Don't matter," said Brandon. "The poor fella who lost it isn't here to tell us."

"What if—" started Conall. "What if it was that fool who the cops chased after in that robbery? What if that's his blood out there?"

"Who did he rob?" I said. "The Chinese triads?"

Conall continued. "Hear me out, yeah? He takes full advantage of this riot out here, and he goes straight for the drawers of all the stores in the whole street, blending in with the crowd—"

"Feckin' hell," said Brandon. "You mean to tell me he gets away with a full hundred thousand or so without a fight? Without any suspicion? Tugging around a full trash bag and the cops stationed at every corner? You're a gas, Conall."

"Pull your socks up," I said to them. "This is a privy treasure, all right. Odds are that unlucky bastard is bleeding to death or on his way to some hospital or nabbed by the cops. He's dropped his bag off so he could run, is what he did. Come back for it later. But you saw that blood. He'll never make it back."

"Cops are too busy out there," said Conall. "Either they've got him or they've not, but he's not gonna spill where he put it. I wouldn't."

An idea hatched in my brain, quick as it did in the old days. "Brothers," I said, "you listen here. I may have a few pints in me, but my mind is sharper than it ever was. We were meant to find this, you hear? Clearly, fortune has left this country behind, but not us. They'll tear their own town apart out there, but we've got a bag of seed and it's time to start planting, by God."

Brandon put a cool hand to his hot head. "Who would have thought?"

"But we can't haul it away like this," said Conall. "There's barneys everywhere. They're looking for the same bag, wouldn't you say?"

"He's right," said Brandon. "Even in this mess, we'll stand out. We can't even divvy it up in our pockets. And we can't leave it here. With all that blood."

"They'll mistake us for the robber," said Conall. "Or his accomplices."

"I got a plan to get it back to the house," I said. "Yours, mine, whatever. Luck is on our side tonight, but let's not treat her with no disrespect. There's three of us. We can guard it, and we can haul it out. So, here's our solution. You two sit tight, sober up a little. Have a smoke and look like you're minding your own business. I run up the road, take a few twenties, and buy the backpacks off some of these hippies. I'll come back, and we'll use these to stow our money. Cops'll be none the wiser."

In silence, the other two considered.

Brandon tugged my jacket. "Stop and get us some liquor, too. I want to celebrate."

Conall had some look in his eyes, like he felt suddenly brave.

"I'll go," he said. "I'm the youngest. I've had the least to drink. It's better if I go."

"Suit yourself," I said. "Now that I'm sitting, I don't think I want to rise again for a hot hour."

Brandon started giggling like some six-year-old. "Look at the bleeding state of us. Have we gone mad?"

"Mad as hell," I said.


With Conall gone, Brandon and I sat and smoked in the dark and talked about what we would do with our share of thirty grand or more. We tried looking like any two bums minding our own business when the city was aflame. I thought of buying me a share in some company that was to capitalize on the pandemic, seeing as how the market is going up and down over it. Brandon had the idea of purchasing a farm. I told him he didn't know anything of farming. He said I didn't know anything about stocks. We were absolutely stocious, but cognizant enough to dream the future and remember the past.

"Remember the old days?" I said. "When we'd do a job every few months or so working for Tommy? And we'd get a cut of it, and you'd always—you'd always try and tell me he was shorting us our share?"

"How can I forget?" said Brandon.

"I think you might've been right. Look at this pile here. Look at what they're doing to our town. None of it's right. But this here, Brandon. This is right."

"God's bones, it's right."

A notion surfaced in my mind that I couldn't help but parley with. In all the anger, the confusion, the thrill—in all of it a notion made certain sense to me, blocked and sober at the same time. It never made more sense than now.

"I think it was Conall," I said. "I think it was Tommy slipping Conall an extra cut."

Brandon was all disconcerted. "I beg your feckin' pardon. You mean on those jobs? Why would he do that?"

"Well," I said, purely reasoning. "You know how Conall always is. Only out to please himself. I think he helped Tommy plan those jobs and had him convinced to the teeth that out of the three of us, he was always the one putting himself most in danger, always the one making the smart decisions. You get me?"

Brandon nodded. "I wouldn't put it past him. But this is our friend you're slandering."

I shook my head. "Ain't no slandering. I always sensed it. And I think you have, too."

I knew Brandon was paranoid at heart. Strangers were never trusted, but in the wrong mood neither could a friend. And when he was drunk, he was as suggestible as a Protestant. All he needed was a trusting hand. I scooted close and hugged his side.

"You know you can always trust me like a brother, Brandon. Now listen to me. This is where our profit lies. These are hard times. What were once thought neighbors—well, you can't turn your back to them. Times like these, they reveal people. You think Conall has gone and volunteered to help us for our sakes?"

Brandon raised an eyebrow. "What are you saying? You saying he wants an edge on us?"

"He's withheld our share before," I said. "He owes us, anyhow. And what is that worth? To his dear and trusted friends?"

"I'd put him in the grave," said Brandon. "Sorry bastard."

"We know what kind of man he is more than anybody," I told him. "He's so cheap he'd peel an orange in his pocket."

"You're not wrong. The ocean wouldn't give him a wave."

"We were the only friends he's ever had and look how he goes and returns it."

Brandon let out a long exhale. "So do you suppose we do?"

I got right down to brass tacks. "Equally divided amongst us three, supposing he doesn't find a way to miscount it, how much would we fare? To win, we'd have to assume he'd cheat us. Maybe took a few extra stacks when we weren't looking and stashed them somewhere already."

"I thought I saw it," said Brandon.

I pointed at the invisible truth before us. "Now, if I found a way to shape it so that the two of us could split the prize, you'd call me a friend forever, yeah?"

Brandon buried his cig in the dirt. "But how? He knows where it's supposed to be and we're watching it. We'd have to leave town because he would rat. You know he would."

"Here's our bargain," I said. "You've got to trust me and know that I would never betray a friend. Not like Conall. Wearing a mask all these years. Calling us friends and hiding the truth."

He shrugged angrily. "What's to be done?"

"We do what's fair," I said. "He got us looking around for death. We've seen it's already due to this town."

Brandon was taken. "Dennis? Are you letting it on?"

"No," I said. "I'm dead serious."

His face went from shock to whimsy. At any other time, he would have refused the thought. But now? The elixir had mixed in perfect proportions.

I said, "There's two of us, and one of him. When he gets back, you go to help him with the packs. You act like you're so thrilled to see him return you go for a hug. Yeah? That's when I whip out my knife."

Brandon shivered. "On Conall."

"Think of how many knives he put in our backs, and we never knew."

He thought on it. He said, "I've got my knife."

I hazarded a grim smile. "We dispatch the man that done us in, friend we thought he was. And you and I—we'll divide it equally, of course. Whatever you want to do with it—gamble with it—I don't care. I trust you to bury it and do the right thing, friend."

"I trust you, too," he said.

We looked out at the night. Smoke rose from a car on fire up the road. It was a pity what had to be done. But tonight, everyone was a miscreant. No sermons about it. Everyone had to be out for himself, was the new law.

# THREE SORRY LANGERS

***

Let's not waste our breath. Conall came sauntering back with three bottles, just like he said, keeping his secrets from us, as if we wouldn't know. The rest happened exactly as we planned it. Brandon went to help Conall fill a pack, I fell on him with my knife. He jumped back, Brandon also fell on him, knives in and out until there was no breath in him that wasn't choked in the traitor's blood.

"Christ on a cracker!" cried Conall in his last gargling breath.

Brandon sneered. "Don't you call the name of Christ, you Judas."

There might have been a hint of remorse had we not reviewed all the years that our false friend had lied to us and stuffed his coffers. So, I might have inflated the truth a little. We took our bottles, tucked his under his dying arm, and we all drank a toast, gulping it down in celebration.

I spit upon our once true friend. "To your health as well, ye bastard."

"What about his body?" said Brandon.

"Drink now, bury the body later," I said. There was some bit of humanity yet in me that was troubled in my gut, but I ignored it outright.

Brandon got up to take a piss on the dying body of our treacherous companion, and only got out a little trickle before he fell over. I laughed at his imbalance.

"Shut up," he said, groaning. "I don't feel right."

"You've had enough," I told him, quite dizzy myself.

"No," he said, totally aghast. "My stomach. My throat."

And when he said it, I felt it. And I knew.

That bastard.

The poison took its time to creep up, and when it did, it began to take us quickly. I fell, feeling the swelling in my tongue. I spat the blood from my gums. Brandon was groaning, I was groaning, and poor Conall's fingers were still twitching around his bottle. I reached for a stack of green paper bills and put them in his hand, that damned viper. Here was a taste of what he'd gone after. I finally had my proof of his deceit in my own lusting belly. My hand rested over his, clutching the same parcel of vanity. One would think we were brothers to the end.

Look at the sorry lot of us. We were lured to perdition, three sorry langers who gave ourselves full permission to be the worst of fiends. Had it coming, we did. We were the devil's clay and damn us if we'd never repent. We received our due. If I could, I'd cough up every penny of it.

# NO REQUEST DENIED
## Travis Richardson

*The Guitarist*

Riding in the back of a hired Cadillac Escalade, Mick Gentry, English guitarist of the progressive rock band Helium Pig, felt like shit. An insufferable eleven-hour flight from Heathrow to LAX put him in a foul mood. The first-class accommodations hadn't made a difference. The idea of working with the lead singer and de facto band leader irked him like an unscratchable itch. That's why he chose to stay at the Château Gardens off Sunset Boulevard instead of living with the band in a rented Brentwood mansion. He needed space from his overbearing, egotistical bandmate when they weren't recording.

Checking into the exclusive hotel in the early afternoon, he couldn't stifle a jetlagged yawn. He asked for the concierge.

"Pierre is the man you need to speak to."

Mick followed the clerk's finger over to a prim middle-aged man with a plaid bowtie and rimless glasses standing behind a podium.

"'ello," Mick said, walking to the man. "Was wonderin' if you could do me a favor."

Pierre beamed. "Absolutely, what would you like?" he said with a French accent.

Mick leaned his lanky body toward the smaller man and whispered. "I'd like some company for a few days."

"That can be arranged." The concierge's face showed no offense. "Can you give me more details on the type of *company* you're looking for?"

Mick's mind buzzed, thinking of all the options LA had to offer. Although he had a wife and kids back in London, she tolerated his philandering on the condition that photos wouldn't emerge with another woman on his arm. Which is why he preferred professionals over groupies. They didn't take selfies. Also, this hotel had a reputation for being discrete and servicing their clients' requests.

"I'd like an intelligent, yet dirty girl."

"When you say girl," the concierge asked in a low, conspiratorial voice, "do you mean of a legal or illegal age?"

Fire ripped through Mick's veins. "Excuse me? I 'ave a fookin' daughter back home."

The concierge held up his hands, his face trying to convey wide-eyed innocence. "Oh, no, sir. It's not what you think. I meant a woman who looks young. I would never think of hiring anybody underage. Tell me what kind of *woman* you'd like."

Mick looked the man over. He didn't trust his reassurance. Slime seemed to ooze off his polished facade. But what could he do? He wanted something illegal, and this man could get it.

"I'd like a woman in her late twenties or early thirties...well-educated...who can discuss history, current events, Orwell or whatever."

"I know the perfect candidate. When would you want her?"

Mick was exhausted. While sex would be wonderful, he needed sleep more.

"How about tomorrow evening? Give her a key to my suite in case I'm not there. If things work out, I might want her company for the next few weeks."

"As you wish," Pierre said with an ingratiating smile. "Her full evening fare is fifteen-hundred a night."

Steep. But if she could alleviate the stress, then it'd be worth it. He nodded.

"Also, can you get me a bag of weed, too?"

"Yes. It is legal here, by the way."

Mick forgot. The laws kept changing.

"Get me some anyway, would you?"

He walked toward the elevator, motioning to the bellhop to bring his gear. A few hours of shuteye would be lovely.

*The Concierge*

Pierre breathed a sigh of relief after the gangly British rock star walked away. The moral lines of the rich and famous were unpredictable. One person's sin was another's delight. His job was to make the clients happy, regardless of the request.

His phone rang. "Hello, Château—"

"Pierre, my belle," a voice drawled over the line. "So good to hear your voice."

Blood drained from the concierge's face. "What do you want?" he asked in a clipped voice.

"I want what I had last time, honey."

Pierre walked away from his podium and into his office, carrying the cordless phone. "You were lucky that you did not get arrested last time," he whispered.

"I want the Sunset Cottage tomorrow," the world-famous actor said. "Oh, and a young boy."

"You can't have it. It's booked." Pierre closed the door and sat at his desk.

"Come on, Pierre. Kick out whoever is there and double the rate. I know you can do it."

"I can't let you come back. Not after what you did."

"Oh, come on. I paid for the cleanup. Didn't I? As well as the upgraded interior financed by yours truly."

"But still."

"And I paid that pimp for his loss. You got a hefty fee, didn't you? Fifty thousand dollars on top of your fee, if I remember correctly."

"What you did is...immoral," Pierre said, tasting bile.

"What you do is immoral, too. Procuring boys and girls for the wealthy. Drugs and firearms too. Anything anyone desires for the right price."

Pierre flushed. "That may be true. There's a lot I do wrong, but I never condone torture and murder."

"Oh, but you do, Pierre. When you cashed my check, you were complicit. We're now tied together. If I ever get caught, you better believe I'll implicate you. We'll both go down together. So why don't you shut the fuck up and do your job. I want the Sunset cottage so I can be as loud and thorough as I need to be without any interruptions."

Pierre felt like vomiting. What could he do without going to jail? "The cleanup will be—"

"I'm taking better precautions this time. Plastic sheets and a body bag. But you'll still need to destroy the bed and sheets, no doubt. Maybe repaint the walls."

With a shaky hand, Pierre booked the cottage under the actor's pseudonym and charged double the rate. Typically hiring a prostitute, even a young one, was a quick phone call in a coded language. But this request would end with a corpse. It took finesse. A one-on-one meeting with a reprehensible pimp.

*The Pimp*

Matt Jordan hated losing talent, especially the young ones. Procuring children while staying off law enforcement and social services' radar was tricky. But big money trumped everything else.

Pierre sat in front of plump man at the back of an East Hollywood dive bar. Loud hip-hop music blared. Nobody could overhear their conversation, which was necessary in Matt's line of work. Especially when murder was involved.

Matt mopped his sweaty forehead, wondering how much he could get.

"I've got a stable of teenagers. Runaways that nobody knows anything about." Matt took a deep swallow of beer and belched. "But your client wants pre-teen. That's a whole other issue."

"Which is why you get to charge a premium."

"Yes, but your client plans to murder him."

Pierre nodded, his eyes downcast. His usual tan skin looked gray. Was he hoping Matt would say no and let him off the hook? That couldn't happen. Not with this much money on the line.

"Fine. I'll get you one. There's a meth head whose son I've been grooming. She'll forget all about him with a month's worth of smack. But this will cost you, and I'll need the money up front."

"How much?"

Matt didn't want to shoot too high and lose out. "How about forty k?"

Pierre pulled out his phone and texted. They sat in silence, sipping their drinks.

"Is this unnamed client of yours a celebrity I might know, or a prince of some kind?"

Pierre waved him away and sipped his cognac. His phone vibrated a moment later.

"You have the same Bitcoin address?"

The pimp nodded.

"You will have the money within an hour. Have the kid go to the Sunset Cottage tomorrow night."

He slid a card key to him across the sticky table and left without another word. Matt chuckled. And here he thought old Frenchie didn't have a conscience.

*The Concierge*

Pierre drove to a nicer bar in Hollywood and ordered a cognac, and then another. He loved his job most of the time. Pleasing people, that's what he does best. Getting close to the rich and the famous used to be a thrill, even with the over-the-top requests. But this was too much. Too fucking despicable. Perhaps the first time had been a mistake. *Maybe.* But not this time. This was pure premeditated homicide. And he was the procurer of the victim. How in the hell had he let this happen? What had he done with his life?

"Another cognac," he yelled to the bartender.

"You sure?" the bartender asked.

"*Oui.* But make it two." His words slurred.

The bartender brought a bottle of Martell over and set it next to Pierre's crimson journal.

"Would it be easier if I gave you the bottle?"

Pierre smiled and dropped a wad of cash on the table.


*The Guitarist*

Mick woke up at two thirty in the morning. Ten thirty London time. He knew he should sleep so he could adjust to Pacific Time, but he felt alive with an intense urge. An urge to create. He pulled out his Stratocaster and strummed it for several minutes. It felt good, but it wasn't enough. He plugged the guitar into an amp. Electric chords vibrated the room. Hell yeah. Mick started jamming. Hard.

The neighbors knocked on the walls, and the room telephone rang for several minutes, but he didn't care. Mick was in the zone, creating wild, new sounds. His front door opened. A hotel employee with two security guards entered his suite.

Mick stopped playing. "What the fuck ya doin'?"

"It's three in the morning, Mr. Gentry," the young man said. "People around you are trying to sleep."

"Well, I'm tryin' to play."

He struck the strings. The sound vibrated off the walls. The employee walked over to the amp and turned it off.

"Bleedin' hell."

"Look," the man said with his hands out. "I know who you are. I've listened to your music for as long as I can remember. My brother got me into it. Your guitar playing is amazing."

"Thank you for all the accolades an' all, but I can't really practice if you turn off my amp, can I?"

"Look. There's an empty cottage you can use. It's away from the main building. We'll move your things over. Okay?"

*The Actor*

When Devin Gaetz arrived at the hotel, he was enraged to find out that he couldn't have the Sunset Cottage.

"I made a reservation—a very expensive fucking reservation—for that cottage tonight."

"I see your reservation," the woman behind the counter said. "It is for a deluxe suite. The Cottage is reserved for the rest of the month."

"That's not what I was told. Where is Pierre?"

The woman blanched. "I don't know, Mr. Gaetz. He didn't show up to work today. We've been calling him."

"Look, miss." The actor's eyes filled with rage. "You obviously know who I am. I suggest you get your manager immediately or I am going to break every lamp, vase, and any other overpriced kitschy bullshit décor in this place."

The trembling woman nodded and disappeared behind a door. Devin pulled out his phone and texted Pierre:

*WTF. I want my cottage now!*

"Excuse me, Mr. Gaetz."

Devin looked up to see a pathetic excuse of a manager. Short, bald, and of some ethnic heritage he couldn't define.

"Tell me who the hell bumped me out of my cottage, or I'll sue you for an ungodly amount of money."

"Warner Brothers," the manager said flatly.

"But I paid—"

"They paid more for longer time. If you want to take it up with the studio—"

Devin waved him off. He had a couple of projects bouncing around different studios. He didn't want to throw a hissy fit with them just yet. Instead, he'd wait until after the ink dried to unleash his revenge.

"The good news is that you have a complimentary suite from us for the next two nights," the manager said.

"I only need it for one night…but hell, I'll take it. Have Pierre call me as soon as you get a hold of him."

"We will," the manager promised.

Devin pointed to the bellhop with his baggage.

"Lead the way."

Although this was not what he planned, he knew Pierre would deliver the boy. The man had never let him down before. Devin felt grateful that along with his ropes and knives, he'd thought to pack a ball gag.

## The Escort

Amanda sauntered down the hall to suite 309. Dressed in designer clothes and carrying an overnight bag, she looked more like a wealthy European traveler than a prostitute. She didn't know who the client was, only that she needed to be discreet. She didn't see Pierre at the front desk, but a card key was waiting for her. Not that it mattered. The door was unlocked. Walking into the hallway, her high heels clattered on the marble tile.

"Hello," she called out.

Something felt off, but she couldn't pinpoint what. She hesitated for a moment, but decided to enter the low-lit, empty living room. She'd been told to make herself comfortable if the client wasn't there, but her instincts told her she wasn't alone. Somebody was there. Somewhere. Moving past the sofas and dining table, she opened the bedroom door. Plastic sheets had been placed around the bed and hung on the walls. What. The. Fuck?

Amanda spun around, ready to bolt. Ten feet in front of her stood that famous actor. The one she'd heard kinky rumors about. He wore a studded leather S&M gear and held a ball gag. His face twisted in disgust.

"What the hell is a woman doing here?"

"I-I think I got the wrong room."

She started to walk around him, but he blocked her path.

"Yes, you got the wrong room. But you can't leave."

"I won't say a word, Mr. Gaetz."

He punched her in the stomach. Air escaped her lungs as she fell to her knees.

"You'll never say another word to anybody. I'll make sure of that."

He shoved the ball into her mouth.

*The Rocker*

Mick returned to the cottage later than expected. Slightly drunk and definitely stoned, he felt high after jamming with bandmates. They loved his new licks, and the studio rented him the cottage for the entire month. Although fatigue was setting in, he looked forward to a nightcap with whomever the concierge had provided.

Horny, he entered the dark bedroom. Squinting, he made on the outline of a form laying on the bed. Smaller than expected, but perhaps the drugs were screwing up his perception. He turned on a table lamp and pulled back the sheet.

"'ello there—Holy shite!"

Mick jumped back. A young boy, twelve at most, clad in only underwear, stared at him. His dark eyes blinked with sad innocence as his body trembled.

"Cover yourself." Mick pulled the sheet over him. "Jeezus."

"It's okay, mister. You can do whatever you want."

The boy started to pull the sheet down again.

"Don't." Mick said, jabbing a finger toward him. "There's been a cock-up of some sort." He patted his pants, searching for his phone. He couldn't find it.

"Please, don't call Mr. Jordan. He'll kill me if I don't do my job."

"Jordan. Who the bloody hell is that?"

The boy tilted his head, confused. "That's the man who brought me here."

Mick wanted to puke. He brought out his wallet.

"Look here. Put yer clothes on an' I'll give you some money to make sure everything's…"

He caught himself. This was bullshit. He wouldn't send that boy back to Jordan, that sack of human garbage. He finally found the phone in his jacket.

The boy scooped up his clothes, his eyes wide with fright. Shit, the kid was going to run.

"How long you supposed to be here with me tonight? I'm a bit drunk and may've forgotten."

The boy, already in his jeans, said, "All night. In the morning, he'll pick me up."

"Sit on the bed for a bit. I'm gonna order room service. You hungry?"

"Sure," the boy said, cautiously sitting on the bed.

"All right then."

The guitarist walked into the living room and called the front desk.

"Is the concierge there?"

"How can I help you?" a woman asked on the other line.

"I want the French fella. Pierre, I think it is."

"He's not here. May I assist you?"

He glanced across the room at the boy watching him.

"Send over some sausage and eggs…with pancakes. Milk and coffee too."

He hung up. Completely sober, Mick felt like one of two things had happened. Either the concierge got the wrong idea of what a dirty woman meant or when he switched rooms the other night, he received another man's illicit order. He dialed another number.

*The Actor*

Twice Devin had choked the woman unconsciousness. He'd punched her face and pounded her body numerous times. One eye was almost swollen shut. This just wasn't working out. Torture wasn't the same with a grown woman. He glanced at the knives spread out on the nightstand. Maybe he should go for the jugular and end the night early.

A light knock got his attention. Excitement filled his body. The boy had finally arrived. He rushed to the front door and threw it open.

"Hello, sweet—"

In front of him stood four pale, long-haired men. One threw a punch straight into his nose.

*The Guitarist*

While the other three band mates gave Devin a worthy beating inside the suite, Mick rushed into the bedroom. He saw the escort tied to the bed. Bloody.

"Oh, God."

He untied her as fast as his trembling fingers could work. She rolled off the bed, threw out the gag, and scrambled to the bathroom, locking the door. Mick called the police.

Returning to the living room, he stepped on the actor's hand. "What did you do to her?"

"It's just a misunderstanding," Devin cried.

"I know because this…evil was meant for a boy. Right?"

Devin's eyes widened. Mick stomped the actor's smug face.

***

*The Detective*

LAPD Homicide Detective Susan Horner stood at bottom of a canyon, looking two hundred feet above at Mulholland Drive. She'd been assigned to investigate Devin Gaetz. The kidnapping, torture, and battery charges were so bulletproof that no high-powered team of lawyers could save that Oscar-winning pathetic excuse of an organism. And even better, the judge denied the sicko bail.

The arrest of the pimp, Matt Jordan, led to an even darker twist, linking Gaetz to a previous murder at the Château. For two weeks, an All-Points-Bulletin went out for Pierre Pelletier. Susan wanted the concierge to corroborate this story, which would ensure a death penalty prosecution against Devin. Today he had been found in his gold Mercedes, crushed at the bottom of the canyon.

"Suicide?" Alex, her junior partner, asked while taking photos of the wreckage.

"Probably. There weren't any skid marks."

Something caught the detective's eye. Six feet away from the car, a red leather journal lay atop an agave plant. She took a few photographs and then donned a pair of gloves.

"What's that?" Alex asked several minutes later.

She flinched, startled by the interruption.

"It looks like the concierge had been keeping a journal going back at least..." She flipped to the front pages. "Twelve years."

"What's in it?"

"Besides damning info about Gaetz, it looks as if he documented rapes, assaults, and a bunch of other crimes committed by the rich and famous that were never reported."

Alex's jaw dropped.

"You'd better clear your calendar," Susan continued. "We're gonna have a full caseload this year."

# RHAPSODY IN BLOOD
## Robb T. White

Not all my cases wound up with me in a gator-infested swamp searching for body parts. This one did. I went as far as to put on the waders, but I had no intention of going into the water. The Indian River County Dive Team was doing fine without me.

"Y'all sure you want to stand there?"

A young deputy sheriff with a blade of grass in his mouth broke my concentration. I was mentally composing a call to the mother.

"Y'all standing right next to a belly drag," he said.

I stepped closer to him. That was all he wanted. The yips and smirks from the deputies behind us confirmed it. Snickers booted me in the ass to the collection tent. "Dumbass city boy," the deputy with janky teeth said. You can be forty-three and still be called "boy." On top of that, I was a relocated Yankee, a snowbird who stayed. Florida is changing. Too fast for some.

"Hey, Sally, how's it going?"

"Oh, fine, considering. How about you?"

"Getting by," I replied. "Providing much-needed mirth for the locals."

"I heard. What did you do?"

"Exposed another hole in my education. Natural sciences, I

think."

"Don't feel bad. Last year, I had a tourist on my table. Parts of him anyhow. He stepped on a log out here. That twelve-foot gator didn't appreciate being a footstool."

"I know the feeling."

Sally Jesperson, masked up and holding tweezers, was bent over the table, picking at something that resembled a femur with gristle hanging from it. They'd found a forearm, and the twenty-two-year-old boy's head so far. His eyes were half-mast, smeary gray.

Sally's was the one friendly face I recognized among the law enforcement gathered out here since my 911 call that morning.

"*Un poco putrido*," Sally said, mostly to herself.

"You said it. Stinks to high heaven."

"Did you know that the olfactory system shuts down in sleep? You could fall asleep on this table and not smell a thing."

I found that hard to believe. The reek of decomp was accelerating in the heat by the second. The stagnant water and rotting vegetation were overpowering enough. Bird calls out in the cypress canopy had a torpor to them. Everything but the mosquitoes and biting flies, which were rabidly energetic. I glanced back at the water. One fallen tree near the bank resembled a bull alligator's back cresting the surface with its snout resting in muck. Only the cueball-sized eyeballs above the water were missing. I hadn't spotted an actual alligator yet.

"Who called in the Bureau?" Sally asked.

"His mother's a state senator," I replied. "The father's a cosmetic surgeon in Tallahassee."

"Ah, important people."

I stepped back from the table, but the air wasn't any fresher.

"The sheriff has my card," I told her. "He can reach me at my office. There's nothing for more for me to do here."

"The mechanics were messing with that dang airboat yesterday. Anyway, autopsy won't be earlier than tomorrow midday," she said. "Call the ME's office. We use an odontologist in town.

He'll confirm when the dentist lab in Ocala sends the X-rays over."

There's an exhilaration when you deliver a son or daughter back to the parents. Family dynamics cause most ruptures. In the son's case, he'd broken with his family when he got involved with climate protesters who traveled up and down the state whenever new construction was announced, or recreational boaters bothered another manatee breeding site. They reacted like bees in an agitated hive, setting off with posters, bullhorns, and their single-minded intention to stop Miami from sinking into the sea or whatever it was from happening.

When a radical element peeled off to commit acts of eco-terrorism, he joined because of a girl he was seeing. She was more committed than he was, so when he told her he was leaving the cell, the self-appointed leader, a fanatical Marxist and his sidekick, a dropout and doper, lured the boy into an abandoned building and beat him to death with two-by-fours. The leader and his doper sidekick dumped the body in that swamp off the highway.

Whatever their scientific credentials were, they weren't the brightest criminals around. Cell towers pinged their trip with the body in the trunk down Interstate 95 and all over Dade County. Toll booths captured their vehicle and time-stamped them coming and going. Buying cinder blocks at Home Depot and tarp, rope, and jugs of bleach at a Walmart supercenter in Gainesville put the sprinkles on the sundae for the prosecution. Say what you will about shiny crap from China sold in Walmart stores, they do have outstanding pixel resolution in their CCTV system.

The Dade County district attorney thought she had more than enough to bury the two killers in Raiford for life, although it's mostly ex-cons who refer to the Florida State Prison in Bradford County by its shorthand name. I met a wrinkled old con in a bar who bragged about doing time there, as though he'd pledged an exclusive fraternity, which, in a manner of speaking, I suppose he had. Another sign of these upside-down times.

My go-bag in the trunk of my rental holds extra clothes and my surveillance gear. I grabbed a clean T-shirt and peeled off the one sticking to my back. I tossed it in with the waders. The smell lingered, prickled my nostrils, until the AC set to morgue temperature blew the last of the stink out the vents.

My cell phone indicated three missed calls, all from the boy's mother, and a text flagged "Urgent." She heard her son had been located alive. Could I confirm?

The Mark Twain quote about a lie traveling halfway around the world while truth is putting on its shoes came to mind.

Every trite expression of condolence I'd ever used stared back at me from the scratch pad. I felt like a dim student unprepared for the essay portion of the exam. I knew something about that because I failed the LSAT three times. And I thought being a lawyer instead of a cop would solidify my crumbling marriage. All that effort accomplished was to remove the block in *Jenga* that sent the tower collapsing.

On top of that, the public relations officer called while I was scribbling to let me know the Sheriff's Office wanted to do the notice. He implied my doing it would aggravate his "feelings" for me. It was no secret he despised me. That was like trying to come back from being dumped, so I called her without looking at my notes.

She listened without interrupting while I summarized the steps I'd taken over the course of my three-week investigation from the day I walked into his dorm room through my interviews with his girlfriend, all of it breadcrumbs leading to that swamp.

She cleared her throat once. No banshee keening as I'd experienced with other mothers in the rawness of grief. She said she'd make funeral arrangements and call the boy's father. She ended by telling me where to email the report and to include an itemized line item of expenses.

"Your toner needs changing," she added.

I gave her the numbers for the Dade ME and the sheriff, and that was it. She didn't thank me or say goodbye. Just dead air.

But air is never dead. It's jam-packed with molecules, trillions of atoms. The screens of old TV sets crackled with a scattering of photons from the beginning of creation, the Big Bang, when the set was turned off. We live in a sea of microbes that want to use us as hosts or kill us. Like that stinking swamp: eating, sex, and death everywhere you look.

I brooded over irrelevancies like that, thinking about her toner comment. Exchanging the frigid North for a warmer climate hadn't knocked the habit out of my head. I was still impressed by the sizes of bugs here.

The woman who came into my office two days after the autopsy said she'd seen my name in the *Sun Sentinel*. My photo, standing around in waders, had appeared in the *Herald*, where I was misidentified as a sheriff's deputy. I didn't recall a reporter being on scene, but they find their way.

Lucinda Gray from Fort Lauderdale had a sister she wanted me to find, Abigail. We spoke for twenty minutes. Family photos of Abby and her older siblings playing in front of small blue tract house showed a blond child squinting into the light. The most recent photo was taken five years ago. The two sisters had arms entwined but no smiles. The chubby little girl's face had been replaced by a slender woman who looked uncomfortable. Like some nineteenth-century rancher's wife who was forced to have her photo taken and could produce only a razor-slit smile.

Lucinda was pregnant with her third child when Abby disappeared shortly after giving birth to her son. Lucinda raised the boy. Lately, he began pestering her about his "real mom" because kids at school mocked him, called him a "trick baby."

She kept bringing up my fee. She wanted to work out a pay scale in advance. I gave her my standard contract and told her not to worry about the bill.

"All I do is worry about bills," she said. She wasn't poor-mouthing.

"There might come a point where I have to stop. You realize that?"

She nodded. "Beaten down" doesn't cover the varieties of abused women. Those who live with a controlling husband give off their own unique scent. She wanted to have me call when her husband was at work.

Once we got past the money part, she gave me the rest of it. Abby, now twenty-nine, was a prostitute and drug addict. Lucinda maintained communication outside the family's knowledge but had not heard from her in two months.

The parents were drug-addled riffraff who had a "come to Jesus moment" and reformed too late to do the older children much good. Most, like Lucinda, were grown and gone by the time Abby graduated salutatorian from high school. Abby was the tarnished jewel of her family. One misstep, and it all came crashing down on her like a house of cards under strobe lighting. Lucinda told me in fits and starts. Abby attended a beach party in Panama City the summer after high-school graduation. She'd won a scholarship to a small private college. A boy at the party slipped GHB into her drink; then he led her off to the shoreline to have sex with her. A group of local boys drawn to the bonfire and beer heard about it when the rapist returned. They gang-raped her. The college provost decided to quash the investigation soon after because of adverse publicity. The boy was never prosecuted, nor were the others discovered. Abby's slide toward oblivion was rapid.

"Did she tell you where she was staying?"

"She didn't say where," Lucinda told me. "Just Fort Lauderdale."

"What do you want me to do when or if I locate her?"

"Have her—ask her if she would please call me. I just want to know she's all right."

I knew many junkie hookers from my cop days. Not a single one of them was "all right" by even the loosest definition.

I told her I'd report progress at intervals.

Fort Lauderdale is a tale of two cities: the one the tourists see in daylight and the other one, the one where street prostitutes, rednecks, and outlaw bikers congregate in the shadows of the tourism industry. About ten years ago, I fetched a runaway girl from Fort Lauderdale. She was addicted to meth, emaciated, smelled like raw sewage, and was barely coherent when I found her in a hooker's motel. We couldn't fly home because of her condition. During the road trip back, we stayed at Bates motels and cabins way off the beaten track. I watched her fight through a fierce withdrawal. Before her fall, she was a piano prodigy, a scholarship student at the prestigious Dana School of Music at Youngstown State. The last time I heard from her was two Christmases ago when she sent me a photo card. She was surrounded by a beaming husband and two young girls, all wearing goofy Santa hats for the camera.

None of the college kids hitting town during spring break nowadays remembered the beach blanket movies that put Fort Lauderdale on the map. Annette Funicello and her beehive hairdo. Tall, handsome Frankie Avalon's bookend opposite was tall, handsome Troy Donahue with his with his blond, wavy duck's ass. The boys still wear the ducktail but with a buzzcut on the sides. Social media platforms overwhelm teenagers like an Alpine avalanche bearing down on a ski lodge. From the gangs of Liberty City peddling drugs and pills, fights and overdoses, to the biker gangs, pimps, and hookers, the drifters, and psychos cruising everywhere, you can watch the chaos on YouTube. Hundreds of college kids get arrested every year, and it doesn't make news. Gunshots near a beachfront hotel on South Beach send the cattle stampeding. The next night, it's the same thing—all for clicks and eyeballs on Instagram and TikTok.

Sordid catastrophes are my income. I didn't leave halcyon for Armageddon. I exchanged office addresses. But Florida suffers from a "toxic positivity" like no other place. People *demand* happiness here. Fort Lauderdale is smack in the middle of this sociological hurricane. I believe in depression and being disappointed. Anything else isn't real life.

Between Las Olas Isles and Home Beautiful Park, the best and the worst neighborhoods, you have the bulk of citizens living mundane lives, albeit in great weather, and doing what people do everywhere. Every city's politicians hate it when the crime stats come out and nowhere more than wherever tourist dollars are affected.

A trail eight years old isn't a trail. I hit the sketchy bars and hooker hangouts first. People tell me I don't look like a cop—more like the last guy in the office to get a raise. It helped to blend in when I'm in dicey territory.

From the I-95 Interstate moving east toward the Atlantic, everything improves, even overall snack availability. But when you're starting with an average annual income of $20,000 and an unemployment rate flirting with twenty percent, it has to, or you're looking at the demographics for Kigali. Small houses minus garages dabbed in cheery yellow set on rectangular concrete blocks from one end to the other. If it weren't for the sandy vacant lots strewn with fast-food packaging, you wouldn't know what street you were on between NW 7th and Andrews Avenue. I had as much chance of spotting her sitting behind my laptop checking Google Earth.

Fortunately, I can still find a cop bar in any city without a map. Raymundo's Tavern bumped up against Rio del Lindo, which was a lower-middle-class enclave fighting to stay out of the top ten worst neighborhood rankings.

Cops are by nature suspicious. Bartender, less so, but you need to grease them. Buying rounds helped. By nine thirty, I had the names of Vice cops who might help. Because crime is mostly a nocturnal phenomenon, I returned to see if the seeds I'd planted the night before bore fruit. Night-shift cops often decompressed before going home.

One name I'd heard more than once was Dru Penfield. Leery of being sent on a snipe hunt, a favorite cop game played on rookies and gumshoes north and south, I tracked Penfield to his off-duty lair, a different cop bar in a tonier neighborhood where they served food and had TVs everywhere you swiveled your head. One of his less-ardent admirers in the PD told me that, if I didn't see him getting sloshed at this bar, he'd be at the dog track in Dania eight miles away.

Stopping a man coming back from the pissoir is a gamble. Bad guys get annoyed. Good guys tend to be more distracted than irked by a stranger popping up in front of them like a jack-in-the-box. They've emptied their bladders, they're ready for the next brew or dirty martini.

Penfield was shitfaced, surly, and highly irritated at nine thirty in the morning. For a moment, I thought he was going to swing on me.

I placated him with a combination of flattery ("Your colleagues at the precinct tell me there's no Vice cop who's got a better inside track…") and greed ("Your time is valuable to me, Officer, and I'm willing to pay for it.").

Free booze is like an offsides penalty to a desperate quarterback when the ref doesn't throw the flag. You can heave one deep and hope the Hail Mary worked.

I waylaid him toward a booth in back.

"Nope. Doesn't register. She's young to be a professional," he said, handing back the photos.

"Most were taken before she hit the streets."

"Yeah, not many skidmarks on her. A thousand blowjobs won't do what dope does in a month."

Ever since that first deputy in the Northwest showed the age progression faces of meth addicts as crank bugs scarred their faces and meth mouth caved in their lower jaws and rotted their teeth, every department in the country did the same thing. Cleveland had its own lineup of "stars" that drew wicked comments from street cops who watched the degradation close up.

"These bitches all use different names. Especially if they got an unhappy john or a weirdo out there looking for them."

"Who's the girl I need to talk to? The one who'd know if anybody would."

"Ask around for Donna. She bounces between Durrs Homeowners and Home Beautiful. She's chummy with all the girls."

"Look, you've earned your money," I said. "Just give me one more name, and the money's yours."

"Héctor Rivera," he said. "Street name 'Sugar Boy.'"

"Thanks."

"Screw that, gumshoe. Fork over."

Public records give something. Nobody lived completely off the grid, but I couldn't afford those cop databases for deep dives that vacuum everything up, including your last credit card transaction.

Pimps walked a line between flamboyant excess and phantom secretiveness. Lucky for me, Héctor belonged in the former camp. A showboat from his puce, high-top sneakers to his yellow Ferrari with the rally stripes, he was the opposite of discreet. The first two working girls on West Sunrise near the Burger King told me where I could find him.

I put that information in my back pocket. First, I had to see what Donna could tell me.

"She old," said the skinny black girl in a blond wig. "Whatchu want wid her, man? She got no teeth." She made smacking noises with her mouth. The chunky white girl with her was negotiating with the driver of a white Honda at the intersection. Her head popped up like a prairie-dog out of a burrow. She laughed at the cheap wit.

"He wants one of Den'al Donna's famous gum jobs," she said and resumed her business with the Honda. The backs of her thighs were pitted like an orange.

I misheard. I thought she said "Delta" like the old country-western tune "Delta Dawn" with the chorus that sounded like "Amazing Grace."

The motel Donna worked from—not to put too fine a point on it—was a shithole. I'd been to places like it in my patrolman days before all the strip bars gravitated toward an upmarket area in the Warehouse District called the Flats. My first prostitution sting was at Do-Re-Mia's on Prospect Avenue, a magnet for hookers, drug dealers, and transvestites. The city closed these places down, often with a sidebar of umbrage in the *Plain Dealer* from the councilman who realized it existed in his own ward. Two weeks later, a new club opened, and business resumed.

This place was rocking on a Tuesday, more like New Year's Eve, and the sun hadn't gone all the way down to the green wink in the Key West. People stumbled into and out of rooms, music blasted every time a door opened—rap, hip-hop, and rockabilly all competing. Most men milling about looked like bikers or the trash that hung around them, like remora fish under a shark's belly. The cell phone in my hand was a stun gun, although not as effective as the tactical one I used to carry with an LED light at the top of the baton that blinded you. But its advantage was that I carried it around in the open like the rest of the phone zombies. It packed plenty of voltage to get me out of a jam.

Donna's room was surprisingly neat, feminine, without being tawdry. She invited me in when I mentioned my interest was strictly in Abby Corhaven and I showed her the money. She didn't recognize the name, but she did the photo. The headboard next door thudded a bass accompaniment to a song I'd never listen to again the same way. Light jazz on a stereo, another surprise. "Mood Indigo" played when I entered. She sat in the only chair, her eyes closed, waving a hand to the melody like a blind conductor.

"Everybody knows her," she said, tapping the photo. These were the first three words out of her mouth.

Nobody in my business had that kind of luck.

"So where is she?"

She laughed. I had the benefit of her gap-toothed smile—everything between the incisors of her upper jaw missing. Then I knew: "Dental Donna."

"She called herself 'Lucky,'" when she come here. She was freelance 'til Héctor convinced her to become one of his girls."

Pimps and their stables. "Is she here now?"

"She ain't here, that's for sure."

"You said—"

"That girl, every pimp before and after Héctor 'til the end of time, he gonna use her as an *essample*."

"Example?"

"Essample what not to do."

"Then she's dead."

"Might could be."

"I'm confused," I said. I glanced at the door where somebody seemed to be standing right outside talking on a cell phone.

"Pay no mind," she said. "Shit goes on all night. Cops don't bother with this place no more. I seen a guy dead on the floor had more knives sticking in him than a got-damn porkypine."

The missing dentals made the sibilants in her speech hiss.

"Do you know what happened to her?"

Donna shrugged—my cue. I put a pair of crisp twenties on my knee.

"Lucky dint like young girls comin' around here. She even went after their boyfriends. Got herself good and messed up over it. Héctor, he had a shitfit. Called her 'Miss Goody Two Shoes' and got his own licks in. He told Quianna to teach her a lesson, but not to mark her up too much. That girl beat the hell out of Lucky in the parking lot. She had to stay out of sight for a week until the bruises healed up."

"Why would Héctor want to damage his own merchandise over something like that?"

"He *wants* them young. Got him a sideline business. Know what I mean?"

"Underage girls."

Lots of pimps sold younger-looking girls. Passed them off as teens for the old degenerates. I knew a thirty-year-old hooker who passed herself off as sixteen. A john had too much to drink, he'd miss the pancake makeup applied with a trowel to hide the crow's-feet and marionette lines around the mouth.

"What's wrong, Donna?"

"It ain't me telling you this, hear me," she said. "Him and this other guy. Raffa from downtown. It's all kinds of sick shit online. I ain't seen it personally. Word is it's murder, torture, rape—I don't know what all. Children, too, I heard. I ain't seen it and don't want to."

"An extreme porn site, the dark web. Is that what you're saying?"

"Héctor don't have the brains to pour piss out of a boot if the directions was written in crayon on the heel. Raffa's the smart one."

She'd taken something before I came in. The doper's nod coming on fast. I added a twenty to the bills. Her eyes snapped to them, cut to me.

"What does it have to do with Abby—with Lucky?"

"She tried to get two girls to go with her to the cops. Not Héctor's girls, new ones showed up a few months ago. She thought they'd all march down to the sheriff's."

"What happened?"

"Them girls told Héctor." She shook her head, saddened at the naiveté in the world.

"Did he sic Quianna on her this time."

"Nope." The head shake again, followed by what I expected to hear: "Gone. Sugar Boy cut her loose. He said he couldn't trust her no more."

As I was leaving, the clarinet glissando of "Rhapsody in Blue" took over and saw me out the door. You can never give up on life when you meet a toothless woman in a shit motel who appreciates Ellington's genius at switching the horns, putting the trombone for the clarinet first, the trumpet in the middle.

I wasted hours trying to get Donna's story confirmed on the street. No luck. If a girl knew of Lucky by name or recognized her photo, she was quick to deny any knowledge of her fate. Donna's story about the website drew blank stares.

I'd missed the first opportunity to call Lucinda and waited until the next "safe hour" rolled around.

"Someone called here," she said. Her voice breathless. A man's voice on the phone recorder left a message telling me to lay off or something might happen to my kids or my husband."

"Report it to the police," I said.

"No, no," she panted. "I can't take that chance!"

She wanted me to send her a bill for "services rendered." I told her I wouldn't do that.

"Why?"

"I'm close," I said. I hoped the small lie would buck her up.

She thumbed off the connection instead.

I had no more reason to do anything the right way now. I was technically unemployed.

Sugar Boy and I hadn't talked.

You know all those cop shows where the detective smiles at the whining scumbucket in front of him, and says: "I just want to hear your side of it"? The suspect could be covered in blood with the axe on him and the cop acts like his only friend left in the world. That's not me.

It cost me a twenty cruising Sunland Park to get a girl in lime hot pants to name Héctor's favorite club.

There's no escape from surveillance. I've done my share of motel peeping, following cheating husbands when there's a whiteout in ten degrees. I keep water and urine bottles, energy bars, and snooze blanket in the trunk along with my Zeiss field glasses. My .45 with the ACP slugs is still in the case it came in. I've never been in a shootout and don't carry. A cop buddy of mine quit the force after his third gunfight. He said it was only a matter of odds before he got killed in one. If I ever made enough, I'd get one of those directional mics that doesn't bounce off glass and some Army-issue night goggles.

Héctor left Poky's Rah-Rah Club on East Olas Boulevard at two-thirteen in the morning with a girl who'd been shoehorned into her skimpy spaghetti-strap dress. My bladder was killing me by then.

I waited for the big engine to rev up. Instead, he threw an arm over the bucket seat and tilted his head back like a man in blissful contemplation of life. She disappeared from view—a perfect time or the worst possible. I got out of my car, not knowing which one.

Trying to stay out of the line of sight of his rearview, I moved closer to the passenger window, and I realized nothing short of an oompah band would have grabbed his attention.

Flinging her door open, I reached over the top of her head to jam the stun gun into his neck. The blue spark arced between the metal prongs, and all the rest of him not stiff planked out after two seconds' worth of voltage dumped into his system.

She, on the other hand, must have been in some kind of narcotic or liquor-induced stupor. I grabbed her hair with my other hand and pulled her off him. She went down on her haunches on the sidewalk. Legs splayed, still in that drug haze. Exposed all the way up to her crotch, she was too stunned to scream.

I lay on top of him, the steering wheel jammed into my spine; his custom stick shift scraped a chunk of skin off my calf. I had a forearm bar across his throat. He began gagging, spewing an oily vomit down his chin and over both of us. He bucked, tried to push me off, but I outweighed him by a hundred pounds.

"You...cock...sucker—"

"Lucky," I said, so close, my spit flecked his lips.

"You be lucky...I don't kill your ass..."

Glancing behind me to check on the girlfriend, I saw she'd staggered to her feet.

"Abby Corhaven. Lucky. One of your girls."

"...fuckin'...kill...you."

I zapped him again. He groaned and went limp, all but the part that didn't get the message the first time.

People were leaving the club. I couldn't see how far his girl had gone. Both his hands were pinned, but his youth and strength would shake off the voltage, and when it turned into a fight inside a phone booth, he'd win. Electricity running through the body isn't abnormal; it's the neural blockage. Hitting him with more might turn him into a drooling vegetable.

"You...puked on me," he said, discovering his own mess on his shirt.

His eyes raked my face, inches from his, for recognition.

"Lucky. Where?"

The edge of the stun gun dug a notch into the skin below his left eye.

"*Chingar*, you used a cell phone?"

"Think, or I'm going to stick this right into your eye socket. Lucky."

"Man, fuck you, I don't—"

"Where...is...she?" I emphasized each word with harder digs into his flesh.

"Dead!"

One word, gasped out.

"Show me where."

Swinging my body over to the passenger seat, I brushed against his crotch. He howled in pain.

"Drive," I ordered. "Remember, Sugar Boy, I'm holding this an inch from your neck."

"Where?"

I named his motel.

He mumbled as he drove: "Dint know the bitch by that name..."; professions of his innocence, excuses, lies. My stomach gurgled from nausea and the aftereffects of the adrenalin jolt. The vomit smell didn't help.

He parked in back.

My luckiest move of the night after taking him down: "Your partner," I said. "I know Raffa did it. Tell me why."

"She...she was gonna tell the cops about the list."

"What list?"

"The client list, fool."

The clients were the "subscribers" to their extreme website, all anonymous online handles. Lucky found it in Héctor's room when he was escorting girls and arranging hookups for his exclusive customers, the ones who wouldn't set foot in that rathole motel. He drove the girls to them or arranged private parties with underaged girls too doped to know where they were going. Some men liked to participate; others wanted to watch. They all paid quite well. Héctor bragged when he told me these were the richest, most powerful men in Fort Lauderdale and Miami.

That list could be matched to IP addresses, and those addresses belonged to men who could destroy three people over him and Raffa. That was how Sugar Boy put it to me.

"You and Raffa killed her for a piece of paper with names?"

"Not me, *cabrón*. Raffa. He said...he'd get it done. 'Don't tell me,' I said. 'I wanna know nothin' about it, man.'"

Every deadass in every interrogation room in every cop precinct in the world has a guy like Héctor Rivera in it. Either asleep with his head in his arms on the table because he was guilty or jabbering away, doing everything to lessen his own guilt.

"I want to see the body," I said. "I don't give a shit about your list of clients."

That was true. Kill them all, every twisted, sick pervert, and a new crop springs up like toadstools after a summer rain. Nothing will change. It hasn't yet.

"Then ask Raffa, *puta*."

I didn't get to ask Raffa. An FBI agent and a detective sergeant had that honor. I wasn't allowed in the precinct when it happened.

The Broward County Sheriff's Dive Rescue Team looked like the one from Indian River County. The mangrove swamp looked the same. It even smelled the same.

Not the same result, though, because nothing of Abby Corhaven was found, either floating in the swamp or submerged in plastic and weighted down.

Héctor finally cracked about Lucky's demise, a bloody one.

His lawyer was good. He reached out for the brass ring and grabbed it for his client, something prosecutors call being "king for a day" when they have a weak case. By the time law enforcement caught up to Raffa, he was already lawyered up with a powerhouse Miami firm and refused to talk. Héctor agreed to plead to conspiracy to manslaughter. He'll do three, maybe five tops, and be out. He assured me of that through the scarred Plexiglass when I visited him in jail. Then he threw a middle finger at me over his shoulder while the guard cuffed him up again. Two men he thought were "Nicaraguans" were hired off the streets in Little Havana. He said Raffa had someone from the client list "handle it." They lured Abby to the motel room. When she walked in, saw the floor and walls covered in plastic painter's tarp, she knew what was coming. The cop said Hector told them "chain saws cut up the body," talking nonchalantly to his interrogators between sips of Evian water. Her remains were supposed to be in that mangrove swamp.

Raffa was never indicted. He denied having a list of names. No list turned up in a search of his condo in Miami, his safe deposit boxes there and in Fort Lauderdale, or anywhere in his six-million-dollar home in his Las Olas. As I said, not every case ended with me in a gator-infested swamp searching for body parts, but too many of them did. After all, this was Florida, a literal and figurative swamp from one end of the state to the other, where dumped bodies provided meals to the resident alligator population and guys like me too often searched for bite-sized morsels left behind.

Lucinda Gray didn't want me to send the report I'd detailed for her. She said she read it in the papers and that was "enough." She sounded the same: full of dread, waiting for the next catastrophe to come around the corner.

Exactly how I felt.

# DINKY DAU
## Michael Chandos

My one-man agency is on Denver's East Colfax Avenue, just down the street from the gold-domed Colorado State Capitol where the BLM rioters camped and the cathedral the Pope once visited. Denver Police Department's District 6 headquarters is located between the flashing lights of Kitty's XXX theater, several hardball bars, and the Fillmore Auditorium. It's Colfax. This is my neighborhood. I fix human problems here.

Mid-April, four a.m. and cold, with just a speck of dirty snow way up under the bigger spruces, still dark gray beyond the city lights. I preferred the streets before the city woke up. They were cleaner and more peaceful without swarming humanity.

I was returning after a pay-the-bills divorce surveillance. I parked my stealth Plymouth in the back and went around front to the second-floor stairway entrance, eyes bleary and my brain crazy after staring at a cheesy motel for eight hours. My bed called for me. Bed later. A quick report to the client, first.

A scarecrow stumbled into me. He had no coat on despite the temperature and was ragged, a character from Dickens. Just an undernourished street guy, I figured, huddling in the narrow pass between buildings. But he looked profoundly lost, vacant somehow, and it stopped me. Asian, I thought, with a few cuts on his face and arms, some fresh, some looking poorly healed. His fingertips were bloody, and his hair matted and…holy shit! No shoes!

"You okay, buddy?"

He turned his head in my direction, but he didn't exactly focus on me. Instead, he leaned against me, bent like someone was pressing down on him. He was young under all the filth, maybe eighteen, maybe younger. The client email could wait a few.

"C'mon, kid. Let me take you where you can get some help. You can warm up at Reverend Paul's mission. Good hot food there, too." He shuffled along like a sick puppy, a lame metaphor, I know, but that's exactly what he was.

I guided him down the side street to my Plymouth and opened the back door. From out of nowhere, we were bathed in headlights and the roar of bad mufflers. I looked up the narrow residential street and saw a rusty yellow sedan racing toward us. I pushed the kid inside my car as I spun like a matador dodging a charging bull. The car's side mirror slapped my overcoat as it raced past. I got a quick impression of an older male driver with a bald head, lots of crap in the back seat, and an old army blanket for seat covers. And what the hell was wrong with his face? Tattoos?

North from Colfax, the street narrowed to one lane because residents of the rooming houses and apartments parked their cars on both sides. My raging bull screeched to a stop, swerving and scraping a couple parked cars. He crammed into an old driveway, attempting to turn his big car around for a second pass. His K-turn was going to be several W's. I could hear him yelling as he landlocked his car between a pickup and a light pole. He smoked his tires in his fury to get back at us. Car alarms rang out and lights came on. I recognized good fortune when I saw it. I jumped into the Plymouth with the kid and sped west on Colfax.

I knew the neighborhood well, of course. There were few other cars to use as cover at this hour, but I knew I could lose any follower no matter the time of day. I made a zigzag route down alleys and up the wrong way on a one-way, and even through a red light. Then, I slowed to boring and legal normality, and headed to Reverend Paul's 24th Street Mission. No one followed. The kid slumped across the back seat.

Reverend Paul was already up. His mission prepared a basic breakfast every morning for the neighborhood homeless. He was still in his faded plaid bathrobe, worn over jeans and tennis shoes. I could see a blue flannel shirt underneath, and an ebony and silver crucifix on a chain. He was tall and angled, and his thinning hair was leaving him with a brotherly bald spot.

Down the main hall, his staff was rousting up the night's residents to groans and laughter as the kitchen came alive. The coffee smelled roasty and metallic, and I needed some desperately.

The kid shivered on a bench in the hall as Paul wrapped him in a gray Navy blanket. "Found another penniless client, I see. And you've been up all night again."

"Just out on another job, Paul." I snugged up the kid's blanket.

"Another case with deep social meaning?"

"Can't eat meaning."

"Come into my office and have some coffee," he said. "The nurse will look him over."

Paul kept his office nice to make a good first impression on visitors and potential donors. One wall was devoted to a large, framed color picture of Jesus. Signed photos of football players, politicians, and local notables were on the opposite wall. The furniture was wood and probably donated. I poured steaming black liquid into the cup with my name on it that Paul kept for me.

"Plan to leave him here, Sammy?" Paul owed me for resolving a few embarrassing problems.

"Yeah, he needs more help than I can offer. Someone very mean and nasty is after him, but I don't know what for. Don't worry about that guy. I lost him comin' over here." Rev Paul fretted over the company I kept. "I think he's Southeast Asian, Paul. The kid doesn't respond to English. Maybe someone from the Vietnamese or Thai community can figure out who he is."

"I'll call Mrs. Tran at the Saigon Cafe. She'll be up already," said Paul.

The nurse brought the kid in and sat him on the couch. She had washed the kid's face, and he looked even younger now, minus the dirt. The Mission had given him fuzzy blue slippers and a second-hand T-shirt, and his fingers and other cuts had been bandaged. The kid clutched a large steaming cup of cocoa like it was gold. I did the same with my coffee.

Mrs. Tran was the polestar of the immigrant Asian community in Denver. She could hide you if you needed hiding, get you off-the-books employment if you needed money, and she knew everything happening in Denver's economic underground. Her voice was smooth and warm over the speakerphone, but it left you no doubt she was a Person-in-Charge.

Paul explained the situation.

"He's in shock, Paul," said Mrs. Tran. "Let me try some Vietnamese. Tell me if he reacts, okay? *Chao An? Anh khoe khong?*" The boy raised his head, and I thought I saw a glimmer of life in his eyes.

"*Khoe.*" Less than a whisper.

"Touchdown," I said.

"*Ban co noi tieng Viet Khong?*" she asked.

"*Va. Lam,*" he said. I didn't understand what they were saying—my Army service was after Vietnam—but I could see his sense of relief. He still sat hunched over, but it was a good start.

"Ask him his name, Mrs. Tran," said Paul. "Is he local?"

"Okay. *Ban ten gi?*" she said.

The boy seemed to have to search for his name. "Lahn." Finally.

"Paul, I might know who this is. Several Vietnamese families moved to Denver last fall via the Philippines. They didn't speak much English, so we placed them in Arvada with another family from Vietnam. They had several children, including teenagers. I'll call to see if they know Lanh. In any case, I'll be over within the hour." Click. The Dragon Lady had spoken.

"Damn it, I was hoping to find out more about this crazy guy in the rusty car," I said.

"Mrs. Tran and her underground family will take good care of Lanh. Do you want to call the police, Sammy?"

"No, not yet. I'd prefer to wait for Mrs. Tran to talk to the boy more, but I must find out what's happening on my streets, Paul. In particular, I want to have a technical discussion with that bald driver who tried to run me over. Lanh's got to be from near downtown because he couldn't have walked far without shoes. Call me on my cell if she gets more info from him, okay? If he needs to see a doctor, call me on that, too. Many thanks, Paul."

My streets can make you crazy in the head, but they are a gold mine of current information. Sherlock had his Irregulars. I had my Central Denver working poor and resident street people. They know what's happening in my neighborhood. If they like you, they'll tell you.

It was after five a.m. and the streets were coming alive. Near the Colfax Mickey D's parking lot, I asked a couple walkers if they had seen a tattooed man. Wrong question: they had seen many. One had seen Elvis, probably did multiple times a day. Another had talked with Jesus, probably did all the time. They just asked for spare change or a cigarette. I don't smoke, but I always carry a pack when I hit the streets. Colorful characters pushing shopping carts stuffed with blue tarps, but not the reliable informants I was looking for.

The newspaper delivery guys were dropping bundles of the morning edition at the FastMart on Colfax. I'd done one of them a favor once. I parked my Plymouth and walked over to their truck.

"Luis, how ya doin'? Hey, I'm looking for a guy in a noisy '70s American car, a big one. Rusty, but looked yellow in bad light. He's an aggressive driver with a crappy attitude. He was near here a couple hours ago. Ya seen him?"

"No, not tonight, Mr. Lagune. We just got here, but, sure, I know that car. White guy, maybe a banger or OG. No joke, but he's bad news. Loco. Yells at people when he drives by and thinks he owns the road. He's just been around since last fall, I think. I don't know where he comes from. You should ask the taxi drivers. They're out on Colfax twenty-four/seven."

A solid suggestion, and it meant Nancy's Diner for a hot breakfast.


Three young taxi drivers were sitting in a back booth at Nancy's. I signaled Nancy for coffee and slipped in. They leaned away until they saw it was me.

"Morning, guys. I'm looking for an angry white man in a banged up American car, an Olds or Pontiac, I think, probably 1970s. Loud exhaust. Rusty and maybe yellow once. Army blankets for seat covers. I think he has tattoos on his face, or maybe a fancy beard. He's burly, maybe sixty-five, might be shaved bald, and he lives within a mile or two of here. Know him and where he hangs?"

"Ooo, Boss, you don't wanna mess with that guy. One hundred percent negative, aggressive, and mean," said Tommy, a twenty-something-year-old from somewhere in the Far East young man, Bronco cap, flashy watch, and no doubt a .45 underneath his jacket. "A couple weeks ago, up on East Colfax near the high school, he nicked my cab while trying to pass me. Skidded to a stop, got out, and started pounding on my roof. He was wearing a faded black T-shirt and camo pants, military boots, too. No beard or tattoos, though. Accused me of interfering with his mission."

"His mission?"

"Yeah, like he was in combat or somethin'. Said I was a gook, whatever that is. When he ran back to his car, I got the hell outta there in case he was goin' for a gun. Stay away from him, Sammy. Nothin' good happenin' there."

"Yeah. I get that, but I still need to find him."

"Well—" Tommy looked at the other drivers. He hesitated to rat out someone local, even a bad guy. He stared into his cup, summoning wisdom from tea leaves. "Try up Washington toward Five Points, but not that far up. Behind a closed car-upholstery shop, I think. Around 17th, 16th? Take an army with you."

"Never needed guns, guys. Just brains and fast feet, and sometimes bear spray and my stunner."

"You want backup?"

"No, I got it. Thanks for the info, Tommy." I picked up their bill and a coffee-to-go in a doubled paper cup. Breakfast was going to become lunch.

Traffic was building, so things were slow, and I had time to think. What did I know and what was I doing? I had a scary bad actor with a temper, maybe a dangerous one, somehow connected to a teen-aged Vietnamese boy, up Washington somewhere. I couldn't be sure of my thin facts. I'd been up since seven the previous morning, and I had that hollow-headed feeling you get when sleep deprived with not much energy left. Had I lost my common sense? The lack of sleep must be making me crazy. What was I fishing for? The meaning and the relevance I lacked in my cases? Justice for a young stranger?

I felt protective of my neighborhood. This guy, this "Bull," this invader, he didn't belong here. I had to find out what was going on before I could sleep. A little investigative diversion up Washington before wrapping up? I had time for that. I owed it to my town.

North on Washington was once a thriving residential neighborhood. Some of the old homes were still there, many converted to basic apartments, two- to three-story frame houses built before there was insulation in the walls or cars in the sheds. Many had been razed to make way for ugly glass-and-stucco office buildings, demolishing heritage to build faceless boxes. As the houses faded along north Washington, small businesses took their places in the form of three-to-five-unit strips. One was the predicted auto upholstery shop.

I didn't see the Bull's rusty sled, so I wasn't sure this was the place. I went up Washington and across 17th a couple blocks but didn't see any other shops that fit the description, so I came back and parked in a vacant lot almost across the street from the target. No lights on, a cut-rate electrician next door and a tall chain-link fence enclosing the yard around the shop. I could see multiple strands of razor wire curling around the top of the fence. Why did an upholstery shop need that much security? Then again, maybe this wasn't the Bull's place.

I couldn't see much from across the street, just common strip mall shops with dirty windows. Most of the older sections of town had alleys between the blocks. I could study the back of the shop from the alley and then make my plan.

The alley was unpaved and rutty, with broken beer bottles, a little garbage and paper here and there. I pulled the Plymouth close under some tall bushes, not minding the scratches, and turned off the engine.

Someone had once attempted to conceal the back of the shop by hanging the usual blue plastic tarps along the alley side of the fence. The ultraviolet at this altitude was murder on cheap plastic so now the tarps hung in strips that fluttered in the early morning breeze. I had a good view of the yard.

I expected to see a green dumpster full of fabric scraps and foam trash from the upholstery shop, and piles of other garbage, but the yard was cleaned up and orderly, military in how things were raked and sterile, and were those white painted rocks around the yard? A low wattage light burned above the wide garage door in the back of the shop, and there was a gate in the street side of the fence I hadn't seen earlier, now chained and locked. Two security cameras were aimed about right to cover the entire area. The razor wire looked sharp and eager.

In the middle of the yard a low rectangular wall, like a concrete house foundation minus the house, protruded three feet above ground level, as if someone had started to build a house, but never made it past the foundation stage. Larger than a three-car garage, the "cellar" was roofed with a shallow tented frame with thick tar-paper waterproofing. Several transparent corrugated fiberglass panels in the roof were installed to pass daylight below. A wire led from a back corner to an alley telephone pole where it joined another wire strung to the next pole, a probable antenna. Light smoke drifted from a small stack in the same back corner with a smaller pipe on the opposite corner, a possible vent. A doorway attached to a downward sloping wedge grew from the corner nearest the shop, fronted by a short homemade step.

I've seen similar "houses" in the Mojave Desert, built by dedicated survivalists and damn-the-government independents. I had no idea what this structure was for, nor did I see anything in the yard connected to the Bull or Lanh. Interesting and weird, but this might still be a miss.

I considered my options. I could wait to see if the Bull came home. But he could be at work all day someplace else, and I'd been up since seven a.m. the previous day. I could tip off the DPD, but what did I have to go on? Of course, I could get a little nosier and go look around closer in. Yeah, that sounded good.

I got out of the Plymouth armed with a strong flashlight, my million-volt stunner (as always), and my digital camera, and toured the fence to see if a different perspective would reveal anything new. I could see tracks in the yard's sandy dirt where a vehicle might park routinely. Faint paths between those tracks and the shop's rear door and from there to the underground house door were scuffed into the dirt. The yard was clean and neat, in a parade ground way, and almost nothing green was growing, not even weeds. There was very little snow. I was about to go sit in my car and call Reverend Paul when I heard it coming.

My stealth Plymouth is sad-looking, even a little bashed, an invisible Everycar, but, underneath, the engine, brakes, and suspension have been "improved" by a talented wrench who owed me for several investigative favors. Ordinary enough to be unnoticed, fast enough to get me away from trouble if needed. And my exhaust was custom made to be super quiet while still allowing the engine to breathe. Stealthy, anonymous, and unremarkable. The Bull's car had no such improvements. I heard it coming from blocks away.

He parked in the driveway, got out to unchain the gate, and drove the car into the yard. It was a 1971 Oldsmobile 98, five thousand pounds plus of American industrial momentum. As he got out again to close the gate, I got my first good look and photos of my target. He was wearing military camouflage pants, canvas military boots, a black field jacket and T-shirt, and a black baseball cap. He was older than I had thought, at least in his mid-70s, but he didn't move like an old man.

OMG. What I thought were tattoos were Vietnam War tiger stripes in black, brown, and green grease paint drawn diagonally across his face. I guess he *was* returning after a mission, just five decades after the fact.

He went into the shop after opening two door locks and a huge padlock. A few minutes later, he came out carrying a plastic milk bottle and a small box. He unlocked the door to the cellar-house and went down, leaving the door open. Even in the dim early morning twilight, no light came from below. I heard two voices, one loud and booming—the Bull—and another that was thin and higher pitched. Was he imprisoning a woman down there?

Five minutes later, he came out, now carrying an M14 carbine and a heavy black bag, perhaps filled with ammo and equipment. He had a Ka-Bar knife in a scabbard on his belt, too. He stashed the bag and rifle in the back seat of the Olds and opened the gate again. He had tried to wipe off the tiger stripes, but I could still see traces. After blocking the door to the cellar with a pipe wedged against the handle, he got in the Olds and roared away, leaving the gate open. Just out for a brief "recon," I guess. I had minutes to see inside.

I pulled the Plymouth up next to the back fence to take a shortcut, literally. Standing on the front fender, I snipped through the wires that held the razor wire to the fence to make an opening in the barrier and I flipped into the yard. That wouldn't work in reverse. I kicked the pipe away from the cellar door and looked down into…what? A Green Hell? A subterranean pot garden gone mad? Man, this place was alive.

The air that floated up was organic, warm, and humid. I heard no sounds. Brandishing my flashlight and my little stun gun ahead of me like light sabers, I went down the steep stairs. The muggy gloom swallowed me. I could see a faint dirty yellow glow from the skylights in the ceiling. Purple grow lights hung from extension cords at regular intervals. A garden fork and a shovel were stacked at the bottom of the stairs, along with bags of fertilizer. Vines, large leaf plants, and tropical trees were everywhere. It was so dark green it was almost black. This guy had his own personal jungle.

Paths meandered through the jungle in two directions. Were there snakes here? I thought I heard birds and insects, too, but maybe it was just in my head. The floor crunched as I walked along the larger of the paths.

I was too young to have served in Vietnam, but I'd been in jungles from the Philippines to Panama during my twenty-four years in Army CID, and they were eerily like this. The smell, the feel, it all came back. I began to sweat, and not just from the heat and humidity.

The main path widened into a small clearing. A partial "hooch," roofed with leaves and with a planked floor, two wooden walls, a chair and table, and a tall bench, was built against the far concrete wall. A dim, compact fluorescent light hanging from the ceiling glowed like an old-fashioned gas lantern. Framed medals, photographs of soldiers, and newspapers hung on the back wall. Pegs in the wall may have held the M14.

A shortwave radio on the bench made scratchy noises amid occasional voices that sounded like troops in the field. Its volume was low. The medals included Silver Stars and Purple Hearts, multiple awards. The photos were of a Ranger battalion, judging from markings on the uniforms. Mr. Bull had been an Army Ranger, training and leading Vietnamese Rangers as they raided along the remote Cambodian border and mined the Ho Chi Minh trail. It was the stuff of legends.

The framed newspaper summarized everything. Mr. Bull, now Staff Sergeant Collins, was the sole survivor after his team had been decimated by the North Vietnamese Army. He had been held captive in a small cage in the jungle for four months before managing to escape during an air strike. He was released from an Army psychiatric hospital and from active duty in 1978.

I think he never left that cage.

The clock in my head screamed that I had been here too long. Time to go. I was trespassing, but that would be a minor problem if Collins returned and found me. I took a couple photos and headed out.

When I reached the bottom of the stairs, I heard a cry and several words from somewhere along the smaller path. The cries I heard before. Damn it, I had to follow up.

Fifteen feet down the path, I came across an empty tiger cage, three feet square by about four feet, built from bamboo lashed together. The open door hung from damaged hinges. My God! The lashings holding the door to the cage had been shredded, and they were bloody. Lanh had been kept here, and he had clawed his way to freedom.

I heard a whimper. Another ten feet down the path, deeper into the claustrophobic darkness, I saw the outline of another bamboo tiger cage. I knelt and turned on my flashlight. Inside was an old Asian man. My flashlight hurt his eyes, so I turned it off. A little work with my pocketknife and the door opened. He shrunk into the back of the cage amid empty sardine tins, a canteen, and a thick smell. No time to waste. I grabbed his skinny arm and pulled him from the cage.

He couldn't walk. He'd been in the cage for way too long, so I picked him up. He was incredibly light, and I could hold him in one arm like a small child.

I guess I missed the Olds the second time. As I started up the steep wooden stairs with the old man, the Bull eclipsed the morning sun. Collins filled the doorway, glaring down at us from his superior position. He raised the M14.

I ducked up the longer path and dove into the non-bulletproof cover of several large-leafed plants. He ran through the entire clip, twenty rounds that pinged their way around the jungle. He yelled as he fired, nothing intelligible, just the roar of the warrior, enraged to find his fortress had been violated and his treasure stolen.

After the gunfire, he continued to yell. I think I heard a couple "bastards" amid the growls. Was he fitting another magazine? If he did, he was sure to come down the steps and get us both. In the relative pause, I rushed the steps, grabbed the garden fork, and threw it at him like a javelin. Flying forks first, it hit the M14 and knocked Collins out of the doorway. Up we came, the old man in my right arm and my cigarette pack-sized stunner in my left hand, buzzing and sparking like a handful of lightning.

The fork had jabbed him in both hands and one forearm. Blood streamed from several ragged wounds. The M14 and a full magazine had scattered on the ground, but he didn't go for them. Instead, he charged when I jumped from the doorway, a bull again. He hit us like a linebacker and the old man flew from my grasp. He left-hooked my face, and I went off in the opposite direction, spinning across his tidy parade ground amid stars and ringing bells.

Ignoring his blood, he jerked me up to throw or hit me again.

He huffed from the exertion, a warrior at heart in a critical battle, but in the body of a seventy-five-year-old veteran who had seen far better days. I pressed the stunner against his temple and pushed the button.

The zap blew us apart. I hit the foundation and rolled onto the roof, my wind gone and my head ringing. If he got to me now, I was a goner. I clawed in the air where I thought his face should be like a dying beetle on its back. My sense of place, time, and pain was all mixed up. I thought I heard voices.

Exhausted, I collapsed against the roof. Soon, hands came to me. I tried to fight them off.

"Sammy, stop it! It's me, Tommy. I thought you'd need backup. Relax, man, you're hurt, but you're gonna be okay."

I believed him and passed out.

I think I was out just a couple minutes. Damn it, I really hate the swirling sensation of regaining consciousness. At least I didn't barf this time, but my stomach thought about it. I sat up to find I was still on the low tar-paper roof. I swung my legs over the edge, but I didn't trust myself to stand. The sun was fully up now, but my vision was iffy.

Tommy stood over Collins. He had his .45 out, but he was holding it without urgency. The old man sat next to the dead-still Collins, who was flat on his back on his beloved parade ground. The old man daubed at Collins's wounds with a rag and water from a plastic bottle I assume came from Tommy. Collins was very pale.

"*Beaucoup dien cai dau*," said the old man. He looked up at me with weary sadness. "I was in the war, too. Seen this many times. *Dinky dau*. Crazy in the head. War makes men love it and it leaves them crazy. Not his fault. Not his fault."

I heard sirens approaching.

\*\*\*

I was late getting to that client email, but I was too tired to care. I'd been up more than thirty-six hours in what seemed like two separate lives, and I was on automatic in my own Dinky Dau moment. Nancy took pity on me and made me some espresso that would raise the dead. I managed to send the email to the client before I collapsed. No broken jaw, but I was gonna be bruised and damn ugly for a while. Yeah, I know, little change there.

Mrs. Tran assumed control of Lanh, and she totally surprised me by letting DPD talk to him. The kid is with his family again.

Collins is back behind the wire. The stunner didn't do him any good, I guess. He'll find some vets in the psych ward to share his war stories with. I don't think he'll ever stop hearing the guns and helicopters.

Turns out the old man had been a Lieutenant Commander in the South Vietnamese Navy. Now, he was a shrimp fisherman in Louisiana. He'd been kidnapped and sold to Collins six months ago. That'll give the DPD and Feds something to think about. Maybe they'll forget about pressing trespassing charges against me.

# UNLUCKY FOR SOME
## Alan Barker

His eyes snapped open.

*"En-ger-land! En-ger-land! En-ger-land!"* came the raucous chant from the cul-de-sac outside. They were the same boorish yobs, surely, who had awoken him every night that week. The racket would soon pass—once they'd taken the cut-through to Beaver Walk and put some distance between them and John's house—but the damage was already done. It would be hours before he could get back to sleep. And his head was pounding.

Almost like a robot, he climbed out of bed, pulled on his joggers and cardigan and clomped downstairs. His parka was draped over a chair in the kitchen. He slipped it on, patting the pockets, and stepped into the garden.

The night was cool and gusty, typical of the summer so far. Clouds scudded across a dark sky, threatening a downpour. Treetops trembled and garden fences creaked. But John barely noticed any of this. Despite the darkness, he made his way across the lawn in a few long strides, eased open the back gate, and stepped down to the towpath that ran alongside the canal.

He could hear the yobs in the distance, laughing and joking. John switched on his pocket torch and set off in the direction of the noise, past the turning for Beaver Walk, where he'd waylaid them two nights before. On that occasion, he'd politely asked them to refrain from singing and shouting each time they went by so late in the evening, explaining about the sleep problem he'd never quite shaken off since serving in Afghanistan. "Suck it up, Soldier Man," one had said. "This is our patch and we're gonna do whatever we want." Barging past him, they headed toward the towpath, taunting him with more brash comments.

The following night, John had taken refuge in his back bedroom, but it made no difference. The chanting woke him yet again, and it took three hours of reading and tossing and turning before he managed any more sleep.

Now, directing the beam of his torch ahead, and with the aid of light shafts from the street that ran parallel to the canal, he picked his way along the towpath. This was his route to the railway station each morning to go to work, as familiar to him as the road he lived on. Reaching the bend, where one end of an abandoned canoe protruded from the stagnant water, a faded number 13 showing on its hull, John spotted the two yobs ambling along the towpath away from him. One flicked a cigarette butt into the canal, and the other kicked out at the undergrowth. John lengthened his stride, until he was almost within touching distance, and directed the beam of his torch on the ground between them.

They turned as one to face him. Recognition dawned in the eyes of the spokesman from two nights before. "Well, well, if it isn't our friend, Soldier Man. In a hurry somewhere, mate?"

Like John, they had short brown hair, but one had a bad case of acne and the other—the lippy one—sported a tattoo of a dagger on his neck. There was an unsavory odor about them, a mixture of sweat, cigarette smoke, and alcohol.

"A couple of nights ago," John said, "I asked you very politely not to do any singing when you go down our road at stupid o'clock on your way home from the pub, or wherever you spend your evenings. I've suffered from PTSD ever since I got hit in the head by shrapnel during the war in Afghanistan. Because of that,

I struggle to sleep, and when something wakes me unexpectedly, I can't get back off again. So, here's me telling you, as nicely as I can, to pack it in."

"Or what? What yer gonna do about it?"

"Throw you in the canal, for starters. That should teach you a lesson."

"Oh, yeah? You and 'oose army?"

He cackled at his own witticism, and his mate responded in kind. John slipped the torch into his left-hand pocket; in the right pocket, his fingers twitched.

The yob inched forward, his nostrils flaring. "You wanna make something of it, then?" John felt flecks of spittle land on his cheeks. "Tell yer what, you can 'ave first shot."

"Fair enough," John said.

He pulled out his pistol and fired once, twice. A couple of birds screeched nearby. There was an urgent flapping of wings and the yelp of a dog as the stricken yobs keeled over like toppling skittles, one falling on top of the other.


He gazed at their motionless bodies, taking in the enormity of what he'd done. He'd killed the pair of them. Just like that.

Should he haul them into the water or maybe the undergrowth, out of sight? He didn't know much about modern forensics, but was sure there were all manner of ways a man could drop himself in it by tampering with the evidence. *Let sleeping yobs lie.*

He swiveled, as if at an unexpected sound. But all he could detect were the dark outlines of the trees that lined the towpath and the rustling of their leaves.

John turned and struck out in the direction he'd been going, power walking. Eventually, he came to the bridge linking the other end of the estate with the canal. He checked the towpath both ways, then, satisfied there was no one else about, tossed the pistol in the water.

A vision flashed before his eyes of the enemy soldier lying prostrate at his feet, John having crept up behind him and catching him with a rabbit punch to the base of the skull. The guy surrendered his pistol like a willing lamb, and John had kept it ever since.

Pulling himself together, he climbed the steps of the bridge and set off home, under cover of the darkness and the trees.

The following morning, a Saturday, John spent at home pacing up and down, bracing himself for a visit from the police. When finally they came, one male officer and one female, he felt a strange sense of relief. He had no idea whether anyone had witnessed his transgressions of the previous night; maybe he was about to find out.

"We're sorry to disturb you, sir," the male officer said, "but a serious incident took place yesterday evening, along the towpath by the canal. You may have heard about it?"

John shook his head and said he'd been on his own indoors all morning.

"I'm afraid two young men were killed in suspicious circumstances. We need to establish what happened and are speaking to all residents. Did you see or hear anything that might be relevant?"

"I can't say I did. Goodness, what a dreadful thing to happen." John hoped his voice carried the right level of concern.

The other officer, a thick-set woman in her thirties carrying a clipboard, produced two photographs. "These are the men who were killed, sir. Have you seen them before?"

She held out the photographs, inviting John to take them. Instead, he kept his arms folded and craned his head round. One of the men had acne and the other a tattoo of a dagger on his neck. He'd had mental images of them all night long. Then he recalled his confrontation with them in Beaver Walk on Wednesday night and chose his words carefully.

"I don't think so. But we get a lot of people walking down our road; it's a handy cut-through to the canal and the rest of the estate. I might have seen them at some point—I honestly don't know."

"But not last night?"

"No. What happened to them?"

"They were shot, sir. That's why we need to ask around, in case anyone saw or heard anything."

John wanted to say, *And nobody did?* but kept his mouth shut and gazed across the road at number 8 *(Garden gate!)* where a Saint George's Cross flag, draped from a bedroom window, flapped in the breeze. The male officer was looking along the row of houses, as if anxious to press on. But the female officer frowned and said, "What were your movements yesterday evening, sir?"

"I had a quiet night in," John replied.

"Does anyone else live here?"

"Just me."

"There's no car in your driveway."

"I don't have a car. I don't drive." John thought about mentioning his condition but decided not to.

"Well, thank you for your time, sir. If I could have your name?" John gave it, and the female officer made a note on her clipboard and glanced up at his front door. "Number thirteen, eh? Unlucky for some."

That afternoon was bright and breezy. The lawn had dried out after the week's rain, so John took the opportunity to cut the grass and tidy up the flower bed.

A prolonged cheer sounded from somewhere nearby, but John was oblivious to it. He was thinking about the female police officer who'd fixed him with a long stare after he declined to handle the photos she held out. He didn't suppose she was trying to trick him into obtaining his fingerprints—in any event, he didn't have a criminal record—but it was just a natural reaction on his part. Nevertheless, there was a shrewdness about her that preyed on his mind.

"A bit chilly for the time of year, John." He swung round to see Catherine, his next-door neighbor in number 12 *(One dozen!)* standing on tiptoe to speak to him over the fence. "You never know what sort of weather the good Lord is going to throw at us, do you?"

"Some of my flowers aren't keen on it," he replied. "The violas are doing their blooming best, but the camellias and salvias are positively wilting. How's Yusuf?"

"The football's on, so he's glued to the television. And Samson is well—aren't you, darling?"

John stepped up to the fence and peered down. Two baskets rested at Catherine's feet, one containing a mound of weeds and the other a sleeping baby boy. Samson was very cute but was another reason for John's sleepless nights.

"Shocking about those two young men who were killed, isn't it?" Catherine said, looking back up. "Did the police speak to you?" His doorbell rang, loud and insistent, causing them both to glance round. "Perhaps that's them now, come to take you away, John!"

He forced a smile and stomped indoors, his heart thumping and sweat forming under his armpits. But it was only Megan, the young lady who lived diagonally across the road in number 7 *(Lucky seven!)* smiling up at him.

"Hi, John, how are you doing? Did you watch the footie?"

"No, I've been busy in the garden. Who was playing?"

She chortled, showing perfect white teeth behind her pale pink lips. "John, you're so funny. England, of course, and they won! You do know it's the World Cup, don't you? Anyway, I thought I'd celebrate by going to the pub tonight and wondered if you fancied tagging along?"

John hesitated. Mixing with a bunch of drunken revelers wasn't his idea of fun. But he quite liked Megan. He had turned her down once before and regretted it afterward.

"Besides, I heard there were a couple of shootings by the canal last night. Terrible, isn't it?" She made eyes at him. "I wouldn't feel safe going out on my own."

John heaved a sigh. "Well, I'm normally busy on a Saturday evening. But I suppose—"

"That's settled then," Megan said. "I'll be round at eight. Don't be late!"

John watched her sashay across to her house, where she glanced back at him and smiled before letting herself indoors. He closed his front door and slumped against the wall. After the tension of thinking it was the police at the door, he didn't know whether to laugh or cry. Was he on a date? He hadn't been out with anyone since before Afghanistan—almost two decades ago. No, he expected Megan simply wanted an evening out, blissfully ignorant of what he'd been up to the previous night.

With a shake of the head, he returned to the garden to fix a trellis to the fence he shared with the middle-aged couple in number 14 *(Valentine's Day!)*


Barely anyone in the Star and Garter noticed the tall, awkward man dressed in a brown cardigan and scruffy jeans as he stepped tentatively into the pub. But many eyed up his attractive companion in the black leather jacket.

"What's your tipple, John?" she asked.

"Tomato juice, please."

"Goodness, don't you want something a bit stronger?"

He thought a moment. "With a dash of Worcestershire sauce, then."

She laughed and headed for the bar, while John searched for somewhere to sit. The pub was packed and noisy, and he found himself having to squeeze past groups of people and duck under pennants of various countries hanging from the low ceiling. He came to an unoccupied table in the far corner and plopped down on a wooden seat. Megan soon appeared, bearing a pint of real ale and John's tomato juice, with two packets of crisps tucked under her arm.

"So, John, tell me what you were so busy in the garden with that you didn't watch the England game." Megan had to raise her voice to combat the noise.

He told her about his flowers that were battling the chilly temperature and the trellis he'd erected.

"I've never been green-fingered myself. I leave all that to Mum." John couldn't think of a suitable response, and Megan said, "What do you normally do on a Saturday night then—watch the telly?"

John shifted in his seat. "You'll probably laugh, but I'm into online bingo."

"Sixty-six, clickety click, that sort of thing?"

"My aunt Edith used to drag me along to the bingo hall during school holidays. Being under eighteen, I wasn't allowed to play, but I became got hooked."

"You are a dark horse, aren't you?"

Megan soon finished her pint of ale, and John swirled the rest of his tomato juice round before downing it. "Same again?" he asked.

"Please, but make sure you get the Ordinary bitter rather than the Special, otherwise you'll have to carry me home!"

He got up and picked his way between the throng of punters to the bar. While waiting to be served, he felt a tap on his arm and turned, recognizing his neighbor from two doors down in number 11 *(Legs eleven!)*. He was a late-middle-aged man of medium height, with graying hair combed back behind his ears. John didn't know his proper name, though he'd mentally christened him Lurch, in view of his unsteady gait and liking for the amber nectar.

"Don't often see you here, John," Lurch shouted in his ear. "You've got a nice bit of fluff over there, though."

John cringed, but offered the semblance of a nod and gave his order to the barmaid. Lurch leaned in closer, reeking of alcohol.

"Hear about those kids getting shot down last night? Bit of a coincidence, don't yer think?"

John swiveled round. "What do you mean?"

The man raised his eyebrows. "Obvious, ain't it? You were talking to 'em the other night, down Beaver Walk. Saw you from me back winder. Looked as though you were 'aving verbals with 'em."

John thought quickly. "You mean, those guys I bumped into were the ones who got killed on the towpath?"

"Course they were! I recognized them as soon as those cops showed me their mug shots. Surprised you didn't put two and two together; I certainly did."

"Well, I'm afraid I didn't."

"What was yer disagreement with 'em then?"

John gritted his teeth. "They were drunk and being difficult, that's all."

His heart was pounding as he paid for the drinks and returned to find Megan chatting with a young couple at the next table. She introduced them, but their names didn't register with John, nor did the conversation that followed.

On leaving the pub, Megan shivered and slipped her arm through his, and they set off home. John spotted Lurch making his way through the graveyard, a shortcut to Otter Close. Darkness had arrived, not just in a literal sense, but in John's mind, too. He barely took in a word Megan said on the way back.

Soon, they reached her house, and she removed her arm from his and said, "Would you like to come in for a coffee? Mum'll be upstairs fast asleep by now."

"I won't," John replied rather quickly. "The stress of work has given me some sleepless nights this week, so I've some catching-up to do."

She smiled and shrugged, then let herself into her house. This time, she didn't look back.

\*\*\*

Lying in bed that night, listening to the rain drumming on the roof, he thought about his confrontation with the yobs in Beaver Walk on Wednesday night and that, unknown to him at the time, Lurch had witnessed it. And he recalled looking at the photos of the yobs, telling the police officers he didn't recognize them. Should he call the police in the morning and tell them he now remembered passing two youngsters that night, who might be the ones killed on Friday? He could make it out to be an honest oversight, but was nervous of drawing attention to himself. On balance, he was inclined to leave well alone, but would have to rely on Lurch keeping shtum. Presumably, Lurch hadn't mentioned the confrontation to the police, otherwise they would have tackled John about it.

Eventually, he fell into a fitful sleep. He groaned when he thought he heard someone banging on the front door. But that couldn't be right, this time of the night, and anyway, they'd more likely ring the bell.

Half an hour later, he found himself wide awake, staring at the ceiling. A glimmer of light was creeping around the curtains as he got up and padded downstairs. On the doormat was a note with a single word on it, handwritten in capital letters.

MURDERER

There was no going back to sleep after that. He tried, but it was futile. Ten minutes later, after thrashing from one side of the bed to the other, he got up again and had a shower, holding his head in his hands under the jet of water, waiting in vain for his headache to ease.

Someone knew. One of his neighbors, perhaps? It seemed odd another person had been using the towpath so late in the day, when it was dark. The yobs had been there, presumably on their way home, but they'd been three sheets to the wind and most likely didn't give a damn.

He recalled the moment he'd stared at the two bodies, wondering whether to haul them into the canal so they wouldn't be discovered immediately. Something had prompted him to look over his shoulder in alarm, but in the darkness, he hadn't seen anyone. Had there been someone in the shadows who'd witnessed the altercation?

And what was going to happen next? Was that someone going to tell the police? Or did they have something else in mind?

John had a good idea what that something else might be.

Later that morning, John sat at his kitchen table by the window, watching his neighbors go about their daily business. Catherine and Yusuf from next door, pushing little Samson in his pram, setting off for Sunday church, no doubt; Megan's mum taking in the week's groceries courtesy of a Waitrose delivery, exchanging pleasantries with the van driver; and the medium-sized, featureless man from Number 4 *(Knock at the door!),* being tugged along by his Yorkshire Terrier. It seemed hard to believe one of his neighbors had witnessed the killings, or maybe seen him sneaking back into his house at the dead of night and managed to join the dots. Or perhaps a stranger had?

John had no plans for the day other than to stay put. He sensed there would be a second anonymous note and wanted to be around when it was delivered, hoping to catch the culprit red-handed or at least learn whom he was dealing with.

But when would that be?

When the doorbell rang early that afternoon, he reached the front door in a few strides. Hovering on the doorstep, his drawn-back lips exposing teeth stained by nicotine, was Lurch.

"How are you, me old mate? Enjoy yer night out with the bird?"

Even sober, there was something odious about this man, John thought. How glad he was Lurch wasn't one of his immediate neighbors.

John didn't reply, and Lurch said, "Wondered if you fancied a couple of jars down the pub tonight? They've got Brazil v Belgium on the box."

"No, you're okay," John said. "I'm having a night in."

He started to close the door, but Lurch carried on speaking. "Those two guys I saw you 'aving a spat with the other night. 'Ave you told the cops they were the ones 'oo got gunned down?"

John's hand tightened on the doorknob. He looked Lurch hard in the eye. "I didn't think it was relevant. It was a different night I bumped into them."

Lurch shrugged. "Fair enough. That information might be worth something, that's all."

"How do you mean?"

"Nothing. Just wondered what yer thinking was. I'll leave it with yer."

With that, Lurch turned and headed back to his own house, and John watched him until he was out of sight.

John stayed indoors the rest of the afternoon, watching the sky turn gray, biding his time. At seven o'clock, he put on a lightweight waterproof jacket and went out via the front door. He turned left at the end of his garden path and headed along the cut-through between Numbers 10 and 11. Reaching Beaver Walk, he turned left again, toward the canal. A light was on in the sitting room of Number 11, and John glanced round to see Lurch, a cigarette dangling from his lips, staring at him. It must have been around here, John reflected, that he'd had his encounter with the yobs on Wednesday night.

John averted his gaze and continued along the walkway to the towpath. Here, a row of trees screened him from the view of his neighbors, and he turned left again, slipping back into his house via his back gate and garden.

He lingered in the hallway, waiting for a note to be popped

through the letterbox, but nothing came.

Presently, in the kitchen preparing his dinner, he saw Lurch lumber past, presumably on his way to the pub.

The second anonymous note arrived the following day, Monday. John, returning from work that evening, swore and snatched it up from the doormat.

ONE GRAND IN CASH
LEAVE IN A BLACK BIN LINER UNDER
RUBBISH BIN IN BEAVER WALK
BY 9PM TUESDAY LATEST
OR THE COPS WILL BE INFORMED

The gloves were off. John could be in no doubt someone had witnessed his actions on Friday night. Now he thought of it, that someone could have seen what happened from the road that ran parallel to the canal. And if that person had followed him home, it didn't necessarily mean the blackmailer was someone who knew him.

It could be anyone.

A little later, having forced down some scrambled egg on toast, followed by a strong coffee, John watched Lurch saunter past his window in that familiar lumbering gait of his. John checked his watch: 7:40. Exactly the time Lurch had gone by the previous evening.

John mulled over what he knew about Lurch. Like himself, he was a bachelor living on his own. Whether or not he had employment, or what he did by day when John was at the office, John had no idea. Presumably he didn't have serious money issues (perhaps he was on benefits?) otherwise he wouldn't be able to afford to get sloshed each night.

If he was the one who'd seen John kill the yobs, would he be the type to resort to blackmail? John couldn't tell one way or the other. But, by Lurch's own admission, he had witnessed John's confrontation with the yobs two nights earlier. What was it Lurch had said to him? *I recognized them as soon as those cops showed me the mug shots. Surprised you didn't put two and two together; I certainly did.* And then: *That information might be worth something.*

John sat very quietly at the kitchen table until the light faded. Then he went upstairs, got changed, and went out via his back gate.

He leaned against the yew tree, listening to the soft patter of rain on leaves and the wind whistling around the tower and roof tiles of the church. Before him, headstones of various shapes and sizes seemed to peer at him through the gloom, looking as if they might creep up on him the moment his back was turned.

A silhouetted figure shuffled along the pathway, struggling to keep in a straight line. John waited, his muscles tensing. Gradually, the figure drew nearer, and John heard the mumblings of a drunken man. John watched as the figure came alongside him, then he took a step and grabbed him in a firm headlock, dragging him behind the tree almost in the same movement.

Lurch's eyes swiveled round. A bead of saliva dripped down his jaw.

"You've been putting nasty notes through my letterbox, haven't you?" John whispered in his ear. "Suggesting I killed those guys on the canal."

A guttural sound came from Lurch's throat, but he said nothing.

"Admit it!" John tightened his grip. "You thought I was the killer and decided to blackmail me. Well, it wasn't me, right? You put two and two together and came up with the wrong answer. So let's not have any more of these grubby little notes. Understood? *Understood?*"

John thrust his face closer, but then drew back and released his grip. Lurch's eyes were staring, but not at him. He lay Lurch on the ground and slapped his face. "*Wake up!*" he hissed. He placed two fingers on Lurch's neck but felt nothing.

He exhaled deeply, muttering to himself. If there'd been a spade to hand, he might have dug himself a grave and put an end to the whole sorry mess.

Instead, the rain trickling in rivulets down his cheeks, he turned up his collar and hurried back home.

He slept in snatches. Most of the night he spent listening to the wind whipping round the house and thinking about Lurch, lying prostrate behind the yew tree, never again going to sample his favorite beer.

John went to work the following day, Tuesday, struggling to come to terms with how things had spiraled out of control. First, he'd lost it with the yobs, and now he'd killed Lurch without intending to. He dreaded another interview with the police and unconsciously found himself working late in the office. On the journey home, though, he felt his appetite gradually return and picked up some fish and chips on the walk from the station.

He was halfway through his meal when the sound of the doorbell sent his pulse racing. But it was only Megan, dressed in dark joggers and a light blue denim shirt, a slightly troubled look on her face.

"Hi, John. Sorry to trouble you, but a couple of panels in our fence have keeled over in the wind. I don't suppose you…?"

"No problem, I can fix it for you. But it's getting a bit late and I'm in the middle of my dinner. Perhaps tomorrow evening?"

Megan brightened visibly. "Thanks, John, you're a star! Why don't you come over at seven and we'll cook you something?" He smiled in agreement and was about to close the door when Megan said, "Did you hear about the chap in number 11?"

John stiffened. "What about him?"

"Oh, it's awful. He died last night. Apparently, the vicar found him in the graveyard. They think he died of a heart attack."

*"A heart attack?"*

His astonishment didn't seem to register with Megan. "I reckon he had one too many in the pub—he was there the other night when we were there—and collapsed on his way home. Mum told me he had a heart condition, so he probably brought it on himself." John stood very still while he digested this information, and Megan said, "At least, he won't have far to go for his funeral."

John had his best night's sleep for several weeks. He dreamed of taking Megan out for a candlelit dinner, holding hands across the table. When they got back to her place, her Mum, presented them with a wedding cake with two figures on top, the groom twice as tall as the bride.

He took a long shower the next morning, humming the tune for "The Wonder of You." He dressed for work and was halfway down the stairs when he stopped, gripping the banister rail. On his doormat was a note in the same off-white color as the previous notes.

> I'M DISAPPOINTED
> YOU NEED TO LEAVE ONE GRAND
> IN CASH UNDER RUBBISH BIN
> BEAVER WALK BY 9.00 PM WEDNESDAY
> OR ELSE

John dropped the note and pressed his hands to his face.

He thought of Lurch—stupid, harmless Lurch—and realized he'd made a terrible, terrible mistake.

An hour later, John set off for the station, his face as dark as the clouds. A steady drizzle fell, but the wind had died down. His normal route to the station was via the canal towpath, but on Monday, when he'd reached the bend where the abandoned canoe was jammed against the bank, he could see the area where he'd killed the yobs cordoned off. So he'd been going the long way round, via the estate.

Wednesday was dustbin day, and the bin lorry was reversing steadily back down Otter Close, its beeper beeping. The nondescript man from number 4 was striding past, his dog on a long leash. The dog yelped as it jumped away from the moving lorry.

Frowning, John stopped and glanced over his shoulder at the dog. It was small and skittish, a typical Yorkshire Terrier. John recalled the scene on Friday night after he'd fired those fatal shots. In the near darkness there'd come the screech of birds taking flight and—yes, he was sure of it—a dog had yelped from somewhere nearby. John felt certain the noise had come from the road that ran parallel to the canal. And he imagined the dog's owner peering through the undergrowth and recognizing his tall neighbor from Otter Close, a pistol clasped in his hand and two motionless bodies at his feet. And the guy had realized how he could benefit.

John's gaze traveled from the dog, along the leash, to the man holding it. As he did so, the guy glanced back over *his* shoulder and for a split second their eyes met, before the guy jerked the leash and hurried away, tugging the dog along with him.

Yeah, I've got your number, John thought.

*Number 4, knock at the door.*


In Megan's back garden, John checked his watch: nine p.m. The time set by the blackmailer for leaving the money under the small black bin in Beaver Walk. Well, John wasn't dancing to his crappy tune. Number 4 was in for another disappointment. But what would happen then? The guy would no doubt threaten to tell the police what he'd witnessed on Friday night, and John couldn't risk that.

Megan's mum—Lynette—had cooked him a nice beef casserole with potatoes and veg. He'd then succumbed to her specialty: apple crumble and custard. It took another half hour for the food to go down while he'd introduced Lynette to online bingo on his mobile phone, before he'd set about fixing the fence.

By the time he hammered in the final nail, it was almost dark and the rain had started again, in earnest. Heading back indoors, he found the ladies lounging on the sofa, watching a World Cup match on TV. "All done," he said. They both thanked him and invited him to stay for a coffee, which he accepted.

While the kettle was boiling, he popped upstairs to the bathroom. On coming out a minute later, he glanced through the landing window and saw a man striding past in the direction of Beaver Walk. He was wearing a dark jacket and baseball cap and there was nothing remarkable about him, but John knew instantly who it was. This time, the Yorkshire Terrier wasn't in tow.

John watched as the guy headed past Number 8 and took a sidelong glance at John's house across the road. No doubt about it.

John skipped down the stairs—he'd always been light on his feet—and put his head round the living room door. "Sorry, must dash. No need to see me out." Megan and Lynette, who'd come in with the coffee things, looked at him with blank expressions, but he barely noticed.

He slipped out through the front door and turned right just in time to see the black-clad figure disappear round the corner into Beaver Walk. Moments later, John found himself watching the guy crouch down by the small black bin situated off the pathway and reach underneath it.

*OK, Number 4, your time is up.*

The guy never knew he had company. John delivered a rabbit punch to the base of his neck, then got down on his haunches and grabbed the guy in a headlock, as he'd done with Lurch, this time with even more force. John dragged the motionless body toward the undergrowth.

"You forgot—" a familiar voice said. He looked up sharply, and there was Megan, her eyes wide and staring, one hand clasped to her mouth and the other clutching his mobile phone. For a moment, they looked at one another, transfixed.

Then, with a stifled howl, she turned and ran the way she'd come. Anger coursed through John's veins, and he felt as if his head were about to explode. Number 4 was already dead, but John gave his head another wrench, for good measure.

*Time's up for you too, Number 13.*
*Unlucky for some.*


John left the body where it was, in plain sight from the walkway, and legged it home. Within minutes, he'd filled his rucksack and left, locking the door behind him.

The rain came down in bursts, blown into his face by the wind. He headed for the canal towpath, but this time didn't have his pocket torch, which he'd left in his other jacket. If the police cordon was still there, he would have to cross it or skirt around it.

John peered at his watch: 10:04. There was a train to London at 10:19 and another half an hour later. Hopefully, he'd make the 10:19.

He ducked his head into the wind and set off along the towpath with his long, loping stride, squelching through the puddles, and straining his eyes in the gloom. A police siren blared, and he gazed back over his shoulder as a bright blue light lit up the sky. He broke into a run but was blinded by the rain, and as the towpath bore right, his left foot caught a patch of mud. He found himself sliding down the bank.

He scrabbled for purchase, but the rain had taken hold, and he tumbled sideways, smashing his head against the hull of the abandoned canoe with a *thunk,* where 13 *(Unlucky for some!)* showed in faded white numbers. Then gravity took hold, and he slithered slowly but surely, inch by inch, into the water's inky blackness.

# SOLID SIX
## Alan Orloff

I sat at the bar, chatting up a Last Call Four. Her name was Patricia or Patrice or something like that, and I'd listened to her drone on about her boring job for the past forty-five minutes. I figured I'd put in enough time, in case I couldn't do any better. A man needed a backup plan.

I waved the bartender over, tossed a credit card down on the bar to pay for our drinks. Once the transaction was complete, I stood, smiled, and gently touched Pat's shoulder. "Nice talking with you, but I need to see a man about a pony. If you'll excuse me."

I went to the restroom, did my business, and when I returned, found a seat at the opposite end of the bar. Scoped things out. First time I'd been to The Watering Hole. On the seedy side, from the looks of the place, the owners took the *Hole* part literally. Clientele a rung lower than most of the bars I frequented. Enough women, though, and many in my league.

I was usually successful at finding companionship. Often in the six range, but I'd land a few Tipsy Sevens. If I played my cards right, I could nail a Desperate Eight now and then. If pickings were slim, I could go home with a Thankful Five, no problem. And tonight, if all else failed, I had Last Call Pattie to fall back on.

I was a six myself, and if I lost fifteen pounds or so, I'd be a seven. With a crisp haircut, I could push eight.

My gaze settled on the bartender. A little scrawny, some acne on her chin, pale skin, dyed red hair, ring in a nose that was one size too big. A decent five, five-and-a-half. She'd seen some action, but the way her eyes took in everything in that first split second intrigued me.

I called her over.

"Can I get you?" she asked, eyes probing.

"Another Manhattan, please."

"Right up." She smiled, then turned around to mix my drink.

She looked decent from behind. A nudge up the scale right there.

A minute later, she spun around and set my drink down on a clean napkin. Gave me a clean smile, too. "You go."

I dug the way she left off the first word of her sentences. And those eyes. Those *eyes*.

All in all, a Solid Six.

I waited outside the bar. On the sidewalk. Under the only working streetlight. Watched the last die-hard patrons leave, then a few minutes later, the staff followed.

When Solid Six came out, she saw me. Came over.

"You again," she said.

"That's right. You're the first bartender in a long time who's made my drink correctly. Kudos to you." I flashed a crooked grin.

"Take pride in my work."

"It shows."

Another bartender, a blonde, came out of the bar, saw us standing there. Stopped. "You okay, hon?"

Solid Six nodded. "Yeah, it's fine, Roz. See you later."

Roz gave me the once over. Nodded. "Okay, then. Have a good time." She hustled off, and Solid Six and I were alone again.

"So, would you like to?" I asked.

"Like to what?"
"Have a good time," I said.
"You have in mind?"
"We could get a drink. Talk."
"Think most places are closed," she said.
"I don't live far. We could go to my place."
"Up for that." She stuck out her hand, and I shook it. "Name's Gigi."

I drove us back to my place. Gigi and I had a good time. A real good time. Twice, in fact.
 In the dark, she was a ten.
 In the dark, everyone's a ten.

Afterward, we reclined, our heads on pillows.
 "Surprised nobody's tied down a guy like you."
 "Not too surprising, really. Didn't like most of the women who wanted to do the tying."
 "Guess most people are assholes," she said.
 "Yeah, we are."
 We lay there, in the dark, in silence, for a while. Then she rolled over, away from me. "Mind if I stay the night? Maybe we can go at it again in the morning, if you're up for it."
 "Sure. Whatever."

I woke with a start. Glanced at the clock. Only an hour later. Movement across the room attracted my attention. I feigned sleep and watched as Gigi rifled through my wallet on the dresser. She removed a wad of bills and stuffed them into her pocket. She'd already dressed, ready for a quick getaway.
 I could have leaped out of bed, confronted her right there. But I was curious. How greedy was she?

She glanced back at me on the bed and must have believed I was still asleep because she opened the top dresser drawer. Felt around. Opened the next drawer and did the same. I watched, surprised but not shocked. Most people *were* assholes.

When she got to the third drawer, my pulse quickened.

She felt around, then pulled out a rectangular jewelry box. My grandmother's diamond necklace.

Before she died, my grandma had given it to me. After my mother drank herself to death, I was all my grandma had left, her pride and joy. And she was all I'd had, too—the last of my family. The only person on Earth who loved me. The necklace was easily the most valuable thing I owned, worth about ten grand, but I'd never sell it. To me, it was priceless.

On the drive to my place, Gigi had talked about hating her job, hating this town, wanting a new start. With my dough, she could buy a bus ticket. With my grandma's necklace, that bus ticket could be the first step in a complete rebirth.

Fat fucking chance.

Gigi checked on me again. Then she tiptoed toward the bedroom door. Still holding the necklace.

I threw the covers off and jumped out of bed. "Hang on, there."

Gigi gave one millisecond of thought—stay or run—then decided to bolt. She made it out of the bedroom, down the hall, and into the living room before I caught up. I grabbed her and swung her around, but she squirmed out of my grasp and darted for the front door. I lunged and snagged her ankle, and she went down.

Unfortunately, on the way down, her head caught the corner of the marble-topped coffee table, then slammed against the hard tile floor.

Her head smashed against the tiles a few more times. I might have helped.

Sprawled there, dead, with the side of her head caved in and blood running down her face, Gigi was no more than a Tragic Two.

\*\*\*

I cleaned up the blood. Lugged her body into the garage. Stuffed it into my trunk. Then I drove her to a place I knew way out in the country and dumped her into a deep, dark ravine.

Last time I dumped a body there, about three years ago—after a vaguely similar incident—things had turned out okay. Nobody had ever found it. Hopefully, my luck would continue.

Still had one problem, though.

I returned to The Watering Hole the next night. Got a two-top in the corner. Watched Gigi's blond bartender friend Roz chat with customers and pour their drinks, smiling widely when it was time to tip. She'd seen me and Gigi talking, and she must have assumed we'd gone home together.

Loose ends sink ships, or something like that.

I waited for Roz to take a smoke break, then followed her outside, making sure I smiled at the enormous bouncer on the way out—just another friendly, satisfied Watering Hole patron. I found Roz around the corner, leaning against a brick wall, facing the half-empty parking lot. I scuffed my shoes along the ground so I wouldn't startle her, and stopped five feet away, non-threatening. "Excuse me."

She glanced around the parking lot, then narrowed her eyes at me. "Yeah?"

"Is Gigi working tonight?" Up close, Roz was a Fine Nine and probably not a thief. Seemed like I'd made the wrong choice last night.

Roz took a longer look at me, and her eyes widened when recognition dawned. "You're the guy she was with. Outside the bar, after work."

"Yes. I was hoping Gigi and I could, uh, get together again. She said she was working tonight, but as far as I can tell, she's not here." I sighed. "I guess I should take a hint, huh?"

"Do you know where she is? I'm worried about her. She was supposed to be here. She didn't show." Her voice wavered. "Which is totally not like her. She never misses a shift. She's saving up to blow this town. All she needed was a big hit on the scratch-off, and she would be history. That's what she always said, anyhow. And who could blame her, right?" She took a drag, exhaled. "She woulda told me if she hit it big, though. She wouldn't have just taken off."

"I hope she's okay."

Roz cocked her head. "Why wouldn't she be okay?"

"She didn't show for work. I just hope nothing happened." I tried to inject my words with as much innocence and sincerity as I could.

Her friend stared at me, and I could almost see the gears turning inside her skull. Had she seen through my false front? "You sure she didn't say anything about where she might have gone?"

"Yes. She didn't say a word." I tried to look concerned, which wasn't very hard. I *was* concerned, just not about the same thing Roz was.

"Seems like you know something. Something you ain't telling me." Roz's tone had shifted, and I didn't like the direction it was heading.

"No. We had a good time last night—or at least I thought we did—and she left. Said she had to wake up early for something."

"Gigi *never* woke up early for *anything*. And I should know. I'm her roommate. And she didn't come home at all last night. Usually, she texts me to let me know what's going on. You know, where she is and when she's coming home, but last night, she didn't."

Roommate? *Shit*. I struggled to keep a poker face. "Oh? Is that unusual?"

"She's a fun girl. So, I usually don't worry if she stays out all night. But something isn't sitting right. I'm getting some bad vibes. Real bad vibes. My horoscope said something like this might happen today." Roz tossed the cigarette aside. Pulled her phone from her pocket with shaky hands.

I stepped toward her. "What are you doing?"

She took a step back. "I need to, uh, text someone, then get back to work. Nice talking to you."

I inched closer. "I'll walk you back inside."

She looked over my shoulder, then back at me. Took two more steps in retreat. "You should leave now, okay? You're making me uncomfortable. I can yell real loud if I have to."

I turned around to see if we were alone. Nobody in view. "You're not calling the cops, are you?"

"What? The cops? Are you crazy?" She ended with the lamest chuckle I'd ever heard.

I sprang forward and slapped the phone out of her hand. Then I grabbed her and dragged her around the back corner of the bar, completely out of sight of the parking lot. "If you make a noise, I'll kill you right here." Her neck was in the crook of my arm, and I squeezed. "Got it?"

She squirmed but didn't make a sound. Of course, it must have been difficult to make a sound while I was choking her to death.

I had no choice, though, so I kept squeezing until she stopped squirming. Too bad. Fine Nines didn't grow on trees.

I drove my car to the back corner of the lot. Popped the trunk. Made sure the coast was clear when I stuffed Roz's body inside.

Drove to the ravine again. Dumped a body again. This time, the car practically drove there itself.

I decided to take a break in my bar-hopping, so I laid low for a couple of days. Let things cool down. Half expected the cops to pound on the door, come crashing in, and throw me to the floor. Dig a knee in my back and slap some cuffs on. Haul me off to prison for what I'd done.

But nothing happened. Until there *was* a knock on the door.

I was eating dinner in front of the TV, a greasy takeout burger and some fries. I got up and peered out the front window to see who it was, but I didn't see any cop cars or flashing light bars. So I figured I was safe.

I answered the door.

An enormous man stood there, as tall and broad as a side-by-side refrigerator. It took a second to recognize him. The bouncer at The Watering Hole.

I almost shit my pants.

"Uh, yes?" I sputtered. In my mind, I was calculating how long it would take me to make it to the back door. How fast could a guy that large move?

"Are you Zeke Malloy?"

"What's this about?"

"I'll take that as a yes." Frigidaire barged right in, slammed the door behind him. I didn't point out that entering uninvited was rude.

I glanced down, noticed the size of his forearms—very large—and hands—also very large. He could crack coconuts with them. Or heads. "Look, what do you want?"

"Two of our bartenders seem to be missing." He growled it out more than spoke it.

I painted a blank look on my face. "I don't think I know what—"

"I know you know them. Gigi and Roz. From The Watering Hole."

"Right, that place on West Maple. I was there a week or two ago. Nice place."

"Cut the shit, asswipe."

I tried not to take offense. "I was at the bar, but I don't know what you're talking about. How did you end up here, anyway?"

"I asked around a bit, and a regular named Patsy gave me your name. Saw it on your credit card after you blew her off. I got a buddy on the force who gets me info when I need it. And I needed your address. So here I am. Paying a house call."

I swallowed. "Well, like I said, I *was* there at the bar. I guess I talked with this Patsy for a while, then left. Alone, I assure you. I am sorry about your bartenders, though."

"Dickwad, I know you slept with Gigi. And then the next night, you came to talk to Roz, when she was on a break. I was working the door, and I saw you follow her out. She never came back from that break." Frigidaire stepped in front of the window, and it was like a solar eclipse.

I tried to gather myself. Speak confidently. Lay out a plausible scenario with authority. "They probably just hit the road. Got tired of this town and left. It really is full of losers."

"Without their final paychecks? Not those two." He flexed his giant paws. "No, I think something happened to them. Something bad. And I think you're responsible."

"I'm afraid you're mistaken."

"I think we'll let the cops decide that." Before I could react, Frigidaire had his gigantic mitts around my throat. "I'm pretty sure they'll find the evidence they need to put you away for a long time. They've got me for a witness, and people usually believe what I say."

I tried to speak, but he had his thumbs on my windpipe.

"Yeah, I think I'm going to turn you in to the cops." He paused, glanced around. One eyebrow rose. "Unless you have something of value that might dissuade me. I mean, this all *could* be a big misunderstanding, right?"

I managed a nod.

"Got anything like that? Anything that might lead me to believe that this is all a mistake?"

He eased the pressure on my throat so I could talk. "I've got about three hundred bucks in cash."

Frigidaire laughed. "A player like you? I hear prison is nice. Full of friendly people. I'm sure you'll get along well there." He squeezed, then let up. "Try again."

"Keys to my car?"

"Pass. One more chance, then it's off to the cops. I'll probably get a reward or something. Maybe I'll get my name in the paper, too. Never had my name in the paper."

A flurry of thoughts sped through my mind. Could I give him the necklace, then smash his head in when he wasn't looking, before he left? Highly unlikely. Could I give him the necklace, then find out where he lived and steal it back? Doubtful. Besides, this goon knew where I lived. A half dozen other dubious scenarios appeared before me. All losing propositions.

Frigidaire squeezed, hardly straining a muscle. I, on the other hand, saw stars. Panic, real panic, clawed at my chest. From the inside.

"As they say in the bar business, last call. If you've got anything worth keeping you out of prison, now's the time to offer it up."

Last call. Something I was quite familiar with. That time to grab whatever lifeline you could. Desperation time. *Sorry, Grandma.* "Yeah, okay. I've got something."

"I'm listening."

"A diamond necklace. Worth about ten grand."

"Now you're talking. Where is it?"

"Bedroom."

"Let's go." Frigidaire perp-walked me—hands still around my throat—into the bedroom.

"It's in a dresser drawer. Top, far right."

He strong-armed me over to the dresser. "Go ahead. Reach in there. But if you pull out a weapon, you won't have time to use it."

"No weapon." I reached into the drawer, removed the jewelry box.

"Open it so I can see."

I opened it. Showed him the necklace.

"Real diamonds?" he asked, hands still encircling my throat.

"Yes," I croaked out. "Real diamonds. And a bunch of them." I pictured the utter disappointment on my grandmother's face. I pictured ten g's walking out of my place.

"Okay, then," he said.

"Now let me go," I said, anxious for this goon to beat it so I could breathe again. "A deal's a deal."

Frigidaire's grip tightened.

# BROKEN ENGLISH
## Sam Wiebe

The photo of Tim Garber on the Tri-Cities College faculty page suited an instructor of English. A boyish round face with a healthy complexion, clean spectacles, hairline on the verge of retreat. An expression equal parts good humor and impatience. Garber held degrees from Brown and McGill, had a book and several articles to his name. "An often-cited scholar of the mid-nineteenth-century novel of manners," according to his self-authored bio.

The man next to me at the ramen bar looked more like a punk drummer on stop thirty of a fifty-city tour. In person, Garber was bedraggled and wan, his shapeless gray hoodie infused with burnt tobacco. He fidgeted with the porcelain sake jar, refilling our cups before placing the death threat on the bar.

A printed-off email from an anonymous sender, it read:
*Mr. Tim I'm soon kill you.*
"How do I gauge if this is genuine?" Garber asked.
"Time," I said. "If they follow up, it's usually pretty genuine."
"Sorry if I don't find this amusing, Mr. Wakeland."
The email had been sent two days before. A server I'd never heard of, the account a seemingly random string of characters. Difficult to trace.

"It's best to treat it as serious until we can write it off," I said. "Do you recognize the account? Have you received anything else from it?"

"No."

"Anyone come to mind who'd maybe want to threaten you?"

"Only one or two hundred," Garber said.

He tipped out more sake. Spun his cup clockwise on the bar, once, twice.

"I'm almost surprised I haven't gotten one of these before now," he said. "I teach four classes a term, three terms a year. Thirty-eight students per class."

"All first-year English?"

He nodded. "The pressure these kids are under—that the government *puts* them under—it would make anyone snap."

Given the haunted look to his face, the way he drank, I believed him.

"Explain to me this pressure," I said.

"Did you go to university?"

"Community college. Briefly."

"Lecture halls, a student union, loads of extracurriculars?"

I shrugged. College had been a means to get on the police force, a career which thankfully hadn't worked out. I'd spent my time drinking in libraries, making the minimum effort to study, and whittling a sizable chip for my shoulder against all things academic. For a private investigator, a healthy distrust for inherited wisdom isn't the worst attribute.

"Tri-Cities College has zero in the way of amenities," Garber said. "What we are is a business designed to take money from the families of broke kids overseas. We pretend to teach them, and in exchange, they pretend they're going to school."

The ramen bar was all but empty at eleven a.m., the two waiters watching a Korean soap on the bar's TV. Through the tinted glass, I could see a looming office tower and a ribbon of SkyTrain track. More malls and more towers in the background.

The door chimed, a trio of young women entering. Garber

greeted them each. "Hello, Ranveer. How's your mother, Eunice? Sara, I'm looking forward to your PowerPoint today." The students nodded and took a table in the far corner. Garber hunched over the bar and spoke quietly.

"Presentation week," he explained. "Everybody's a bit stressed."

"You were talking about the college."

He nodded. "The school recruits from rural areas overseas. Pakistan and India are big right now. Before that it was Mongolia, Mainland China. The schools partner with a recruitment agency that works out the visas, sets the kids up with a place to live while they're over here—and also a place to work."

"Doesn't sound like a bad deal," I said. "Make some money between classes. The North American way, isn't it? Unless you're rich."

"I'm not talking about washing a few dishes, Mr. Wakeland. These kids are working forty-, sometimes fifty-hour weeks. Night shifts much of the time. Warehouse jobs, fulfillment centers. They're so overworked they're falling asleep in class."

Our waiter swapped sake jugs, asked if I wanted more tea. I held my hand over my cup, still good.

"It's their choice to work, though," I said, still not understanding.

Garber filled his cup again, quaffed it, wincing at the heat. "The families scrape together everything they have, sometimes taking out mortgages, to get the kids over here. The kids work themselves silly for minimum wage, which is big money back home. Then the school gets rich off international student fees, and the government wets their beak and gets to tout how well the economy is doing."

"And you get a job out of it."

He nodded. "True, I'm no innocent, but I'm not teaching them, either. They're not learning. The placement tests for English are a joke, and instructors are, let's say, 'encouraged' to pass as many students as we can. As long as the kids keep a C average, their visas are good, they can stay, and the whole corrupt enterprise keeps moving."

"What's the class dynamic like?"

"Resentful, and rightfully so. Students come to class unable to write a sentence, let alone a five-paragraph essay. And I'm supposed to mark their research papers. These are good kids for the most part, but by midterms, when they're either flunking or on the precipice of doing so, they get desperate. They cheat, or they plagiarize, or they buckle down and try their best. Whatever they do, I fail a great many of them. The system fails us all."

I tapped the death threat. "But what's any of that got to do with this?"

"Have you any idea how many students I've failed? Say ten per class, which is conservative. Forty a term. A hundred twenty a year. How many of those *don't* wish me dead?"

The question lingered after Garber left to teach, not quite rhetorical but impossible to answer. It was my job to answer it. I read over the note again. *Mr. Tim I'm soon kill you.* Despite the grammar, or maybe because of it, the sentiment was clear.

Tri-Cities College was stuffed into a floor of one of the office towers I'd spied from the restaurant. The lobby looked like the waiting room of a prosperous dental clinic. Students lined the hallway, groups of them laughing or discussing classwork with life-and-death gravity, the few loners on their phones. A polyphonic gauntlet of Punjabi and Mandarin, Korean and English, Cantonese and Spanish and Russian. I picked my way through the ranks to the front desk.

The school's vice president, Jane Campbell, escorted me to a cubbyhole office with a sliding door. Campbell was in her late fifties, slender and well dressed. A Blue Jays pennant and a business degree from Carleton hung behind her.

"The school doesn't have a dean per se," she told me. "The head of Tim's department is on leave, so I guess, yes, technically,

I'm his supervisor."

"Good employee?" I asked.

"We've had no serious friction. Many students appreciate Tim's approach."

"But some don't?"

Campbell studied me before answering. If I'd known I'd be studied, I might have dressed better—more collegial, anyway. A flannel shirt and reasonably clean jeans would have to do.

"Let me put it this way," Campbell said. "We give our instructors great latitude in how they manage their classes. If the students are happy, generally so is admin."

"Does that mean encouraging teachers to pass students who might not make it through the same class at a"—I scanned my brain for a euphemism, found none that I was happy with—"a real college?"

Campbell set her mouth in an approximation of a smile. "Every uni in the Lower Mainland has an international college attached to it. Ours happens to be private. Which means we have to be twice as good, and we get none of the government assistance those public institutions rely on."

"A teacher failing, say, ten students a class, is that high?"

"It's not unheard of."

"But is it high?"

"Of course, we'd prefer zero failures," Campbell said. "What self-respecting postsecondary wouldn't? But we deal in reality here. And the reality is, some students are ill-equipped. We cut them what slack we can, keeping in mind they're being educated in their second or third language. Our classes are small."

"Thirty-eight is small?"

"Compared to the two or three hundred in first-year English at a uni? Absolutely. More facetime with the instructors is one of our selling points. We know our students."

And they know you, I thought. "Has anyone else received threats?"

"This office deals with emotionally charged students all the time."

"Have the police ever been involved?"

"Not that I'm aware."

"This threat that Tim Garber received doesn't seem to bother you."

"Mr. Wakeland," Campbell said, "this morning I spoke with a student who missed her Spanish midterm because her mother had died. She was busy viewing the funeral over Zoom. The school requires proof to reschedule an exam, so the student had her hometown's coroner send me a video of the cremation in process. Would you like to see that?"

I declined.

"Tim's situation is serious. Of course it is. But there's only so much bandwidth administration can spare. We try to reserve as much of it as possible for our clients."

"You mean students," I said.

Campbell smiled. "Yes, students, that's what I meant."


I poked around the college in the late afternoon. The impression I came away with was of a once efficient machine, now straining to keep pace. Classrooms were small and low-ceilinged, converted from office space with partitions. The department offices were repurposed storage rooms. Tri-Cities College had leased some square footage on the floor above, and classes continued over the whine and drone of drilling from upstairs.

In college, I had worked at a butcher's and been shocked a fresh side of beef smelled like an animal. The meat-smell of supermarkets was something artificial, created by the absence of hot blood and viscera, the presence of cellophane. Tri-Cities College gave me the same feeling of shock. I'd never taken to college, but I'd gone to one with a large cluster of concrete buildings, with fields to walk, with a cafeteria and a proper library. Hell, I had a locker. The closest these students had to lockers were the trunks of their cars, if they could afford cars.

I was supposed to meet Garber again at four, after his office hours ended. He wasn't in the office, or the break room, or any of his assigned classrooms. The lone security guard hadn't seen him. I took the elevator down to check if Garber's car was still there.

The underground parkade held the Nissans and Accords of the poorer students, the BMWs and Audis of the wealthier satellite kids, and the sensible mid-priced sedans of the faculty. Tim Garber drove a maroon Kia. He was sitting in the passenger seat, no seatbelt, head lolling back. I called. He didn't answer.

The passenger door was unlocked, the window cracked. Up close, I saw a bib of dark crimson clutching his throat. In his lap was a butterfly knife.

Looking down at the dead man, that butcher's smell of hot blood rolled back at me.

"No prints on the handle of the knife except Garber's own. No prints on the door. There's a camera above the gate showing Garber keying in the faculty code and driving in, probably right after your lunch meeting with him. No cameras inside the garage, unfortunately. A rough break for us."

Sgt. Grant Wong from IHIT, the Lower Mainland's homicide task force, had caught Garber's death. About thirty, stout, with an expression between perplexed and amused, Wong entertained my questions from the courtyard of the mall opposite the college. I'd given him a copy of the email.

"You think it was suicide?" I asked.

"Can't say for certain just yet, but that would be consistent with what we know."

"C'mon," I said. "The same day Garber hires me to look into a threat on his life, he cuts his own throat?"

Wong gave me a shrug, what can I tell you? "All we can go by is the evidence we have. Which doesn't rule out murder, but it sure doesn't point to it, either."

"No suicide note," I said.

"Some people don't leave them."

"A PhD of English wouldn't pen a few lines? Recall a John Donne poem or something?"

Wong didn't volunteer a response.

"Garber was sitting in the passenger's seat," I said. "His window was rolled down. You need a key in the ignition to activate automatic windows. So where were Garber's keys?"

"Turned into the lost and found this morning." Wong sipped his Starbucks and consulted his phone. My question held the remaining third of his attention. "Our theory is the keys fell out of the deceased's pocket and were kicked under one of the other vehicles. When the driver of that vehicle left, the janitor or whoever found the keys and turned them in."

"And sitting in his car, Garber didn't notice that he'd lost them?"

"He was distraught. As you said yourself."

Wong wouldn't treat this as a homicide until the lab analysis was complete. A sensible approach, but it left me with nothing to go on. Maybe Garber had been killed, and maybe, if the forensic lab was prompt and didn't muss up the chain of evidence, I could expect a clue within the year.

Or sooner, if I decided to meddle.

Garber lived near Burnaby Lake, about ten minutes from the college. His condo was on the ground floor of a low-rise building with a mansard roof and a high weathered fence. A man and woman dollied a washing machine through the gate, getting pelted by March rain. I slipped past them through the propped-open door of the building.

The police had gone through Garber's flat yesterday. The door was locked, a seal affixed to it, but by going out the building's back entrance I worked around to Garber's patio. A Maxwell House can full of cigarette butts caught runoff from the drainpipe. The ancient sliding door was easy enough to jimmy open.

I didn't know what I was looking for, or why I was risking a trespassing charge. Any information I could glean wouldn't be of much use to my deceased client. But Tim Garber *was* a client, and I'd found him dead, and I held strong opinions on how he'd ended up that way.

The closets first. The kitchen drawers. The file cabinet of tax forms and papers. I moved thoroughly, thinking the killer might have taken Garber's keys and come here after the crime. Why? To remove something? What?

I was looking for an unknown—worse, an absence of an unknown. If I'd been here directly after the killer, maybe this object would be easy to locate. But the police had moved and removed Garber's things as well. I saw a rectangle of dust on the table where his computer had been.

This was hopeless. I gave up. And the moment I did, I found something.

Garber was a bachelor, tidy but working with limited space. On the top of the fridge was a fruit bowl repurposed to hold odds and ends. Paperclips, gym pass, USB cable, a pair of off-white ear buds, coins, a stamp book with one last portrait of the Queen inside. A condom. An Allen key. And lighters, four of them, Bics of all colors.

Make that three. One of the lighters was a bit too squat, its sides flat where the others were rounded. The striking wheel was plastic and lifted off. Below was the connecting port of a USB drive.

At home on my couch, in my own ground floor palace, I loaded the drive into my MacBook. No password. In a folder labeled SCHOOL, Garber had backed up his grading and correspondence with his students. The files went back a year, spreadsheets showing thirty-six failures in the spring semester, twenty-four the previous fall, and forty from last summer.

An even hundred failed students. Were all of them suspects? How many were still in the country?

The correspondence was just as bleak. Students begged, cajoled, deployed flattery and veiled threats, hinted at the certain doom which would befall their families if the good professor didn't bump them up from thirty percent to fifty, from fifty-four to sixty.

*Dear Sir I need C for my to remain in this Vancouver.*

*As you might not aware my Mum having trouble with her breath.*

*Because of car accident I am late for presentation and am not concentration very much. Please to do make up this Thursday?*

*Mr. Tim I am so grateful if you are helping me achieve C I need C I am BEGGARING!!!!*

The grammar of most emails was proof its claim was undeserving. English is an art; art is subjective; but nothing is that subjective. Students raised on the rules of texting now had to write formal requests in a second language, pleading their cases as sincerely as they could, but rarely on the grounds of merit. These were pleas for mercy.

I shut the laptop for a moment and thought of what that kind of gatekeeping would do to a person. Who devotes years of their lives to earning a graduate degree, forgoing better pay and sunshine to stay inside hacking through whacks of Victorian prose and post-structuralist theory—who becomes a college instructor in order to ruin students' lives?

Judging from his replies, Garber had done his best to tread the middle path, cutting the students what breaks he could, without making the grading process ridiculous. The one time I'd met Tim Garber he appeared scooped out, hollow inside. Now I understood why.

Saved on the drive among the presentation schedules and attendance sheets was a text file, UNTITLED-2. A letter Garber had started writing to the president of the college, concerning a student named Arliss Cho.

*...At the end of the exam, I said 'Pencils down.' The student did not comply. I repeated my request. The student hurled her pencil in my direction, storming out of the classroom, and slamming the door forcefully...I believe Ms. Cho's final grade of 33% is more than fair.*

A name.

Arliss Cho had made a lateral shift, flunking out of Tri-Cities College, enrolling at The New Cambridge, a strip mall institution on Terminal Avenue. New Cambridge had more room to work with than Tri-Cities, including a canopied courtyard in front of the building. Even so, it didn't seem like it would give the old Cambridge an academic run for its money.

How many of these schools are there? I wondered.

Cho was in the computer lab, playing the kind of top-down shoot-'em-up that makes video game battle look like televised lacrosse. She clicked a cursor, and a phalanx of armored warriors rushed at the walls of a castle. Cho scowled when I held up Garber's threat but didn't deny writing it.

"He only pass the boys," Cho said. "The boy behind me? He pass. The boy here?" She indicated to her immediate left. "*He* pass. Not many girls. Not fair."

"Other students feel that way?"

"Everybody."

In sentences fired off between castle assaults, Cho explained that yes, she'd been pissed at Garber. Her car had broken down on the Patullo Bridge, a frightening experience. Try calling a tow truck while stranded on a narrow bridge at the height of rush hour, in a community you've only lived in for four months. Cho had arrived at school only thirty minutes late. Garber hadn't given her additional time.

When Cho petitioned to rewrite the final, Garber refused, sending her through the labyrinth of administration, to the president of the college, and finally a conference with all parties involved. This felt to her like a mob sitdown. Cho pressed her case and was allowed to retake the exam, improving her score from thirty-three to forty-six. Garber bumped this to fifty, but that was still ten percent below what she needed.

"Why threaten a former teacher?" I asked.

"Still angry."

"Did you kill him?"

She didn't even look up.

"Where were you yesterday?"

"School. Home. Here." Meaning the computer lab.

"Proof?"

Cho shrugged, immersed in her clan's scaling of the battlements.

"Can you think of anyone who hated Garber more than you?"

"Ajit."

"And who's he?"

She didn't say. On the screen, carnage raged outside the castle. I left her to the wars.

Ajit Singh Sodhi had been registered in the same block of English as Cho. Ajit was no longer a student. He'd repeated the class three times, twice with Garber, each time bettering his grades only marginally. He now worked at the Braid Station Fulfillment Center, a windowless complex with a guard at the gate. Employees were bussed in and out of a gate with an advertisement for *Jack Reacher* on it. Ajit was on graveyard shift, would come off work at eight. I parked by the gate and waited.

Imagine this is your experience of North America. An apartment near nothing but malls and other apartments. A company bus which takes you to the warehouse where you slip garden gnomes and action figures into brown envelopes. Your piss breaks are timed. Your meals are eaten at yet another mall. And in the afternoons, dog tired and aching, you go to college in a renovated office space and try to stay awake.

Not slavery exactly, but you couldn't call it much of a life.

At 8:04, Ajit Singh Sodhi came through the gate with the others, still wearing his high-vis vest. The bus awaited. Before he boarded, I approached him, earning a baleful glare from the driver.

"Step away, sir," the driver said to me.

"Permission to speak with one of the prisoners, commandant?" I snapped off a salute that earned me another scowl. The laborers only looked confused.

"Can we talk a bit?" I asked Ajit. Suspicion, fear—I don't know if he understood he didn't have to speak with me. To my shame, I didn't inform him of his right to refuse.

As I drove him home, puttering along behind the bus, Ajit looked around my Cadillac's beat-up interior. He ran his hand over the cracked dashboard. I told him about Garber's murder and asked for Ajit's thoughts.

"Mr. Tim was very nice."

"He failed you, didn't he? A couple times?"

Ajit shrugged. "I'm sad he's dead."

"Did you feel he was unfair?"

"No."

"Treated you different from other students?"

"No."

"What do you remember about him?"

Ajit worked the automatic windows up and down, letting in the right amount of breeze. Eyes closed, enjoying it.

"He make us laugh," Ajit said. "Nice man."

I tried several approaches but couldn't pry loose a disparaging word for the dead man. No longer in a position of power, Garber no longer mattered. Ajit would work another month before his visa expired. Double shifts when he could get them, as much money as possible to take home.

"Anything you're planning to do before you leave?" I asked. "Trips, tourist stuff?"

"Work."

"Nothing you want to see?"

He thought about it. I pulled into the roundabout behind the bus, a crescent of six identical apartment towers. Card swipe entrances and one potted tree per tower. Ajit undid his seat belt.

"Water," he said. "I'd like to see the what do you call it. With sand."

"Beach," I said.

He nodded. "Before I go, I'd like to see a beach."

Over the next week I spoke with two dozen more students who'd failed Garber's class—or been failed by him, however you wanted to put it. Some had tried again and passed, moving on to a proper university. Others had resigned themselves as Ajit had, to work as much as they could before their visas ran out. Still others had litigated their grades and were in the process of dispute resolution with the school. I gathered Tri-Cities College wanted to keep its customers happy, or at least within the cycle of failure and reapplication.

The classrooms of the college were continuously in use. Instructors left nothing behind other than dry erase markers and reams of composition paper. The English department office was similarly busy. Garber's personal effects were in a Bankers Box under the table he shared with six fellow instructors. Inside, some lecture notes and overhead slides, a box of granola bars, annotated copies of *Wuthering Heights* and *A Christmas Carol*.

Garber's colleagues shared their own horror stories. The school had scant resources for its students, next to none for mental health. Two academic counselors, both with business backgrounds, only one of whom spoke a second language. There had been suicides, workplace accidents caused by lack of sleep. Car crashes.

As a result, the instructors had issues of their own. The department head, I was told in confidence, was on extended medical leave. Some fought depression, anxiety. Others found the role of gatekeeper so repellent they simply passed every student who showed up. A few had doubled down, calculating grades to a maddening level of precision. This essay garners a 56.25 mark and no higher.

As far as I could tell Tim Garber was liked by his colleagues and had done his job unremarkably but with decency. He smoked and drank too much, but he wasn't alone in either. Garber hadn't acted maliciously. He hadn't deserved to die.

From the perspective of Arliss Cho or Ajit Singh Sodhi, though, Tim Garber had been the face of a system that was duplicitous, uncaring, and corrupt. A system set up to extract labor from them and money from their parents. A system which had worked on them exactly as designed.

Step back from the question of who. Why was Garber in the passenger's seat? Why were his keys missing and then handed into the lost and found? And was the knife his, or the killer's?

You might sit shotgun in your own car if someone else was driving. Or if you were sleeping, reclining the seat. But there was no indication that anyone else had driven the car, and Garber had been sitting upright.

I thought about my meeting with the dead instructor, and about the students I'd interviewed. The impossible situations they all found themselves in. Combatants rather than partners in learning. To kill Garber required rage, motive, a reason to be close and alone—

And then there it was.

Sara Kang volunteered at the school library, a small cloakroom with one shelf of books and a photo backdrop for snapping school IDs. The temple of knowledge was empty save for Kang, whom I recognized. She and two friends had been in the ramen bar while I'd spoken with Garber.

I eased the door closed and told her I knew what happened.

"Do you want to tell me about it?" I asked.

Sara Kang didn't look like a murderer. A useless thought, since who does? Slender, short, a bit older than the average student, maybe twenty-four. She wore a pearl-colored blouse with washed-out ink stains visible on the left cuff, a button at the throat that didn't match the others. She was perspiring. Sara Kang looked like the type of person who'd sit with her back to the lobster tanks at a seafood restaurant.

"How did your presentation go?" I asked her.

She gnawed her bottom lip and shook her head.

"What was the topic?"

No answer. I felt foolish. The Great Detective, ready to explain how he'd brilliantly deduced the identity of the culprit, and I had no idea if my audience would understand.

"You did your makeup presentation for Mr. Garber. A PowerPoint slideshow. But the school is too busy, so where could you go to find ten minutes in a quiet space?"

Sara Kang looked over at her feet. I peered over the counter. A few textbooks and a MacBook peaked out of a green Herschel backpack. Her laptop looked no different from my own.

"No free classrooms and a department office full of others. So you presented in the car. With Garber in the passenger's seat and the laptop in front of him on the dashboard. Not exactly ideal. How badly did it go?"

"Very bad," she whispered.

"Was the knife yours?"

"I took from the lost and found. For protection. I walk home at night."

"And what happened with Garber? Did you finish your presentation?"

"No. He stop me."

"Why did he make you stop?"

She inhaled, remembering the desperate anger flooding back. "Mr. Tim said it wasn't my words. He said I plagiarize. But I *didn't*. I only ask my friend to help with the language."

"And then what?"

"He told me my grade…"

There were tears now, for Garber and what she'd done to him, and for her own shattered future. One moment of lashing out and two lives smashed to bits.

Her laptop had been open on the dash when she'd stabbed him in the throat. Garber had been in shock, hadn't struggled, had died looking at a presentation slide. Particles of his blood would have settled on the keyboard and screen.

In the moments after her outburst, Sara Kang had the presence of mind to wipe the knife, the seatbelt clasp, the door. She'd taken out the keys and wiped them, too, pocketing them absently, only realizing later what she'd done and dumping them in the lost and found. She explained how she'd done this in a daze, outside herself.

"The authorities need to know what happened," I said.

She nodded, mute.

"Assuming you burnt the clothes you wore, the only physical evidence is there." Pointing at the laptop.

She looked at it, at me, and nodded. I stepped outside to phone Sgt. Wong.

Why handle it that way? Why help her? My own tenderhearted, foolish nature. A pushover for kids, small dogs, and murderers under the age of twenty-five. Maybe I'd done it because I guessed that's what Tim Garber might do. I very much doubted the justice system would cut Sara Kang more breaks than the educational system had. Welcome to North America, now pay up.

Mercy was in short supply these days.

# BARSTOW
## Tom Milani

Spencer lived by himself during the pandemic. His family was distant—geographically and emotionally—and his few friends had hunkered down with their significant others, binge-watching Netflix, and getting their groceries from Instacart, their connections to him broken. To Spencer, the country had turned into a nation of introverts overnight, their collective fear writ large in the form of death-toll chyrons parading across the nightly news broadcasts. Breathless uncertainty and terror became the principal emotions conveyed by the talking heads, reassurance left to gnome-like government officials.

When Spencer attended Zoom meetings, his screen background was a photograph of the supermassive black hole M87 taken by the Event Horizon Telescope. The image was simultaneously beautiful and terrifying, the red-orange annular glow like the inside of a glass-blower's furnace, the event horizon at its center an unforgiving emptiness he didn't want to comprehend.

A year into the pandemic, his company consolidated the individual division editors into a publications group answering to a VP whom Spencer had never liked. No matter, because the consolidation, done in the name of "efficiency and effectiveness," resulted in Spencer being laid off, not even offered the opportunity to give his former colleagues a virtual farewell.

Tired of looking at his walls and laptop screen, Spencer stopped the mail, got the oil changed in his Corolla, packed a few pairs of jeans and his favorite bowling shirts, and headed west.

After four days of driving, he finally swung south, taking the Bobby Troup route through Gallup, Flagstaff, Kingman, and into Barstow, where the Corolla's engine made arrhythmic noises even the radio couldn't hide. He pulled into the first garage he saw, stopping at an open bay door. A mechanic in coveralls and a railroad conductor's hat emerged from the bay, shaking his head. "Dale" was stitched onto an oval patch above his chest pocket.

"That doesn't sound good," he said, his flat affect causing Spencer to assume the worst. He went on, "I've got three oil changes ahead of you, and I'm the only one working since the pandemic. You can leave it here overnight, and I'll get to it first thing in the morning."

Spencer looked around. "I need a place to stay."

The mechanic pointed over Spencer's shoulder. "The Barstow Inn has good food."

He crossed the street and checked in. The boot-heel-sized dent next to the lock didn't give Spencer much confidence in the security of the door to his room, but the mechanic had been right about the bar: it served the best al pastor tacos he'd ever eaten. Even better, given the impending hit to his finances, Mike, the bartender, comped his last beer.

Spencer woke to a headache drilling above his right eye, the pain precise and unrelenting. The room spun, stopping only when his bare feet touched the napless carpet. His unpacked rolling suitcase stood by the bed, handle extended. From it, he retrieved a bottle of ibuprofen and dry-swallowed four tablets.

He staggered to the shower, running the water as hot as he could stand it, the alcohol wafting from his pores. When his headache dialed back a notch, he turned the water full cold, the shock making him gasp, but a few minutes later, his headache was mostly gone, and he emerged from the shower shivering and hungry.

He made his way to the breakfast room. Eight tables ran down the middle in two rows of four, and four booths lined each wall. A guy sitting at the table opposite Spencer's had elaborate facial hair—mustache, angled sideburns, soul patch—that belonged on a jazz musician.

Spencer's waitress wore a nametag that read "Emily." Her dark hair, not quite black, was piled on top of her head. Heavy on the eyeliner, in tight black jeans and tight black T-shirt, she reminded Spencer of the girls he'd danced with at hardcore shows before the pandemic. He tried not to stare.

At the sound of raised voices, he looked up. The jazz guy was pointing at his plate and glaring at Emily. She started crying. Spencer had been served by polite waitresses, surly waitresses, angry waitresses, and indifferent waitresses, but he'd never seen one driven to tears by a customer.

When she brought him his scrambled-egg burrito, he asked, "Is everything all right?"

"No, everything's not all right. My boyfriend's an asshole."

Spencer nodded at the jazz guy. "*He's* your boyfriend?"

She straightened. "What's that supposed to mean?"

"He made you cry."

"You've never been in love?"

Spencer wasn't sure he wanted to answer. His high-school girlfriend had broken his heart when she went away to college. The relationships he'd been in since had run hot for a few weeks before sputtering like the engine in his Corolla.

"It's been awhile," he finally said.

She looked over her shoulder at her boyfriend, who was absorbed in his phone. "I don't recommend it. Can I get you anything else?"

Spencer didn't want to spend another night drinking at the motel, with only Mike the bartender for company. "Have dinner with me tonight."

She cocked an eyebrow. "You must think you're something."

Spencer wasn't surprised he'd blown it, but at least he'd tried.

The twenty-five hundred miles of interstate between here and home would give him time to think about what was next.

His waitress slapped his tab face down on the table. "You pay up front."

Spencer turned the bill over. Below the total, she had written "Emily" and a phone number. Spencer grinned, telling himself the road trip had been worth it, despite the problems with his car. He headed across the street to the garage. The railroad cap low over his eyes, Dale grimaced as Spencer approached.

"Bad news?" Spencer asked, his voice calm.

Dale explained what was wrong with the engine, using terms Spencer, who couldn't open the hood of his Corolla, didn't understand.

"If we're lucky, I'll have the parts tomorrow, the day after at the latest," Dale finished.

With nowhere to go and no time to be there, Spencer said, "That sounds good."

"About now, most people would be telling me how I was wrecking their plans," Dale said.

"Some people like to vent," Spencer said. "I'll check in with you tomorrow."

Even after Emily agreed to have dinner with him at the bar—Spencer explained the situation with his car—he wasn't sure she would show. He couldn't read body language in a string of texts, and he'd been ghosted by girls before. Still, he put on his favorite bowling shirt, a vintage black-and-white King Louie number made for the UNLV Running Rebels. His coworkers thought he wore it ironically, but in truth, Spencer, with his dad bod and lack of athletic ability in any other sport, had bowled weekly until the pandemic shut down the lanes.

When he walked into the bar ten minutes early, Emily was already there, talking to Mike. She'd let her hair down, and it shimmered in ochre waves. Her lipstick was a maroon slash against her pale skin. She wore black yoga pants and a spaghetti-strap top that matched her lipstick.

Mike nodded at Spencer, and Emily turned and smiled. One of her teeth was chipped, the flaw making his heart lurch.

"You look great, Emily," he said.

"Call me Em," she said.

"No nickname for me, I'm afraid."

"What's your story, no-nickname Spencer? Do you always ask out crying waitresses, or am I special?"

Spencer thought about it. "You're the first—the last and the only," he said.

Em cocked an eyebrow. "That's a good answer."

They took their drinks to a table. When she asked about his car and how he found himself in Barstow, he gave her the short version, beginning with his layoff and ending with Dale.

"Dale's honest," she said. "The shop's not cheap, but you won't have to bring your car back there because they didn't fix it right the first time."

Spencer knew he'd gotten lucky in finding the shop and lucky a second time when he went with Dale's recommendation to stay at the Barstow Inn. If things turned out how he hoped tonight, he'd get lucky a third time.

While they ate, Spencer answered Em's questions, telling her about himself and his life, which until the last week hadn't included much adventure. His father, long out of the picture; his mother, a decent woman who deserved better; an older brother he hadn't seen or heard from in half a decade; his last job, editing reports that no one would read. When he finished, Em seemed to be taking his measure, and he wondered how her judgment of him added up.

"That doesn't sound so bad, Spence. Most people have some family drama, and everyone has had a shitty job."

"What about you?" he asked.

"What about me?"

"How did you end up in Barstow?"

"I didn't 'end up' here—I grew up in town, never lived anywhere else. My mother raised me, waitressing everywhere. When

I was eighteen, she hired on as a dealer in Vegas, said I was old enough to live on my own, the way she had. So I moved into a shithole efficiency north of town and got a job working here, the apple not falling far from the tree."

Spencer wasn't usually comfortable on first dates, but Em had put him at ease. At one point during the evening, they switched to tequila shots. He didn't remember paying for dinner or getting up from the table, but they ended up in his motel room.

While Spencer peeled down the straps of Em's top and cupped her breasts, her lips were hot on his neck as she unbuttoned his shirt and pants. She pushed him onto the bed. He watched her take off her clothes, her body lean and shadowed in the room's silver light. She climbed on top of him, and Spencer lifted his hips to meet hers. Their breathing grew ragged as they moved together until Em threw her head back and bit her lip. He came as she collapsed on top of him, his heart pounding in counterpoint to her own.

Spencer woke to the sound of someone retching in his bathroom. The last few hours slipped in and out of focus, his recall fragmented, refusing to coalesce. Em walked naked from the bathroom, bent at the waist, her phone in her hand.

"Don't look at me," she said.

She slid into bed, her back to him. The sheet glowed as her phone chimed. Spencer felt Em's shoulders move as she texted. He wanted to take her phone and throw it across the room. Instead, he pulled the covers up and Em close. She coughed as she settled against him.

He woke up alone.

At the garage, Dale said the parts had come in and he'd be done installing them by the end of the day. Spencer spent the rest of the morning wandering through town, the interstate never beyond his sight. The heat rose quickly, and soon his shirt was soaked with sweat. He sat on a bench, the sun at his back, his shadow foreshortened.

His phone showed no messages from Em, but Spencer

couldn't say he was surprised. For all he knew, she was having makeup sex with her asshole boyfriend, her hookup with Spencer a bad memory.

Before that image could take root in his mind, he texted her: "Had a great time last night. Can I take you to dinner?"

His phone chimed, and Spencer read Em's reply: "Glad you weren't planning to leave without saying goodbye."

Em's apartment building was painted a shade of tan that matched the dirt shoulders and sandy ground flanking it. Open block walls bordered a cracked asphalt parking lot. The complex looked like a medium-security federal prison, minus the warmth. As Spencer pulled up to her unit, Em stepped outside. She wore a rose-pattern peasant blouse and denim skirt, a barrette holding her hair in place. Through her briefly open door, Spencer glimpsed a Navajo rug hanging on one wall, its colors reflecting the landscape.

Em got into his car. "Hope the damage wasn't too bad."

The hit to his credit card had all but maxed it out. "At least it's fixed," he said. "Where to?"

"Stay on this road."

A few miles later, she directed him into a parking lot for a restaurant. Painted bright red, Rojas was a scarlet drop on the beige landscape. The main roof pitched steeply like an ersatz chapel, but the color made Spencer wonder what god had been worshipped there. Still, the full parking lot suggested good food and low prices. Inside, the air conditioning was just north of freezing, the place loud with conversation and shouts from the kitchen, the sensory overload jarring.

The hostess knew Em and led them to a two-top by a window. Four palm trees, evenly spaced like sentinels, ran the length of the building. Spencer ordered a beer, and Em a mojito.

"So, Spence, it must feel good to know you're not stuck here anymore."

"It wasn't such a bad place to be stuck."

"When are you leaving?"

"Tomorrow, I guess."

Em's lips went down at the corners, and he regretted what he'd said.

Her smile returned. "You guess?"

He rubbed his eyes and leaned back. "To be honest, I hadn't thought about anything beyond seeing you tonight."

She cocked an eyebrow. "That's a good answer."

Spencer brushed ice off the bottle and sipped his beer. He told himself her texts last night didn't matter because Em was with him now. For the first time, he felt out of the pandemic's shadow.

"What's your favorite thing about living in Barstow?" he asked.

"I love the desert," she said. "From the car, it all looks the same, but if you walk it, you can see where the colors change. And I like how radical the temperature is—from freezing cold at night to triple digits at lunchtime. And the stars, Spencer. My God, have you ever seen the Milky Way?"

"Only in pictures."

"Well, you owe it to yourself to go into the desert at night, lie on your back, and look up at the sky. It's magical."

Their food came, and as he dug in, Spencer pictured himself with Em on a blanket, the constellations above them all but unrecognizable there were so many. Barstow was everything Virginia was not: dry rather than lush; open instead of crowded. Now he wondered if Em was reason enough to stay.

"How about we skip the dessert and go back to my place?" she said.

Spencer couldn't signal for the check fast enough.

When he parked in front of her door, the sun was down, just a band of red narrowing like a cut along the horizon. He followed Em inside. She hit a switch, and a single floor lamp came on, the shade glowing like fire. A small counter divided the kitchen from the main area, and shoji screens hid her bed. There was no clutter, and besides, the rug hung on the wall, no decoration of any kind. He sat on a stool on one side of the counter, while Em pulled glasses from a cabinet.

She ran a lime wedge around the rims and salted them. "Margaritas are my specialty," she said, before adding tequila, lime juice, and triple sec to a cocktail shaker, along with a few ice cubes, and shaking the mix. As she filled the glasses, the color rose like the fog he'd seen from his window this morning.

Em put her hands around his neck, her glass cold against his skin. They kissed, her lips tart. She broke their embrace and went behind the shoji screens, where she lit votive candles on her nightstand.

"Would you get the light?" she asked.

Spencer hit the switch above the counter, and Em's shadow danced on the screens as she pulled down the bedcover. They slipped out of their clothes without last night's frenzy, and now her touch felt electric. She led him to the bed, her taut skin pliant under his fingers. For an instant, he saw them from above, Em's head arched back, his own bent forward, their movements soundless, the moment broken when she grabbed his hair and bore him down upon her.

Afterward, Spencer lay back, the candles wax pools. Em was on her side, one arm and leg across his body. The ceiling was the color of smog, and it darkened as the candles dimmed, Em's weight dovetailed against his own.

When he woke, she was sitting on the edge of the bed, her phone screen glowing in her hand. Spencer sat up, and she closed the display.

"I think you should go."

"What's wrong?"

"I can't sleep with you here, and I have to get up early."

"Was that your boyfriend?"

"Let's leave Damon out of it."

"You're always texting him."

"It's not what you think."

"Tell me what it is, then."

"What difference does it make? You'll be on the road tomorrow, and I'd rather say goodbye now."

Spencer gathered his clothes and began putting them on. His phone, which he didn't remember taking out, was on the floor. Em sat fully on the bed now, looking straight ahead, the woman in Hopper's *Morning Sun* brought to life. Her phone lit up, a flare beneath her face. He walked to the door without looking back.

"Spence," she started.

He turned. Behind the shoji screens, Em's form was amorphous, her voice disembodied. When she didn't go on, he left.

Too wired to sleep, he drove back to the motel. In the bar, baseball played silently on the TV overhead. He took a seat, and Mike brought him a beer. Wanting something stronger, he asked for a tequila shot to back it up.

"No Emily tonight?" Mike asked.

Spencer downed the shot. "She said she had to get up early."

Mike nodded, his expression unchanging.

Spencer remembered watching pandemic baseball, cardboard cutouts of fans filling the seats, crowd noise piped in, the virtual and the real merging into something that was neither. Until the vaccines, he'd believed that was the future, technology allowing for connections that lacked only humanity.

"Ready for another round?" Mike asked.

Spencer didn't remember finishing his beer. "Sure."

Sometime later, he paid his tab and went back to his room. After he showered, he drank a quart of water, hoping to ward off a hangover. He put on boxers and a Fugazi *Seven Songs* T-shirt and crawled under the covers. The room wobbled but didn't spin. He fell asleep, reaching for Emily, unbalanced without her.

The impact of the door bursting open jerked Spencer awake, his heart a jackhammer in his chest. Hallway light filled the doorway, momentarily revealing a short man, before the door rebounded shut behind him. Spencer scrambled across the bed in search of a weapon, but the lamp over the nightstand was bolted to the wall, and the single chair was out of reach.

A pistol cocked, and he froze.

"That's right," the man said.

The wan light that leaked through the curtains illuminated Em's asshole boyfriend—Spencer recognized his jazz musician sideburns. Damon took a step backward toward the switch on the wall. The light came on, and Spencer felt exposed in his boxers. Damon grinned at him, his eyes unfocused, the gun he held aimed at Spencer's chest. He wore a JanSport backpack over one shoulder. Mildew stained the vinyl like camouflage, and what looked like a shovel handle protruded from the top. Spencer's guts churned.

"Put on your clothes," Damon said. "We're going for a little ride in your car."

"Where?" Spencer asked.

"You'll see soon enough. Now get moving."

Spencer stepped into his jeans and pulled on his boots. At the sound of a door opening and closing, Damon's gaze shifted, and his gun wavered. Spencer snatched the handle of his suitcase and flung it sidearm. It bounced off Damon's chest, knocking him into the wall. Spencer charged forward, but he was too late in ducking Damon's backhand. The pistol caught him square on the jaw, the pain that followed a cattle prod to his brain.

Spencer found himself on the floor. A lump rose from the right side of his chin, and his ears buzzed the way they did after a concert, but without the accompanying good feeling. Damon's mouth moved soundlessly until Spencer's synapses re-fired, and the words took shape.

"You've got guts," Damon said. "But if you try anything like that again, I'll shoot you without a second thought."

His eyes were focused now, and Spencer realized his best chance to get out of whatever was happening had come and gone. His stomach roiled, and he thought he was going to puke. The feeling passed, leaving his forehead sheened with sweat.

"All right, let's go," Damon said.

The hallway outside Spencer's room was empty, early morning noises apparently so common here they didn't raise any alarm. The parking lot was similarly devoid of people, the night air cool. Damon made Spencer get into his Corolla through the passenger-side door, prodding him with the pistol as he climbed over the console.

"Start the car and do what I tell you," Damon said. "Maybe you'll live."

They headed north, which set off warning bells in Spencer's mind. North was the desert. North was dry lakes and dirt roads. Far enough north was Death Valley. The lights of Barstow receded in the rearview mirror. When they were gone, Spencer leaned forward and craned his neck. Stars sprinkled the sky like spilled salt.

"What are you looking at?"

"Nothing," Spencer said.

Damon stiffened. "I see Emmy's been feeding you her romantic bullshit about nighttime in the desert."

Spencer returned his gaze to the divided highway, the broken yellow lines a continuum marking time and distance, but surely not infinity.

"Don't feel bad," Damon went on. "I'll bury you face up so that you'll always be looking at the sky."

Spencer jerked the wheel, his involuntary motion carrying the Corolla across the double line.

"Easy, Spencer," Damon said. "I was kidding. This is about teaching you a lesson to stay away from other guys' girls."

"Isn't that Em's decision?"

"Not tonight, it isn't."

Spencer couldn't wrap his head around the idea that his life had turned into a tabloid story. And for what? No one deserved to die for hooking up.

"You're not going to get away with it," he said.

"Here's what's going to happen," Damon started, his voice so matter-of-fact it unnerved Spencer. "I'm going to leave you in the desert and drive your car back to the motel. If you're smart, you'll start walking before the sun rises. You can't get lost because there's only one way out. You'll be dehydrated and hallucinating by the time you make it into town, but you'll have learned a valuable lesson."

The gun and backpack suggested something more permanent than dehydration, but Spencer clung to Damon's words with a hope borne of desperation. He checked the rearview mirror and sensed a shift in the darkness behind them. Damon turned in his seat. Spencer considered grabbing for the pistol, but before he could act, Damon faced him.

"There's no one back there," he said. "Slow down and take that right."

Spencer braked as he steered onto a dirt road that was barely distinguishable from the surrounding desert. When he flicked on his high beams, red eyes glowed at the edge of his vision, before whatever animal he'd illuminated sped into the darkness. He dimmed the headlights, and the landscape ahead faded from view.

"Stop here and leave the car running," Damon said.

Spencer put the car in park. Damon waved the pistol. "Get out."

The early morning air was a cold shot to Spencer's chest. As Damon rounded the car, he pulled an entrenching tool from his backpack and tossed it at Spencer's feet.

"Start over there." He pointed his gun at a bare spot of ground illuminated by the Corolla's headlights.

"I'm not digging my own grave."

Damon shrugged. "If you don't, I'll gut shoot you and let the coyotes finish you off."

Spencer grabbed the entrenching tool and locked the blade open. He imagined hurling it at Damon's throat.

"What the hell is wrong with you?" he shouted. "Do you think killing me will make Em come running back to you?" He blew snot from his nose and wiped his tears with the back of his hand.

"You're pathetic," Damon said.

Over Damon's shoulder, at the far edge of Spencer's vision,

headlights dotted the road. He allowed himself another moment of hope until they winked out like shooting stars.

"I'm not telling you again," Damon said.

Spencer jabbed the shovel into the ground, and it rebounded as if he'd struck asphalt. The earth here was pocked and ridged like corduroy. He angled the blade into a fissure and drove it forward with his boot and tossed the dirt aside. At this rate, it would take him hours to dig any kind of hole. But he continued to work, never turning his back on Damon. The pile of dirt grew, and his palms began to blister. As sweat from his armpits drizzled down his sides, Spencer smelled tequila and something rank. Fear, he guessed, though before today he didn't know it had an odor of its own.

He stopped digging, needing to catch his breath. Damon's boot heels scraped the desert floor like sandpaper, and his pockets jingled whenever he spun and leveled the gun at Spencer. The ground lit by the Corolla's headlights was shaded brown and tan and russet, but on either side of the cone of light, the landscape was formless and without hope.

Spencer jabbed the shovel into the earth, and it sparked against stone, sending shocks the length of his forearms.

"I see what you're doing," Damon said. "In fact, if you don't stop fucking around, I'll kill you now and bury you myself."

Spencer clamped down on his outrage and worked the blade under the stone he'd struck. When he looked up again, the headlights he thought he'd seen before were no longer pinpricks on the horizon, but the oval smears from a pickup truck. Damon turned, but kept his pistol pointed at Spencer's chest.

The truck swung a wide arc so that its high beams crossed those of Corolla and set Damon's features in relief. Em sat behind the wheel. The truck's personalized license plate read DAMON1. She got out of the truck, leaving it running.

"What the hell do you think you're doing?" she shouted at Damon.

Damon looked confused. "Did you follow me here?"

"After you texted me last night, I was afraid you'd do something stupid, so I shared Spencer's location with my phone. When I saw he was headed to the desert, I figured you had to be involved."

"So you stole my truck."

"You said I could borrow it anytime I needed to go somewhere."

Spencer looked from Em to Damon and back again, trying to piece together what was happening.

"I'm tired of your shit, Emmy."

"Don't call me that."

Damon faced Spencer. "She was just using you to make me jealous. This isn't the first time it's happened, but it's going to be the last."

"Don't be an idiot," Em said.

"You killed my love," Damon said, the ache in his voice surprising Spencer.

Em sputtered. "No, Damon, you did that yourself."

Spencer's thoughts spiraled outward, a nebula of fear spurred by the shimmer in the distance he recognized as the coming dawn.

Damon pointed his gun at Em. "I told you this was going to be the last time."

"You want to shoot me? Go ahead." She threw her arms wide.

Damon's gun hand wavered. In one motion, Spencer grabbed the softball-sized stone he'd worked loose and sidearmed it at Damon. The stone was infused with some mineral that sparkled like a comet as it crossed the headlight beams.

Damon brought up his left arm to shield himself as he fired, the sound impossibly loud. The stone caromed off his arm into his head, and he toppled like a statue. His gun lay on the ground a few feet from his twitching, outstretched hand.

Em had fallen, and Spencer ran toward her. She pushed herself upright and sat against the truck's front tire. One side of her shirt was wet. Crimson motes dotted her collarbone. Spencer put his arm around her and pulled her close. With his other hand, he took out his phone to call for help.

"Don't bother." She coughed, and blood fountained from her mouth. Her head lolled forward until her chin rested on her chest. When she grew limp, Spencer laid her down on the earth. He brushed her hair off her forehead.

Em's phone was outlined in her back pocket. Spencer held it to her face until the screen opened. He read the texts between her and Damon. She complained that he took her for granted, and Damon replied that she was too needy. Back and forth they went, an argument that surely was rote to them by now. Em's last text was a photo of naked Spencer asleep on her bed. He turned away from the screen, finally recognizing the part he'd unwittingly played, before reading the threats from Damon that followed.

A noise made him look up. Damon was crawling toward the gun. His movements were jerky and robotic, his head dented where the stone had struck.

Spencer rushed forward. They reached the gun at the same time. He pinned Damon's wrist to the ground with his left foot and kicked him under the chin with his right. Damon's eyes rolled up until only the whites showed, and his body stilled.

Spencer wrenched Damon's arm until the gun was above his face. His eyes fluttered, and his body bucked as he tore at Spencer's wrists with his free hand. Spencer dropped onto Damon's chest and drove the gun between his lips. Damon thrashed beneath him.

The blast blew out the left side of Damon's skull in a shower of bone and blood that sent Spencer reeling. He stood, his ears ringing, and turned away from the wreckage that was Damon's head. To the east, the horizon had begun to glow like embers. Spencer didn't know how far sound carried in the desert or if someone would investigate the gunshots, but he figured he didn't have much time.

Damon's phone was beside his body. Spencer put it on the ground, next to Em's, and smashed both phones with the stone.

# BARSTOW

He buried the pieces under a California juniper beyond the throw of the Corolla's headlights and wiped down the entrenching tool's handle with a Red Man T-shirt he found in the truck's bed. He went back for the stone and heaved it into the scrub, far from the scene at his feet.

On the desert floor, Damon and Em faced each other, their bodies lit red in the morning light. Spencer drove east, into the unforgiving sun.

Photo Credit Amber Bracken

**MICHAEL BRACKEN** (CrimeFictionWriter.com) has edited or co-edited thirty-two published and forthcoming crime fiction anthologies, including the Anthony Award-nominated *The Eyes of Texas: Private Eyes from the Panhandle to the Piney Woods.* Additionally, he is the editor of *Black Cat Mystery Magazine* and an associate editor of *Black Cat Weekly.* Stories from his projects have received or been short-listed for Anthony, Derringer, Edgar, Macavity, Shamus, and Thriller awards, and have been named among the year's best by the editors of *The Best American Mystery Stories, The Best American Mystery and Suspense, The World's Finest Mystery and Crime Stories,* and *The Best Mystery Stories of the Year.*

Also a writer, Bracken is the Edgar Award- and Shamus Award-nominated, Derringer Award-winning author of fourteen

## ABOUT THE EDITOR

books and almost 1,300 short stories, including crime fiction published in *Alfred Hitchcock's Mystery Magazine*, *Ellery Queen's Mystery Magazine*, *The Best American Mystery Stories*, *The Best Mystery Stories of the Year*, and *The Best Crime Stories of the Year*. In 2016, he received the Edward D. Hoch Memorial Golden Derringer Award for Lifetime Achievement in short mystery fiction, and in 2024, he was inducted into the Texas Institute of Letters for his contributions to Texas literature. He lives, writes, and edits in Texas.

# ABOUT THE CONTRIBUTORS

**K.L. ABRAHAMSON** (KarenLAbrahamson.com) spent seventeen years working in the Canadian Criminal Justice System. Author of the Detective Kazakov Mysteries and the Phoebe Clay Mysteries, her short fiction can be found in *Black Cat Mystery Magazine*, *Ellery Queen's Mystery Magazine*, *Mystery Magazine*, and anthologies. Her short stories have been finalists for the Crime Writers of Canada Award of Excellence and the Derringer Award for short fiction.

**ALAN BARKER** has been writing creatively since taking early retirement in 2018. He has short stories published in various magazines (*Café Lit*, *Crystal Scribble*, *Ireland's Own*, *Your Cat UK*, and *Yours Fiction*) and in anthologies, including *Godalming Tales 3*, *The Second Black Beacon Book of Mystery*, *Tales from the Surrey Hills*, and Christopher Fielden's *Writing Challenges*. He is also a certified proofreader and copy editor.

**MICHAEL CHANDOS** is the pen name of a working private investigator. Michael is a member of Mystery Writers of America, the Private Eye Writers of America, and the Short Mystery Fiction Society. He is published in the US and England, in both fiction and nonfiction. He is a Macavity-nominated author, and he has stories in the anthologies *Fresh Starts*, *More Groovy Gumshoes*, and the Anthony-nominated *The Eyes of Texas*.

**CALEB COY** is a freelance writer living with his family in Blacksburg, Virginia. His stories have appeared in *Coachella*

## ABOUT THE CONTRIBUTORS

*Review, Mystery Magazine, Mystery Tribune* online, *Shotgun Honey,* and elsewhere. He is the author of the 2015 novel, *An Authentic Derivative.*

**EDDIE GENEROUS** (JiffyPopAndHorror.com) is a Canadian author of numerous books. He owns and operates Unnerving and *Unnerving Magazine,* and is a big fan of cats.

**NILS GILBERTSON** (NilsGilbertson.com) is a writer and attorney living in Texas. His short stories have appeared in *Cowboy Jamboree, Ellery Queen's Mystery Magazine, Mystery Magazine, Prohibition Peepers, Rock and a Hard Place,* several previous volumes of *Mickey Finn: 21st Century Noir,* and others. His story "Washed Up" was named a Distinguished Story in *The Best American Mystery and Suspense 2022.*

**JAMES A. HEARN** (JamesAHearn.com), an Edgar Award nominee for Best Short Story, writes in a variety of genres, including mystery, crime, science fiction, fantasy, and horror. His work has appeared in *Alfred Hitchcock's Mystery Magazine, Black Cat Mystery Magazine,* and numerous anthologies, including *Monsters, Movies & Mayhem.* James is a two-time finalist for the Writers of the Future contest and has appeared in *The Best American Mystery and Suspense.*

**HUGH LESSIG**'s short fiction has appeared in three previous volumes of *Mickey Finn: 21st Century Noir,* plus two other anthologies from Down & Out Books: *Groovy Gumshoes: Private Eyes in the Psychedelic Sixties,* and *Prohibition Peepers: Private Eyes During the Noble Experiment.* His debut novel, *Fadeaway Joe,* is available from Crooked Lane Books. A former longtime newspaperman, his assignments have ranged from local government meetings to post-earthquake relief in Haiti. He lives in Hampton Roads, Virginia, with his girlfriend Shana, and their two dogs, Gus and Daisy May.

# ABOUT THE CONTRIBUTORS

**SEAN MCCLUSKEY** is a professional cop and semi-professional writer who likes crime better when he gets to make it up and enjoys having his stories appear in anthologies because it's like joining a crew for a big score (as long as he doesn't have to be Mr. Pink). His work has appeared in *Mickey Finn: 21st Century Noir,* Volumes 3 and 4, *Ellery Queen's Mystery Magazine,* and *The Best Mystery Stories of the Year 2023.*

**TOM MILANI**'s (TomMilani.com) short fiction has appeared in *Black Cat Weekly, Groovy Gumshoes: Private Eyes in the Psychedelic Sixties,* and *Illicit Motions,* among other places.

**BILL W. MORGAN** has published stories with *Out of the Gutter Online, Shotgun Honey, Yellow Mama Magazine,* and *The Reno News and Review.* He's had five books published and was a 2017 Eric Hoffer Book Award finalist for his book *Suffer Head.* In 2022, his chapbook *Static* was chosen to be part of the Ghost City Press Summer Series. He lives in Carson City, Nevada, and is currently working on a collection of short fiction.

**ALAN ORLOFF** (AlanOrloff.com) has published eleven novels and fifty short stories. His work has won an Agatha, an Anthony, a Derringer, and two ITW Thriller Awards, including one for his story, "Rent Due," from *Mickey Finn: 21st Century Noir,* Vol. 1 (Down & Out Books). He's also been a finalist for the Shamus Award and has had a story selected for *The Best American Mystery Stories.*

**TRAVIS RICHARDSON** (TSRichardson.com) has published more than fifty short stories. He won a Derringer flash fiction award and has been a three-time nominee for the Macavity and a two-time nominee for the Anthony short story awards. He has two novellas, *Lost In Clover* and *Keeping The Record,* and a short story collection, *Bloodshot and Bruised.*

# ABOUT THE CONTRIBUTORS

**JOSEPH S. WALKER** (JSWalkerauthor.com) lives in Indiana. His short fiction has appeared in many magazines and anthologies, including *The Best American Mystery and Suspense* and three consecutive editions of *The Mysterious Bookshop Presents the Best Mystery Stories of the Year*. He has been nominated for the Edgar Award and the Derringer Award, and he won the Al Blanchard Award in 2019 and 2021. Follow him on Twitter @JSWalkerAuthor.

**ANDREW WELSH-HUGGINS** (AndrewWelshHuggins.com) is the Shamus, Derringer, and International Thriller Writers-award-nominated author of the Andy Hayes Private Eye series and editor of *Columbus Noir*. His stories have appeared in *Alfred Hitchcock's Mystery Magazine*, *Ellery Queen's Mystery Magazine*, *Mystery Magazine*, the anthologies *The Best Mystery Stories of the Year 2021* and *Private Dicks and Disco Balls*, and many other magazines and anthologies.

**ROBB T. WHITE** lives in Northeastern Ohio. Many of his stories and novels feature private investigators Thomas Haftmann or Raimo Jarvi. In 2019, he was nominated for a Derringer for "God's Own Avenger." "Inside Man," a crime story, was selected for inclusion in *The Best American Mystery Stories 2019*. A collection of revenge tales in 2022, *Betray Me Not*, was selected for distinction by the Independent Fiction Alliance in 2022.

**SAM WIEBE** (samwiebe.substack.com) is one of the most acclaimed crime writers in Canada, and the author of the Wakeland series. His standalone thriller *Ocean Drive* was released earlier this year.

**STACY WOODSON** (StacyWoodson.com) is a US Army veteran, and memories of her time in the military are often a source of inspiration for her stories. She made her crime fiction debut in

## ABOUT THE CONTRIBUTORS

*Ellery Queen's Mystery Magazine's* Department of First Stories and won the 2018 Readers Award. Since her debut, she has placed more than thirty stories in anthologies and publications—two winning the Derringer award.

Made in United States
Orlando, FL
02 January 2025